The Heart of the Spring Everlasting

A Bennett Spring Novel

Book 4

Laura L. Valenti

Cover Art & Photography by Bailey Reid
Publishing Coordinator – Sharon Kizziah-Holmes

Indie Pub Press

Springfield, Missouri

ISBN -13: 978-1-964559-40-7

DEDICATION

Dedicated to each and every one who has come home after a time away; to all who have struggled to find their way and return to or establish a new life they can love and be proud of; and most of all, this book is dedicated to those who have come home to the valley of Brice and Bennett and the Osages' Sacred One and fallen in love, with a place, with a spirit, with the heart of Bennett Spring.

And with gratitude to God for the gift of this beautiful place, that many of us may visit for a day, a week, or that some have even been blessed enough to call their own sweet home.

AUTHOR'S PREFACE

It is absolutely amazing to me that just five years ago in 2010, I was blessed to introduce the original *The Heart of the Spring* novel to my readers, telling the fictional story of the history of Bennett Spring State Park and how it came to be. Over a thousand copies of that first book have been sold and it has been followed by two equally popular sequels, *The Heart of the Spring Lives On* and *The Heart of the Spring Comes Home.*

That first book, *The Heart of the Spring* (Book 1) introduced the Darling Family living in the village of Brice in 1924 before there ever was a park. Eighteen year old Becky Darling heard the rumors of the park to come and was thrilled at the prospect. Her father, Zeb, the local mail carrier, was equally appalled and fought briefly, as did some actual residents at the time, against the proposal. Fortunately, for all of us, those who welcomed the coming of the park prevailed and more than ninety years later, we are still enjoying the benefits.

The first sequel, *The Heart of the Spring Lives On* (Book 2) is set in 1935 when the Civilian Conservation Corps (CCC) was at Bennett Spring building many of the features we still love today, like the Dining Lodge and the beloved triple-arched bridge. Becky's younger brother, Ben, is a new deputy for the local sheriff's department and this story centers on him and his times during the worst Depression this country has ever known.

The Heart of the Spring Comes Home (Book 3) the next sequel, picks up the story at the end of World War II in 1946 as folks return to the Bennett Spring valley, including

Esther Darling, a Navy nurse and the youngest Darling sister. As local people struggle to rebuild their lives after the world's most devastating war, they unite around their local church that is in danger of being wiped out by a clause in the very contract that established Bennett Spring State Park.

In each of these books, I have blended historical fact with fictional stories, gifts from God, representing local folks, their histories, their loves and lives. The results have been three novels that I've been blessed to present to those, like me, who have long loved Bennett Spring. Even more satisfying are the many blessings I have received from the readers who also love the stories and let me know they are eagerly awaiting the next sequel.

And now, finally, I am pleased to present *The Heart of the Spring Everlasting*. In 1967, Tabby, Becky's youngest daughter, like so many others in those tumultuous days, has run away to the teeming streets of San Francisco. She comes home, her head down in shame, to discover the love of Bennett Spring still runs strong and may ultimately save her in more ways than one.

While the individuals, situations and conversations as related here are completely fictional, there are a few kernels of truth sprinkled throughout, such as the construction of the Catholic church known as the Sportsman's Chapel at Bennett Spring. That effort was spearheaded by the late Father Clem Ilmberger, the pastor of Lebanon's St. Francis de Sales Catholic Church in the early 1970s and completed through the efforts of many volunteers, several of them known as the Sugar Creek Gang. There are also several actual members of the Bennett Spring community of that time, mentioned here such as Ralph and Willa Jean (Evans) Ursery and George K., who are mentioned throughout the book but all of their situations and conversations are fictional. While I placed a family campground, along Highway 64A, just before the actual main entrance to Bennett Spring Park and approximately across from the Sportsman's Chapel in the summer of 1967, there was no campground along that stretch until the late 1970s. I found that Rolla and Maxine Pearson did have a campground in that location in the late 1970s and people still remember the Made Rite burgers they sold there. They must have been really good!

Likewise, I thought of the Baird family farm, located on that same road, a bit closer to Highway 64, as my make-believe model for the old Schultz Farm, which became J.C., Becky, and Tabby Shine's family home and farm. Both locations, like the property once belonging to the Ursery's, are all now part of the lands that make up Bennett Spring State Park property. All the structures and manmade things are now gone and the land has been returned to nature and the animals who live there. The Baird family are actually the true benefactors of the Sportsman's Chapel who donated the land for its construction in the early 1970s.

All of the true people and locations I mention here, I do as a tribute to their contributions to Bennett Spring over the years—their delightful company and friendship, their stories, and even the buildings they left behind like the Bennett Spring Church of God, in the case of the Userys and George's major project, the Bennett Spring Nature Center as well as a lifetime of service to the people of Missouri.

For the purposes of historical fiction, times, dates, and places must sometimes be altered to fit the story line. While this story takes place in 1967, the actual construction of the chapel was between 1972 and 1974 and was entirely accomplished with funds raised specifically for that purpose. I took the liberty of using Father Clem's name as well as that of the Sugar Creek Gang as a way of honoring their efforts, the beautiful benefits of which we still enjoy and appreciate. No disrespect of any kind is or was intended in doing so, quite the contrary. Their efforts are further mentioned in the *Historically Speaking* section at the end of this book.

For me, history has always been a wondrous story book, just waiting to be explored and yet for reasons I will never understand, it is at times reduced to a list of hard dry facts with no life at all, leaving a bad aftertaste for those who do not share in the adventure and romance of days gone by. My purpose here is to once again remind one and all that our history has been written by living, breathing men and women, who, like us, struggle with circumstances that threaten to overwhelm. Their stories help us in our challenging times, whatever they may be, to remember that with faith and love, we can also triumph in the face of adversity.

Once again, I have to say this is not my story, but rather one given to me by the good Lord to pass on, and for that I am most thankful. While several have asked why this one has taken so long to reach print, like everyone else, I also face life's struggles from health challenges to the high pressure of the needs of my family and so for the delay, I do sincerely apologize.

I am also most appreciative to the many others who have so graciously lent their talents to make this book complete, including:

My three faithful proofreaders, Debbie Blades, Francesca Rich, and new this time, Sandy Musice, all of whom have greatly helped to refine and improve this book for your enjoyment;

Eric Adams, Laclede County's own photographic wizard

and high school teacher who generously shares his incredible skills and talents with our community as well as his students in more ways than any of us can count, for once again producing an incredible book cover for this latest sequel;

Jim and Carmen Rogers for their continued generous material support, as well as Ginger Clark of Lebanon Books, and the gracious ladies of Pierced Book Store and Bistro, all of Lebanon, Missouri;

Diane Tucker, Bennett Spring Park Naturalist, for her willingness to share history and photos of Bennett Spring State Park and to her and Sue Eckmann, well-known presence at the front counter of the Bennett Spring Park Store, for their inspiration that started this whole series and their ever-present encouragement, even when I've not been so sure;

Larry Peace, Jennifer (Vogel) Long for sharing their memories of Bennett Spring to further refine this story;

Eddie Lopez of Sarasota, Florida who is of Dominican Republic and Cuban descent, and his dear 'aunt', Carmen Corriazo-Cannon, of Doral, Florida, both of whom were kind enough to share a few joys and facts their family's beloved heritage to enhance and enrich the characters here, just as those coming from so many other places, have helped to enrich all of our lives in America today;

Clayton Boggs, proprietor of Boggs Family Automotive of Bennett Spring, a local mechanical marvel who helped to design J. Junior's renovated Jeep;

And as always, my love and gratitude to my husband, Warren and his patient support of my dream of writing novels, is overwhelming as it is to my children, Francesca and Jón, Lisa and Clayton, Ricardo, Tiffany, Emmanuel and Beth, and theirs, Cooper, Tyson, Austin, Dante, Dominic, Dillon, Derick and Jessica, for these are my loved ones who have taught me what is truly important in life.

I must also once again mention here my admiration and appreciation for the late Ellen Gray Massey, a dear friend, fellow writer, mentor, and editor, who as a great Ozark writer, read and critiqued the first three Bennett Spring novels, encouraging me at every step to complete this journey. Sadly, we lost Ellen in the summer of 2014 at the young-at-heart age of 92. She is still greatly missed but lives on as a treasure of the Ozarks in the 30 books she wrote over the last 30 years of her life. She published her first book after she retired and was past 60 years old, so never think it is too late to complete a dream. She didn't and now we have all of her wonderful books that live on as a lovely tribute and memory of her.

Like many others who now claim Bennett Spring as home, I came to this valley over 45 years ago as a result of a career change, my husband's, with the Missouri Department of Conservation. Warren worked over 21 years as the assistant manager of the Bennett Spring Trout Hatchery during the 1980s and 1990s. As a result, we were blessed to live in the park our first eight years here and then moved to our own home a couple of miles up the road. We raised our children at Bennett Spring and I know wherever they go in this world, like me, they will always think of Bennett Spring fondly.

I sincerely hope this book will be received in the same spirit in which it was written, an offering from one who loves Bennett Spring and the folks who call it home, whether for a few years or a lifetime. I hope, too, it will be greeted in the same way as the first three have been. While all of us who toil as writers hope to make a few coins to fill our pockets from our efforts, without a doubt the most satisfying of the accomplishment of writing such a book are the notes, emails and personal comments from readers who let me know that something I have written has brought a smile, a tear, or a delightful memory to mind. That is the true music to a writer's ear and balm to our souls for which there is no substitute.

May you and yours enjoy *The Heart of the Spring Everlasting* and likewise, always love Bennett Spring, both in person and in your fondest memories of life.

Laura L. Valenti, author
Bennett Spring, Missouri

Darling-Shine Family Tree

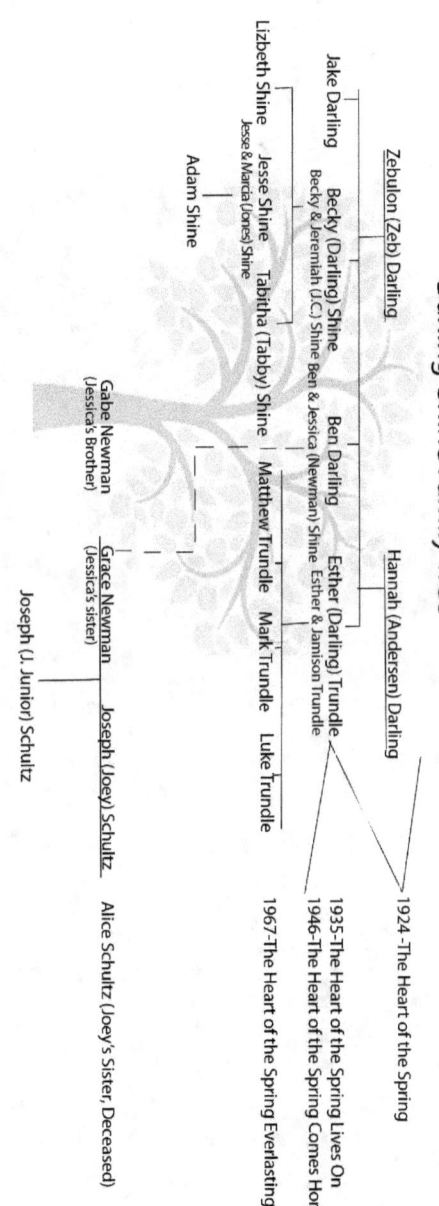

Zebulon (Zeb) Darling   Hannah (Andersen) Darling

Jake Darling

Becky (Darling) Shine
Becky & Jeremiah (J.C.) Shine

Lizbeth Shine

Adam Shine

Jesse Shine
Jesse & Marcia (Jones) Shine

Tabitha (Tabby) Shine

Ben Darling
Ben & Jessica (Newman) Shine

Esther (Darling) Trundle
Esther & Jamison Trundle

Gabe Newman
(Jessica's Brother)

Matthew Trundle

Mark Trundle

Grace Newman
(Jessica's sister)

Luke Trundle

Joseph (Joey) Schultz

Jesse Newman (Jessica's twin)

Akira Hamamoto (Japanese)

Hana   Gina

Joseph (J. Junior) Schultz

Alice Schultz (Joey's Sister, Deceased)

1924-The Heart of the Spring

1935-The Heart of the Spring Lives On
1946-The Heart of the Spring Comes Home

1967-The Heart of the Spring Everlasting

CHAPTER 1

She opened her eyes, vaguely conscious of the noise around her, but found she could focus only on the face in front of hers. His skin was so smooth, especially around his eyes. The raggedy beard growth and his wild dark hair appeared to be pasted across his forehead. A slow realization dawned, something was wrong, terribly wrong. There was a timbre to the voices, an urgency, and she didn't like it. She sat up from the pallet on the floor that she and Seeker had shared the night before. Her attention was still riveted on him and she wondered why he didn't hear it, too. Why wasn't he beginning to stir as well? She reached out to his shoulder in an attempt to roust him but when she pushed, he only flopped onto his back. The strange way he moved further alarmed her. His face, still rimmed with those damp curls, was a flat gray, with no color whatsoever to his lips. Her anxiety continued to build and yet she could not concentrate. Her head felt so woozy, so unfocused.

"Come on, step back now!" The first distinctive voice she could discern was issuing orders. She stayed seated, her hand to her head. An upward glance took in the psychedelic peace sign still splayed across the window where the morning sun was pouring in. Last night her drawing had appeared so vivid in its colors, moving, as if it had a life of its own. But now it was only a faded, washed out version of what she remembered. Which was what?

Seeker's smile was so sweet. "Here, just take a little. See? I crushed up your sugar cube for you so you could take half. I know you've never done this before so you don't want too much at first." She gave him a funny look because he also held three cubes for himself. "It's okay," he reassured her. "After a while, you can do more, too, but not at first. You'll see. It's really great stuff and...."

The angry man's voice was still barking in the background. What was his problem? Didn't he know this was a place of peace? That's what Seeker had called it. "Come on," he told her the day he found her, sitting on the curb, crying. "Come see for yourself. Nobody makes you do anything you don't want to do. No one will demand anything of you. We have a large second floor apartment, some friends and I, and we all just crash there. It's a place of peace. You'll like it, I promise, and if you don't, you can come right back to your spot here on this curb." And she had followed him to his promised land of peace. Last night, Seeker had been laughing, making her feel so loved, snapping pictures with the little camera his brother gave him. Above all else, she had heard Seeker say, no one will demand anything of you and now there was this angry *demanding* man.

"Out of the way now, girl. Is this the one?" The uniformed police officer pointed at her comatose companion and another younger officer kneeled down beside her and Seeker. "Geez, it stinks in here," the barking man continued. "What is that awful smell? It ain't marijuana." He waved his hand in front of his face in a futile effort to banish the offensive odor.

"It's incense, Man," one of the many gathered in the apartment crooned in a sing song manner. "Just incense. Nothing illegal about that."

The younger officer was kneeling on their private sleeping pallet and doing a poor job of concealing his amused smile, listening to his partner's frustration. He poked at Seeker. "Another dead one, I'm afraid."

Dead? She heard the word but it made no sense to her. Dead? Who was dead? Seeker?!

The others in the apartment crowded in and the louder of the two officers ordered them back again. Who was he to be yelling at them? Her disconnected thoughts kaleidoscoped around her. They all slept here. Like her, for the moment, they all lived here, in this tiny oasis of peace on the chaotic streets of San Francisco in 1967.

Reality was slowly taking hold. How could Seeker be dead? She struggled to her feet.

"All right." The Demanding Man was now speaking to all of them. "This man, who knew him? How long? What's his real name? What do you all know about him?"

The multitude shuffled and muttered amongst themselves.

"Okay, who's been here the longest?" The sergeant tried a different approach.

"Bear, get the Bear." A murmur went through the group. A large young man, who appeared to be as wide as he was tall, ambled reluctantly to the front of the pack.

"Bear?" The officer raised an eyebrow in the new arrival's direction as he put a pen to the notebook he held in his right hand. "That your street name? What's it say on your birth certificate, boy? How long you been here?" He waved a hand in a vague arc to take in the apartment where they were standing. Two men arrived with a hospital gurney to take Seeker to his next destination and the sergeant sidestepped around them, still focusing on the Bear.

"Six months, I guess," came the unsteady answer. "My name is Tim Grizzly. Me and Seeker—we rented this place together. He had some money, sent by his dad, I think."

"Whose name is on the lease then?"

"His. I was with him, but I didn't sign anything."

"And what is his name? And don't tell me any of this Seeker nonsense. I need his real name and address."

"Uhh…" He hesitated and looked around as if he were being asked to reveal some deeply held secret in front of a crowd of witnesses.

"Come on, Bear." For the first time since entering the premises, the man's voice softened ever so slightly. "If I have to go roust the landlord again, I won't be happy about it, if you get my drift. I've already talked to him once." He stopped speaking and looked the younger man straight in the eye.

"Oh, well, the name that he put on the lease was Michael. Michael Miller."

"And where's he from? Who do we get in touch with, about his death?"

"I dunno. The check he had was from John Miller. Out of South Dakota, I think."

The sergeant hesitated. "Michael Miller from South Dakota." A deep sigh escaped him. "And he comes to San Francisco to become, who? Seeker?"

"Seeker of Truth," Tim 'the Bear' Grizzly finished weakly.

"Seeker of Truth." The officer shook his head. "Well, he didn't find it in multiple doses of LSD, now that's a fact." He turned his attention back to the other officer who was speaking to Seeker's female companion. As the petite blond began to cry, a couple of the other girls in the crowd surrounded her. One put a blanket around her shoulders and held her in half an embrace as the sergeant approached.

"We'll have to see what the coroner thinks but I'd say your friend had more than his share of the drug of the day last night. What do you know about this? You share it with him?"

"Yes…" She looked down in confusion. "No!" She scrambled for answers as the girl next to her squeezed her shoulders tighter in an unspoken warning. Her mind was so compromised, both by the shock of his death and by the unnamed malady that had somehow scrambled her brain. "We were just partying, quietly, like everyone else, no problems, no trouble. We weren't bothering anyone."

"Yeah, well, your private partying, so to speak, usually involves what? Marijuana? LSD? Heroin? Pretty hardy stuff, young lady!"

"No!" She blurted out again, which only made her head hurt worse. "It wasn't like that. He, we were happy. The colors on the window were so pretty and he even crushed my cu—"

The girl next to her stumbled forward as if she had tripped on the blanket and gave her a sharp look as she straightened back up.

"Oh, I just don't know. I don't remember." She finished miserably.

"Is that the stuff from the Unicorn? I told him not to buy stuff from him anymore. He's wacko! You never know what you're gonna get!" The hoarse whisper from one of the others standing close to the Bear apparently came out louder than he intended.

"The Unicorn, heh?" The sergeant glanced at the other officer. "Not the first time we've heard that name, now is it? The Unicorn." He made another scribble and then flipped the notebook shut with a clap. "Come on, Skip." He gave the other officer a knowing look. "I think we're done here. You boys got this?" He raised his gaze and voice toward the two ambulance attendants who had finished strapping the remains of the late Michael Miller beneath a white sheet.

The ambulance fellows nodded silently and began to make their way out of the apartment with their cargo. The younger officer, approximately the same age as most of the others in the room, started to follow the senior officer out.

"Oh yeah." The sergeant turned back at the last minute. "Miller here, Seeker as he called himself, was the only name on the lease. The owner, the landlord downstairs, says no one else has a right to be here. You all are going to have to find a new place to live. Forty-eight hours. Got it? And take a bath, will ya?" He waved his hand in front of his nose again. "And you, girlie...." He looked directly at Seeker's companion. "What's your name?"

"I've got it." Skip consulted his own notes. "Tabby, Tabitha Darling. Sweet name, huh, Sarge?" He looked over at the tear-stained face and emerald green eyes once more. "Tabitha Darling of Bennett Spring, Missouri. She says as soon as she finds the bus fare that's where she's going. Back home to Bennett Spring."

She stared at them both in silence. She had lied but she had no idea why.

"Smart girl," the sergeant muttered under his breath as he led the way down the stairs. They took no notice of the two dark-suited men in sunglasses sitting in the navy blue sedan across the street from the apartment building.

* * * * *

The afternoon sun sparkled off the spring branch waters of Bennett Spring, making Father Clem squint as he took in the beauty of the place. Tall white-limbed sycamores, fully laden with their early summer greenery, lined the water's edge, reminding him of comforting arms reaching out to embrace all who made their way to this blessed place, whether for sport or rest or a little of both. After a silent prayer of gratitude for time spent in such a majestically green palace, the white-robed priest stepped back from the water's edge and began to set up his portable altar, a folding table with a table cloth. He fanned out imaginary wrinkles in the simple cotton cloth with his hands, in what had become his regular practice on summer Saturdays in preparation for afternoon Mass.

From the nearby town of Lebanon, Father Clem came to southwest Missouri's renowned Bennett Spring trout park with his traveling worship service to say Mass for fishermen, visitors, and locals alike. Each weekend eight months of the year, the park was filled with fishermen and tourists, some of them good Catholics from St. Louis and Kansas City. The priest knew many struggled a bit between taking time from their short weekend break from city life to drive into town to attend Mass or skip the weekly sacrament altogether. This was one way of doing as the Pope had instructed his clergy in Vatican II, a few years before, to reach out beyond the church and extend a hand to the community at large.

"G' afternoon, Father." Frankie O'Donnell approached, also coming up from the stream bank, but from the opposite direction. "Need help setting up this afternoon?"

The young man's well-built physique bore mute testimony to his regular job as a construction worker. His rust-colored curls shone in the bright sunshine and added to his youthful appearance as did the non-descript T-shirt and jeans he wore. The slight but distinctive limp and a taut expression around his dark eyes hinted at more life experience than his years might indicate. Originally from St. Louis, he had spent the past several months working for his uncle's construction company out of Lebanon.

Father Clem handed Frankie a plain woven basket, the last item to be set out before the worship began. "We've collected enough now to start construction. Did you know? I've talked with your uncle and some others and very soon, if all goes well...." He left the thought unfinished but the twinkle in his eye spoke volumes.

"Very soon? Very soon what?" A dusting of freckles covered Frankie's wrinkled nose, his curiosity piqued.

"Well, let me just say, with God's blessing, very soon we will have a permanent spot to celebrate our Mass," the priest continued, enjoying his moment of intrigue. "I'll say no more for now. I wouldn't want to jinx anything." He let his smile do the rest of the talking.

Frankie shook his head, knowing he would get no more information for the moment. "Are you ready? I'll get my guitar." He walked a short distance over to a working man's truck as he liked to call his faded red pickup, one that bore the bumps, dents, and splatters of many a day on a construction site.

The crack of gunfire had him on the ground in a split second, striking his chin on the rocks as he scrambled to inch under his pickup truck. And just as quickly as the loud backfire of the truck on the nearby road spewed a nasty little black cloud, he realized he was in no danger at all.

Feeling incredibly foolish, he climbed to his feet while rubbing his chin. Visions of rice paddies, helicopters, and men in guerrilla fatigues flitted through the back of his mind as he cast an awkward eye around. He was relieved to see that apparently no one had noticed his belly flop in the gravel. Instead, those who were not focused on the fishing were watching the noisy rattle trap pickup make its way across the wooden bridge, just above the confluence where the spring branch meets the Niangua River.

Back beside Father Clem's table, a still trembling Frankie began to strum the sweet notes of a familiar hymn on his guitar, visibly trying to calm his frazzled nerves. Father Clem watched him, wondering, but his attention was soon distracted by those gathering. Some walked up from the stream while others arrived in their vehicles, parking nearby.

"We come together today in God's beautiful, natural cathedral," Father Clem began, "the perfect setting to worship our Lord and Savior. Before we begin today, I want to share with you that very soon we will be meeting, still in God's lovely outdoors but on a parcel of land that has been donated especially for the purpose of a place to worship here at Bennett Spring. As you turn onto the road that leads into the park, on the left side you'll see a lush green meadow, just before you begin the descent into the valley. The land there has been donated to us by the man who owns it. So next Saturday, look for us there at this time. We won't be next to the water but rest assured there, like here, you will be welcomed to come to the worship of God in your fishing gear and waders. I have it on good authority that the Lord Jesus Christ has a special tenderness in his heart for fishermen. Come now," he continued, as he raised his hands up high, "let us worship God."

While Father Clem and his followers prepared to worship, cars continued to roll past on their way across the wooden bridge with the tranquil blue-green water of the spring branch swirling below. J.C. and Becky Shine and her mother, Hannah Darling, crossed over on their way to the Bennett Spring Dining Lodge after an afternoon drive. Hannah and her daughter were life-long residents of the area, from the days before there ever was a Bennett Spring State Park. Back then, it had been simply a picturesque valley, more isolated than not by distance and geography, home to the village of Brice, Missouri, which had long since faded into history.

"What are those people up to now?" Hannah piped up from the back seat in a tone that Becky had come to dread since her father's death several months before.

"What people?" Becky asked, twisting around to catch a glimpse of the ongoing Mass.

"Those people." Hannah hissed. "Can't they worship on Sunday morning in a church building like everyone else? Honestly!"

"Ma, what's the problem?" Becky knew she was headed into dangerous territory but she couldn't help herself. "Can't think of a prettier place to hold worship than right out here in the open. We've held many a church service on the spring branch, like every spring and summer for baptisms."

"Hmphf!" came Hannah's reply. "That's different. We only go out there once in a while and for a very specific purpose but they are out here every week, like they don't even have a proper church home."

"Well, that's not true," Becky continued. "The priest is from the Catholic Church in Lebanon, St. Francis de Sales, and some of the worshipers are his own but many are here visiting from other places, so this way they still attend worship, even while they are on vacation. Frankly, I think it's kind of sweet. You know, Jamison has always welcomed fishermen and visitors to our church right here in the valley, anytime they want to come."

"It's just different," Hannah repeated, practically whining at this point. "They're different, that's all. I guess we should be thankful they are at least speaking in English these days and the priest is no longer going on in Latin like they did years ago. How is anybody supposed to get anything out of a message when they can't even understand it? It's just, more and more different sorts of people keep coming into our valley and I'm not so sure...."

"Not so sure of what?" Becky bristled at her mother's implications. "I swear since Pa died," she muttered under her breath to her husband, who had kept his eyes on the road, maintaining his silence during the conversation.

J.C. Shine had come to Bennett Spring over forty years before as a young aide to the state senator originally sent to the area to explore the possibility of establishing the state park. Despite a short return to Jefferson City, he had followed his heart back to Becky and Bennett Spring where he had remained ever since, with the exception of a World War II assignment to Washington D.C. In the many years since, he had served as the local newspaper editor. In more recent years, he had published several books and also helped his brother-in-law, Ben, in raising cattle on the side.

"Oh, I don't know." Hannah's words continued to wander. "So many changes here of late. It's like the whole world has gone crazy. You know they are tearing down the old museum? Your father helped to build that, Becky. There was no good reason to tear it down. I heard they were going to build a new one but who knows when that will be or if they will even do it. I don't like it, not one bit. And yet there doesn't seem to be any stopping it either, all these strange people, all these changes." A heavy sigh escaped her.

"Ma, the old museum was just that, old. The park superintendent told me the roof had leaked so bad over the years, some of the beams were rotted. It was cheaper to tear it down and build a new one. It is not that surprising, all things considered!"

Hannah ignored her daughter's comment. "J.C., what do you think?"

J.C. waited a moment longer before answering, as he carefully wended his way along the narrowest part of the road that passed along the left side of their own Bennett Spring Church of God. He glanced up Highway OO that led up the hill, past the gravel drive to the little house where he and Becky had lived the first years they were married. Now, like most of the year, the house was invisible, tucked out of sight in the leaf-laden trees, but he knew it was there and he always thought of it when he passed this way, even if he couldn't see it.

"My guess would be you are not be the first person to feel that way here, Mamá." He used the Spanish form of mother to address his mother-in-law, left over from his childhood days in Panama and Cuba, where his father had been an engineer and then a hotel owner. "And I know you are not alone right now. Many others feel the same." He glanced in the rearview mirror at Hannah, who was as dear to him as his own late mother. J.C. spoke slowly, like he was forming his thoughts in the same way, but Becky recognized her husband's tone as the one he employed when simplifying the most complicated concepts.

"I imagine the Sac and the Osage, the last of the tribes to leave this valley just before the arrival of James Brice, the first settler here, felt much the same way," he concluded, as he pulled into a space in the Dining Lodge parking lot. "So many changes, so many strange people and there doesn't seem to be a thing we can do to stop it. I'm sure they must have felt those very same things."

* * * * *

The jarring ring of the phone cut through the quiet hours of the early morning. Still in his pajama shorts, Ben Darling, not so many years ago Sheriff Ben Darling, stumbled to the clanging thing. Drowsy recollections slipped through his mind of the many nights in years past, when a ringing phone in the wee hours of the morning meant a call to work.

"Uncle Benji." The weak voice on the line, thick with static, snapped him to full wakefulness.

"Tabby! Tabby, is that you?"

"Oh, Uncle Benji!" The voice grew fainter yet, but this time clouded by tears, not electrical interference.

"Tabby, where are you? Are you in some kind of trouble? Tell me where you are and I'll get help there fast. I can get sheriff's deputies to you wherever you are, little girl. Just tell me and—"

"Uncle Benji, I'm okay, really. I'm on my way...." She sounded a little stronger but then hesitated again. "I'm on my way back to you all. I'm somewhere in western Kansas, I don't know. On the bus. This is just where we stopped for some gas and food, is all. I'll be in Lebanon tomorrow around noon. I'm sorry to wake you but I wasn't sure when I would get a chance to use a phone again. I was just wondering...can you pick me up at the bus station? Can I go home with you for a little while, first? Is that all right?"

"Well, of course," he stammered, caught by complete surprise. "But your mother, does she know you are

13

coming? She'll be so happy, Tabby!"

A strange woman's harsh voice cut him off. "Please deposit another seventy-five cents to continue." He heard the mechanical clink as Tabby dropped more coins into the pay phone.

"Uncle Benji, can you still hear me?" Ben heard her faint voice in the background once again.

"Yes, I hear you, Tabby. Your mama and your dad, J.C., they've both been so worried about you. Have you called home?"

The silence on the other end of the phone gave him the clear answer.

"Tabby, are you there?"

"I'm still here, Uncle Benji," came the somewhat distracted answer. "I'm just watching. I think they are re-loading the bus. I've got to go. I don't want to lose my place. I don't have any more money for another ticket or another phone call. I'm sorry to bother you, Uncle Benji. I just couldn't call my mother right now...."

"Tabby, don't worry. Listen, you get back on that bus, quick now. I'll be at the bus station tomorrow, today really, right? Later today. We'll be waiting, you hear? Me and your Aunt Jessica. Go on now, don't miss that bus. We love you, little girl. Get here fast as you can!"

"Thank you, Uncle Benji." He heard her quick reply before the line clicked to silence.

He hung up the phone reluctantly but as his hand turned loose of the receiver, he sprang to life. Forgetting the hour, he sprinted back to the bedroom. "Jessica!" he whooped. "That was Tabby and she's coming home!"

CHAPTER 2

Flashing neon lights burned through the gray light of dawn, waking her as the bus pulled into another early morning stop, allowing the passengers to find some coffee, doughnuts, and other much needed relief from the long ride across the western states. She swiped at her eyes but they remained swollen from the hours spent crying herself to sleep, the only way she had managed any rest on this trip.

Before packing up her few meager possessions, she had gathered Seeker's things into a couple of cardboard cartons for his friends to send to his relatives. She had looked for some little momento she might hang on to as a remembrance of their time together but there really was nothing that held any special significance for her. It was one more reason she found Seeker so intriguing, his lack of interest in material possessions. He not only preached it, he lived it. Then she saw the skinny little camera. His brother had dropped it off to him a few days before in a clandestine sort of late night visit. Seeker laughed about it when she asked but then he used the camera the next day to snap several pictures of the two of them together. That's the only thing she wanted, those pictures.

She stuffed the camera into her bag but thinking of Seeker

only sharpened the pain of losing him and his kindness, like the first day he had found her. She had come to California with one of her dormitory suite mates from college, Margie Dolan. They had been such close friends for over a year in Springfield and then on the road to San Francisco. Even the first couple of weeks in California had been good but then, everything changed. Diablo, they all called him, although Tabby knew from the beginning that was not his real name. It didn't matter. Margie fell madly in love with him and the two girls quickly ended up living in the cubby hole of an apartment he called home. Tabby felt like she could manage but did her best to avoid Diablo as much as possible. Something about the dark and swarthy yet ominous way he looked at her set her nerves on edge. And then, early one morning, he was in her room, slipping into bed beside her. He covered her mouth and she didn't scream but he didn't do much either, except whisper and threaten while he lay there beside her. And then suddenly he was gone.

She tried to tell Margie the truth but she could see even before she was halfway through her explanation the anger and disbelief on her friend's face. She stopped as the tears welled up as she tried to describe the terrifying moments he was in her bed. The words stuck in her throat. Margie stood up stiffly from where she sat on the end of the bed. Tabby started out the bedroom door after her but then she saw Diablo, standing by the front door. The smirk on his face as he looked down at his hands, holding onto both sides of the doorknob, said he had seen both their expressions and he knew. He was waiting for Margie and the two of them left together. Tabby was out the door shortly after that, her packed bag on her back.

At this point on the bus, she wasn't even sure what she was crying about anymore. There were so many things. The death of someone she had dared to care about and the loss of a dream, nothing more than a pipe dream, some would say. Yet, she certainly wasn't alone in her search for meaning for her own life, as the packed, tumultuous streets of San Francisco proved every day with the arrival of more lost young people like herself from all across the country. And then, there was the embarrassment of begging money from her new friends, and there was still the hole where her heart was supposed to be, broken when her Grandpa Zeb died, but perhaps what she hated most was the shame of returning home, empty-handed, once again, feeling like such a complete and utter failure.

Tabby shifted in her seat, turning from the window. She didn't even bother to get off the bus this time. She had made her telephone call at the last stop and she didn't have enough money left for a cup of coffee. The grim gray interior of the bus smelled of stale cigarettes and too many bodies in close proximity. She tried to ignore the rumbling in the pit of her stomach as she closed her eyes once more, in search of the only peace she could find at the moment.

* * * * *

As good as his word, Ben and Jessica Darling sat at a table in the Lebanon Greyhound Bus Station, waiting on the arrival of the eastbound noon bus. Jessica kept an eye on her nervous husband as she sipped a cherry Coke from a glass bearing the same insignia. For a man who had faced down trouble in many forms and dealt personally with more than one crazed man with a loaded weapon, she found it amusing that the arrival of his niece from parts unknown had him more agitated than any situation in recent memory.

"Ben." The former sheriff's wife could maintain her silence no longer as he shredded the paper wrapper she'd taken off the straw a short time before. "It'll be fine. She called you, didn't she? The bus will be here soon. Didn't Fred tell you it was on time?"

"Yes, he did," Ben admitted with a sheepish grin. "I just wish it would hurry up is all. I don't know what I was thinking to come in here without saying anything to Becky or Ma. Becky will hang me out dry over this, when it's all said and done." He shook his head in disbelief.

"Ben, we talked about this. As upset as Becky has been about Tabby taking off the way she did with that other girl from the college, there was no point in saying something to her and J.C. until we are sure Tabby really is on that bus. Once she's here, home in Lebanon, then you can talk to your sister, but until then, it just seems like there's been enough to deal with in these last few months, with Zeb's passing and with what's happened to J. Junior. And now Becky and J.C. working to move your mother into their house. Becky Shine is, without a doubt, my best friend and I just can't bear to lay one more emotional burden at her feet right now. You've heard of the straw that broke the camel's back. Well, I'm afraid our whole family is about there. So, for heaven's sake, take a deep breath. Have a piece of pie or something but please try to calm down a little because you know...." She didn't get to finish her thought. Ben leapt to his feet as the Greyhound bus lumbered into the parking lot, with all the grace of a gleaming silver pachyderm.

Jessica joined him as they moved outside into the bright sunshine. A people watcher's smorgasbord of individuals tumbled forth as fast as the bus door snapped open. The driver followed, moving to the underbelly of the traveling beast to begin unloading passenger luggage. A perplexed Ben Darling gave his wife an alarmed glance and started toward the still open bus door. As he reached the lowest step, a waif of a young woman in a long colorless gauzy dress with a thick blond braid wound around her head began her descent down the bus stairs.

She was a long way from the freckled face, giggly girl Ben always thought of when Tabby's name was mentioned. Becky and J.C.'s youngest child looked lost and alone, her lovely green eyes squinting, all but hidden by bright pink puffy cheeks, as she stepped into the blinding sunlight from the dark bus interior.

"Tabby!" Her shabby appearance didn't dampen her uncle's enthusiasm as he scooped her up in his arms. "I was afraid you weren't on the bus after all."

"Oh, yeah, I'm here, Uncle Benji. Aunt Jessica." She gave a weak wave to her aunt who still stood several paces behind her husband.

"Come on, Tabby. Let's get your luggage." Ben turned toward the bus driver who was still sorting out the various items belonging to the other passengers.

"I don't really have anything, Uncle Benji." She hesitated. "Just this." She swung around a long cloth bag on a shoulder strap that had been more hidden than not behind her back.

"That's it?" An astounded look crossed Ben's face. "I didn't think a woman could go for a night in Kansas City with less than three bags. You've come all the way from— where have you been anyway, girl?" He put his hands on his hips in a mocking motion, bringing a faint smile to the distraught face that had seen too little to eat and drink and too little sleep in recent days.

"San Francisco," she answered with a downward glance.

"California! And that's all the luggage you've got? Now that is amazing! Well, come on then."

Jessica stepped forward to give her a welcoming hug. "We're so glad you're home, wherever you've been,

Tabby. Everybody here has been pretty worried about you, you know. Are you hungry? You want to go inside for a bite to eat?"

"Oh, Aunt Jessica, I just don't know." She looked around as if she were seeing the place for the first time. "I mean, I don't want to see anyone or maybe I don't want...."

"Don't want to be seen just yet?" Jessica finished the thought for her.

Tabby bit her trembling lower lip, casting a nervous look over her shoulder.

"It's not a problem. You're home and you are safe now. Come on. We'll sit in the back. Ben, go ask Fred to bring us...what would you like?" She slid a protective arm around the thin quaking shoulders as she guided her in the front door. "How about a cheeseburger and a milk shake?"

A silent yet compliant Tabby Darling nodded, walking beside her aunt and uncle.

"Here, you go on to the rest room in back there and wash your face," Jessica continued. "That's bound to make you feel a little better. We'll get the food. You want it to go? We can take it along with us if you'd rather. Ben, will you get that?"

As soon as her husband rejoined her at the table where they waited, Jessica began to lay out a plan. "That girl is exhausted and about half-starved, too, from the look of her. What do they feed people in California these days? Or do they? I bet she hasn't eaten in days. Oh, Ben. I remember all too well what it's like to be young and on the road all alone. We'll get her something to eat and take her home to get a bath and a nice long nap in a good comfy bed. Then you go out and see Becky and let her know she's here and safe and...."

Tabby rejoined her aunt with a scrubbed face and a shy smile as Ben picked up a white paper sack at the front counter. "Come on." He ushered the two of them toward the door. "My new pickup is right out back, Tabby. Let's go home."

* * * * *

"What do you mean she's here?" Becky all but screamed at her brother across the front counter of the Darling Family Campground. Despite covering the camp office for her grown son, Jesse, while he worked on the addition of more camping sites on the far north end of their campground, Becky was ready to pick up and go as fast as her brother told her. "When? Where is she, Ben? Is she all right?"

"She's fine, Becky, she's just fine. Pretty tired from what I can tell but that's probably just from riding on a Greyhound bus the last couple of days and nights."

"Oh, poor thing! How in the world…." She shook her head, her eyes filling with tears. "How long have you known? Why didn't you tell me—you know, we've been worried sick."

Ben Darling held up his hands in mock surrender. "Honestly, she just called me last night…well, early this morning, really. Felt like the sheriffin' days again, getting a call at that hour. I started to call you but you know, *your friend, Jessica*…." He grinned as he hesitated to let his words sink in. While his older sister might fuss at him, he knew she would say a lot less about anything Jessica decided. "She said we'd best make sure she really was on the bus before we got your hopes up for no good reason and after I thought about it, I couldn't say she was wrong."

He glanced around, thankful there was no one else in the camp store with them. He motioned his sister out from behind the glass counter, filled with a variety of candies, toiletries, and small travel trailer repair items.

"Listen, to be honest, she just looks wore out. We took her to our house where she got a hot bath and was laying down for a nap in a real bed when I left. Jessica said she would stay there with her and suggested I come tell you so you'd know where she is and that she's safe. She's been with some bunch out there in San Francisco. That was about all I could get out of her. I didn't want to push too hard with her just getting home and all, but the main thing is she's here and she's all in one piece. I've seen a lot of young ones passing through here over the years that looked a lot worse, if you know what I mean. She was hungry. I'll say that. We bought her a cheeseburger and a milk shake at the bus station and I think she had inhaled it all by the time we passed Highway 5 going toward Lake of the Ozarks!"

He reached out and embraced his big sister before she could start to cry again. "Relax, Sis. She'll be fine. I'm sure of it."

"From your lips to God's ear." Becky sighed with a tentative smile. She leaned back against the front of the counter. "Now, let's see. I've got so much to do. I need to get home and change the sheets on her bed and put it all right for her, you know? Where is Jesse anyway? He told me he was just going down to those new camp sites to look over where they were putting in the electrical connections. Marcia had to take the baby to the doctor this afternoon and he said he didn't have anybody to watch the store, but honestly, I need to get home so I can—"

"Hold on, Sis. Tabby is good where she is. There's no reason to get in a big fuss. It'd be my guess she'll sleep right through the night where she's at. Let's give her that. She'll be fine with me and Jessica, you know that." He plowed on despite the dubious look he saw cross Becky's face. "Give the girl a little breathing room is all I'm saying. She's not going anywhere for now. Listen. I've got to go. I've got some cows to check on yet this evening, a couple more are ready to calve and I'd best give them a look before the day is over."

He leaned over and gave an unconvinced Becky a quick peck on the cheek. "Don't worry. I'll call you tomorrow, early, I promise. Maybe even this evening if I find out anything more. For now, just know she's fine and most important of all, she's safe." And with that, he was out the front door.

Back in his truck, he was hopeful that everything he had said was true. He knew Becky was anxious to bring her daughter home but he had also seen on more than one occasion that like so many mothers and daughters, the two were not always good together. He couldn't understand it really. He and Jessica had finished raising her younger sister and brother, Grace and Gabe, years before, but they had not had any children of their own.

Married during the Depression years while he was already working for the sheriff's department, there had never seemed to be a good time nor enough money to actively pursue having their own babies. It wasn't like there weren't kids in their home. He felt like their nieces and nephews, Becky's twins, Jesse and Lizabeth, in addition to Tabby as well as Esther's three boys had grown up in their house as much as in their parents' homes. Grace and Joey's son, J. Junior, also loved staying at Aunt Jessica and Uncle Benji's house when he was growing up and then, of course, on more than one occasion, Jessica had stepped forward and kept different prisoners' kids briefly when their parents had landed in jail. Still, he wondered. Grace, for all practical purposes, was his daughter and now he worried her heart was broken as her son, J. Junior, had come home from Viet

Nam in a wheelchair.

Ben banished the thought, trying to concentrate on the next best move concerning Tabby. Obviously, she shouldn't be allowed to avoid her own parents for any length of time, although he got the definite impression, she wouldn't mind doing so. He thought about his father, Zeb Darling. How Ben wished he was here right now so he could ask his advice. After all, he and his mother, Hannah, had raised four children at Bennett Spring. Jake and Becky were grown, ages nineteen and eighteen, when the park was first established more than forty years ago. Ben still remembered much of the controversy at that time, even though he was only eleven when officials from Jefferson City arrived to look over the area, including the now long gone town of Brice, Missouri.

J.C., Becky's husband, was one of those officials who first came here in 1924. Benji, as he was known by his family and neighbors back then, was most impressed by the flashy car that his future brother-in-law drove, although it actually belonged to a state senator. The baby of the family, Esther was born later that same year. Yes, his folks had raised four kids over the course of more than twenty years. His dad would have known exactly how to best handle this situation, he mused. It was still hard to believe Zeb Darling was gone and that, too, Ben was certain, was part of Tabby's problem.

As the youngest girl, Tabby held a special place in Zeb's heart and the two had spent much time together hunting, fishing, hiking, or just 'hangin' out', as Tabby characterized it. Zeb died in the woods, a heart attack while hunting late in the season, "just where he would've wanted to" as his wife, Hannah, put it when he was found.

He passed away right before Christmas and it was after the holiday when Tabby and her friends were supposed to be on their way back to college that things took a detour. After another row with her mother, instead of returning to classes, these college kids had simply headed west. He had resolved a lot of puzzling investigations over his years as the county sheriff but young people and the things they did would always be the unsolvable mystery. He didn't understand it but maybe the fact that he and Jessica had never had any babies of their own wasn't such a bad thing after all.

* * * * *

A few days later, a brilliant afternoon of warm sunshine found three men in a field, just above the entrance of the state park. "So what do you think?" Father Clem spread his arms wide and turned around slowly, like a child showing off a new suit of clothes. "This is it!" He looked beyond the two men standing in front of him with an expectant smile.

"Well, it certainly is out here in the open, I'll say that." The elder more portly of the pair replied with a happy shrug as he stepped around gingerly in the high grass. "You say, he says we can have it, just like that?"

Father Clem laughed out loud at his companion's incredulous grin. "Yes, pretty much, just like that. The land belonged to his grandfather, Joseph, who left it, along with the larger farm across the road there, to Joey Schultz, our benefactor. The older Joseph died years ago and is buried up there on the hill on that same farm." He waved his arm in a northeasterly direction. "Joey sold the farm to the Shine family years ago and they still have it, but this little piece, a little over three acres, literally, was an oversight somehow. You know the Lord does work in mysterious ways. When Joey heard we were in need of a place, he remembered his grandfather was raised Catholic and the rest, as they say, is history."

"I think it's great!" Frankie O'Donnell's enthusiasm was unabashed. "Look at this, Uncle Bob," he addressed the third man. "There's some trees up here close but the majority of them are back aways, especially over there to the far left, leaving us a great area to work, to build. What do you think, Father? An altar? A shelter? A small church?"

"A shelter, a small chapel, let's call it, Frankie, but we can begin with an altar," the priest answered, enjoying the younger man's fire for the project. The cleric proceeded to take a wider walk around, followed somewhat more reluctantly by Frankie's uncle.

"Well, if you are sure, Father, this is what you want to do. I know we've been collecting funds for some time now but like I told you from the beginning, I'll get you whatever you want in the way of building materials. It won't cost you anything…."

"No, Bob, that's not the point. People are willing to donate and to work, too. That's the beauty of it, don't you see? Everyone contributes and then it belongs to everyone. That's what we want. In doing it this way, it helps pull the people back to the Church, back to God and that is what it is really all about. You know St. Matthew wrote, *where your heart is, there will your treasure be also.* That's the whole idea, to have people bring their real treasure, their hearts back to God."

"I guess I see what you're saying," came the dubious answer. "I just know it would be a whole lot easier to…"

"Ah, but the easier way isn't always the best way and the fact is, it's not usually God's way. Now you know that surely?" The priest's spirit was infectious.

"Yeah, you're right," Bob McCleary grinned. "Man, there's

nothing more aggravating than a priest who is always right."

"Always? Hardly." Father Clem snorted. "Every now and then will do, thank you."

"Well, it's a wonderful site." Frankie rejoined the two and the conversation after a short walk around. "First thing, we'll need to get a lawn mower out here and cut the grass. Let's see, where? Is this the general area you are talking about for the building, right?" He turned away from the two others as he indicated an area a bit closer toward the park. "You've got the plans there in your office, Father. I've seen those papers you keep all rolled up by the door."

"Well, there is a set of plans one of the couples from Sugar Creek, a little town up by Kansas City, had brought by some time ago. They had an architect friend draw them up. Nothing fancy but we don't need anything too dramatic. Just a simple place to worship with a roof so on the rainy days we could still have Mass. Your uncle's seen them."

"Oh, many a time. Yes, we've got plans. Now look, Father, right over here would probably be your best bet, what with the lay of the land, so as to get the best drainage. That way, your drive could come right along this way...."

The two older men walked together but a quick movement across the road caught Frankie's eye. She was moving fast, too fast. Even from a distance, he could see she was upset, her full length blond hair flowing down her back, but the question was why. Was it an emergency of some sort? He wasn't sure but for some reason, he had to know.

"I'll catch up," he called after the other two who seemed to take no note as he peeled off in a new direction. Despite his imperfect gait, he could still cover ground at a respectable rate when he wanted. He reached the road at the westernmost end of the new tract, just as she started down the hill toward the state park.

"Hey." He crossed the road but she barely seemed to notice. "Is there a fire or something? You seem to be in a pretty big hurry."

"What?" She glanced at him, dragging the back of her hand across her eyes as she did so. "What fire?"

"That's what I was asking you," he continued, falling into step beside her. His longer legs allowed him to keep up without too much effort. "You were walking...let's see, how did I hear one of my uncle's friends put it the other day? Like a house a-fire." He was surprised but pleased he had managed to recall the colorful bit of Ozark phrasing.

She laughed softly despite her still serious expression. "Yeah, like a house a-fire. That sounds like somebody around here."

"So?" He asked again. "Is there one? A house on fire somewhere?"

"What? No." She snorted, glancing down at her feet and his and then, deliberately slowing her stride, as she took in his small but noticeable limp. "There's no fire. I was just aggravated really." They continued walking.

"Which way?" he asked as they approached the fork in the road, one road leading to the spring and the other toward the Bennett Spring Park Store and Dining Lodge.

"Oh, I don't know. I don't care!" She spit out the words. "I just had to get out of that house for a little while." She stopped without warning which left him almost stumbling. "Where are you going? And an even better question, why?"

"Why? Well, now that is a good question. Here, let's go this way." He pointed to the left and she complied but more slowly now, contemplating him with a new wariness. "I guess the best answer would be the truth." He hesitated, afraid that the truth might sound too creepy to her. "The truth would be I saw a pretty girl headed out in a hurry and for just a minute or two, I thought she might be in some kind of trouble."

"Trouble? What does that mean?" She frowned, continuing to watch him closely.

"I don't know exactly," he admitted with a sheepish grin. "You looked—well, upset, I guess would be the best way to put it and I just wanted..." He frowned and heaved a small sigh. "I just wanted to see if there was anything I could do."

She laughed again and he relished the sweet sound of it, like a newly discovered brook bubbling over rocks in a stream. "Well, that is kind of you, but no, there is nothing you can do. Nothing anyone can do really." They reached the spring branch and she bent down and scooped up a couple of small rocks. She fired the first one into the stream, her agitation still apparent. She was about to pitch the second into the water when she pulled herself up short and glanced around in a guilty fashion.

"Oh, good grief, what am I thinking?"

"What?"

"What?! Throwing rocks in the spring branch, that's what! Fortunately, there are no fishermen close by right now." She took a second look around, like a child caught with her hand in the proverbial cookie jar. "My father would have a fit if he saw me right now." She giggled with the back of her hand to her mouth as she continued at a more leisurely pace toward the spring. "He's a big trout fisherman and as anybody in my family can tell you, *you do not throw rocks in the spring branch.*"

"I see." He nodded in mock seriousness, a grin tugging at the corners of his mouth.

"You don't fish?"

"Well, not since moving here."

"Moving here? You live here? I thought you were a tourist, a visiting fisherman, like everybody else."

"No. I moved here a few months ago. And you? You said a house, so you're not in a tent or a camper either, are you?"

"No." She shook her head, with a little smile. "I just like the spring. It's a good place to go when you need to figure things out. You know what I mean? Ever since I was a little girl, I've always loved to come down here when I've got troubles and of course, it's right on the way to my grandma and grandpa's house...." She stopped speaking and swallowed hard.

"Your grandparents live close by?" Frankie was impressed. "You really do live here, don't you?"

"Raised right up the road you just came down. Our farm is right up the hill there." She pointed over his shoulder. "So what were you doing up there, across the way? If you're not a fisherman...."

"We, my uncle and I, we are over there helping Father Clem figure out—"

"Oh, my gosh, you're one of those Catholics!" she blurted out and then immediately clapped her hand over her mouth.

CHAPTER 3

Arms tightly folded across her chest, Becky Shine stood on the back deck of her family home and stared at the woods behind the house. She tried taking a couple of deep breaths. Her husband, J.C., joined her, full coffee mugs in both hands.

"Here," was all he said as he handed her one and sat down in a nearby lawn chair to take a sip of his own. After several more moments of silence, he spoke again. "Find something new out there?"

That brought a smile to her face. She pulled up a lawn chair next to his. "I just don't know, J.C. It doesn't seem to matter what I do or say, as far as she is concerned, it's wrong. She came out yesterday afternoon and it all went well. You were here."

"Yes," he nodded slowly.

"And then she went back to Ben and Jessica's and she came back today. I took it that she was thinking of moving home, where she belongs, mind you. At some point I asked her about Jake, if maybe she had checked around and tried to find out anything about him while she was out there in California. It's been so long since we've heard anything, even when Pa died, we didn't hear—well, anyway, that didn't set well with her. I didn't mean anything by it but I could see just the question upset her so I let it drop." She frowned into her coffee as if there was something there she didn't like.

"Then Ma said something about her house and I didn't realize that Tabby didn't know Ma's move here with us was permanent. When Ma told her we were selling the old house to the park folks, Tabby really got shook up. She's been gone for months now but it certainly never occurred to me she'd get that upset about it. I don't understand. First, she's gone to school, then off running in California so what does she think, that we are frozen in time? Things change here, just like everywhere else. Oh, maybe not as fast as at the college in Springfield or in busy California but nothing stays the same. Why can't she see that? The next thing I know she stormed out the front door and I've got Ma, sitting here asking what's going on. I tell you, J.C., sometimes I just don't know."

J.C. leaned back, continuing to nurse his coffee. "I'm thinking the reaction you saw has a lot less to do with you and a great deal more to do with Tabby's own guilt."

"Guilt?"

"She's a bright girl, Becky. We've always known that but for some reason, she's often found herself in what she views as a difficult position. She's the baby of the family, eight years younger than the twins, a place she has long both resented and yet often milked for all it's worth." He grinned at silent memories, an expression that brought a smile to his wife's face as well.

"Yes, you're right."

"The only one who ever seemed to know exactly how to

handle Miz Tabby, as he called her, was your father. He had her figured out from day one and she was the same with him. When he died, I'm afraid it left a mighty big hole in our girl's heart. She was still so upset over J. Junior going off to Viet Nam. There are a few years between those kids but I swear, most of the time, you wouldn't know it. Half the time, he was a friend she grew up with and half the time, she was his babysitter. Still, when he left for the Army, it was pretty difficult for her. I don't even know if she knows he's back and I certainly don't think she knows any more than that."

"And does she think she's the only one who's hurting?" Becky's voice rose in exasperation. "We all miss Pa terribly. Look at my mother, sitting there in our living room. She's absolutely lost. Ben and Esther and me. Zeb was our father! And now J. Junior? I don't even know what to think! It's been a heck of a year is all I can say! Does she think she's got a monopoly on heartbreak? I mean, at least my father, got to live his whole life to the full, but J. Junior, he's barely twenty-one years old, for heaven's sake." Becky's emotions rose in her throat, cutting off her words.

"She isn't thinking, Becky." Her husband leaned forward and rested a hand on her knee. "That's the whole point. She wasn't thinking when she lit out for California. She just saw a quick escape, an adventure perhaps, something to take her away from all of the pain she felt here. Add in what she views as the pressure of college and…"

He hesitated for a moment before continuing. "Let's face it. Our baby girl has never been the best when it comes to the high pressure situation. That's when Miz Tabby tends to fold and I'm thinking that's just what she did this time, running off the way she did. And then what? We don't know the details yet, but I imagine we'll learn more later. I know Ben's already told me he's going to contact some different ones out there in the San Francisco area to see what he can find out. I think it's pretty plain, she didn't find California to be the promised land she expected and now the prodigal, if you will, has come home. Maybe your question about Jake had her feeling like she was somehow a disappointment to us. Who knows? She may not have even thought of him or looked into his situation. And maybe she did and there was nothing to find. This is Jake we are talking about." He added that last with a gentle squeeze to her knee.

"Yes, it's Jake." She shook her head, a frown knitting her brow at the change in the conversation. "I keep hoping maybe he'll turn back up like he did once years ago after crossing Kansas during those dust bowl years." She heaved a deep sigh. "And maybe he'll never turn up again. I would just like to have something to tell Ma. To lift her spirits, even a little."

"I know." He stood up and pulled her to her feet as well. "It's just not meant to be right now, my love."

A ringing phone from the house interrupted him before he could say more.

"I've got to get that." Becky hurried inside, calling back over her shoulder, "Ma will never hear it."

"Yes, yes, just a moment, please." She walked back out on the deck. "J.C., it's the state department and they are asking for you. What in heaven's name? Surely, they are not calling you back to work after all these years." The fear and concern contorted her face in a way that pierced his heart.

"What? Oh, surely not. I'm sure it's some sort of mistake." He threw a protective arm around her shoulders and walked her back inside. He picked up the corded phone from where it lay on the kitchen counter.

"This is J.C. Shine. How can I help you?"

He sounded so official, Becky thought. So much in charge and right now she was so thankful for that attitude because she had not felt this "out of it," as Tabby liked to say, since *she* was a teenager. What was it about life in general lately? For years, she had been the one in charge of her household in so many ways, during the war years when the children were smaller and J.C. was in Washington D.C., working for the government in areas she still wasn't sure about. He had written a couple of moderately successful spy thrillers but he assured her they were totally based on what others had told him in his years there and on "a lot of imagination," he always added with wink. She never knew exactly how much to believe him and decided it was just better to leave it at that.

They had managed to raise the twins, Jesse and Lizbeth, through their teen-aged years but then there was Tabby. Becky thought the late 1950s were a headache with Lizbeth and her friends all crazy about Elvis Presley and Jesse with his head constantly stuck under the hood of a vehicle that he was fixing. Did she ever see that boy without his hands black with car grease? But then came Tabby and a bunch of British boys, the Beatles, the Rolling Stones, the Dave Clark Five, not to mention her love for the Beach Boys. Nothing ever seemed to be quite in control again, the way it once had been. But now J.C.'s answers to the mysterious voice on the telephone were a much bigger concern.

"Yes, sir. Yes, I do know him and his father, the whole family really. We were friends in school years ago. Yes, I was back there, let me see, several years ago, before Castro and his government took over, it would have been...." He covered the phone. "Becky, when were we last in Havana?"

"Nineteen fifty-seven, exactly ten years ago. I was just thinking about that the other day. Why?"

"Looks like it was in fifty-seven, we were last there, just visiting old friends. I remember her, Maria Consuelo Rios. I've kept an eye on the news over the years as the occasional fishing boat was mentioned that had made it to Florida but it never occurred to me..."

He was quiet, listening intently for more than a minute before replying.

"Yes, sir. I did work for the department but that was twenty years ago, during and right after the war. It had absolutely nothing to do with my connection to Cuba. That is all family related, due to my father's work when I was growing up. He was involved with some of the hotels, way back around nineteen hundred eighteen and twenty, long before anybody had ever heard of Fidel Castro. My work during the war was much later, in the European theatre, mopping up the German mess. They are two totally separate and unrelated circumstances. Just makes for a lot of explanations for me but nothing more. You are welcome to check it out, which I'm sure you have or you will. If you contact retired General Horace B. Griswold, he can clear up any doubts you might have, I assure you. Now what about Coni, uh, Consuelo? How is she? What can you tell me about her?"

He listened a few moments more, as Becky fluttered around in the kitchen, wiping down the table, the counter, straightening a nearby collection of pens and pencils and notepads that were already in perfect order.

"All right then. Yes, of course, she can. A couple more days? Fine. You'll be in touch and let me know the next move. Can I talk to her? Uh, huh. I see. Well, yes, please let me know. You have this number. Have her call here and

36

reverse the charges, if that makes it easier or faster. Or if you'll be so kind to call back with a number where I can reach her that would work, too. Thank you. I look forward to hearing back from you soon."

He hung up the phone, still deep in thought.

"Well—" Becky could stand it no longer. "What was that all about?"

"Maria Consuelo, Miguelito's daughter. Remember her? The family's nickname for her, Coni, sounds like 'Connie'."

"Well, of course, I remember her! She was such an adorable little thing when we were down there, daughter of your best friend from school. Where is she? Is she all right?"

"Yes, I think she is but apparently we are not the only ones with a runaway daughter. She's in Miami. The Coast Guard picked her up with a boat full of Cuban refugees yesterday. The man on the phone, a Jeff Dugan from the state department, says she had a plastic bag with my name and address and a couple of pictures in it. She said her father and grandfather told her if she made it safely to the US to find me and I would take care of her. Becky..." He stopped speaking for a moment as the full weight of the situation came to rest. "Becky!" He scooped her up in his arms in a jubilant hug and swung her around, her feet off the ground. "She's in Miami and they want to know if she can stay here with us!"

* * * * *

What is it with this day? Tabby scrambled to pull together a coherent thought that didn't make her sound like a complete dolt. First, her mother and now this guy. Yeah, this guy. Who was he anyway?

"Oh, my gosh," she stammered. "I didn't mean that to sound…or at least, I didn't mean anything by it…oh, that's not right either…."

He shook his head as a wide grin spread over his face at her discomfort. "Well, let's see. I've been called a lot of things in that regard. Fish head, fish eater, Latin chanter…so, *one of those Catholics*, all things considered, is not so bad."

Her face flushed with such heat, she felt certain she might burst into flames at any moment. Maybe that would be just as well if she did, she thought as she hung her head.

"I am so sorry," was all she could manage to whisper. "I certainly didn't mean anything bad."

"Of course, you didn't. I'm Catholic, but don't take on so. It quit being a bad thing around the time the country finally elected John Kennedy as President, right?"

She looked up and saw that his smile was genuine, his dark eyes twinkling.

"This is the spring, huh?" They stopped to contemplate the blue hole with its ever moving waters, bubbling up soothingly from unknown depths.

"It is." She snatched the chance to talk about something else. "I love it. The water just comes up so gentle like, always the same, even in flood times. If you come here then, you can see it, underneath it all. It's so steady, so reliable. There aren't many things like that in the world anymore, you know?"

"What do you mean?"

"I dunno. Watching the news, right now, it just feels like maybe the whole world is coming apart at the seams. All the protests, people marching in the streets, blacks and whites fighting in some of the cities, the government types keep lying to us, saying whatever they think people want to hear, and then of course, so much of it is about this war. A war that is clear on the other side of the world. Our young men are dying over there, coming home in boxes while over here, we are all freaked out, fighting one against the other in our own streets."

His thoughts riveted back to the bustling streets of Saigon. "Wow, that's some pretty heavy stuff you're talking about there. What do you know about it all?" He wasn't often caught by surprise but this girl had done exactly that.

"Too much," she sniffed. "And in another way, probably not enough. I've always been able to come here when I couldn't figure things out and then of course, go on up to my grandpa's house and talk to him but now…." Her words drifted off but in such a way that he didn't feel he dared ask anything more.

The two of them silently watched the water, both held captive by their own private thoughts, holding their restless spirits far from the peace offered by the waters of the blue spring before them.

"I'm sorry," she apologized once again. "You must think I'm a complete freak."

"No, no that was not what I was thinking at all," he answered evenly. "But it did occur to me that my uncle and Father Clem might be waiting on me. We were over there trying to figure out exactly where and how to build a chapel on the land donated to us by Joey Schultz. You probably know him, with living around here all your life? I moved down here from St. Louis a few months ago to work for my uncle's construction business so I still don't know a lot of people."

"Joey? Joey gave you the land? Well, how about that?" She

rolled that pearl of newly discovered information around for a moment. "I've known Joey all my life. He's the mail carrier here, drives the gold-colored Jeep, stuffing the mail boxes all around."

"Oh, I see. Well, I probably ought to be getting back. I just sort of wandered off and they may be wanting to go back to Lebanon."

"That's fine." She brightened up as she turned to face him. "I should go, too." It wasn't really true but she liked talking to him. It was so easy, so natural. "Come on. I don't think the spring has any specific answers for me today. Besides, it will always be here. That's the nice thing about it. It's always here."

They walked together, back the way they had come. The steep grade of the hill coming out of the park precluded any further conversation and while both were young and in good physical condition, neither was inclined to slow their pace, climbing in almost silent competition, one with the other. As they reached the place where they had first met, Frankie could see his Uncle Bob and Father Clem, standing at the edge of the narrow ribbon of highway, watching the two of them as they approached.

His uncle wore a slight frown but Father Clem's face held a bemused smile. "So there you are! Well, now I understand why you disappeared."

"Uh, well, yes." Now it was Frankie's turn to blush. "Uncle Bob, Father Clem, this is…" He was still huffing a bit from their uphill hike as they came to a stop. "This is…" He stopped, further embarrassed by the realization that he did not know the name of the young woman beside him.

"Tabby." She held out her hand in the time-honored gesture of friendship. "Tabby Shine."

Frankie managed to complete the introductions without further stumbling.

"Tabby. Tabitha?" Father Clem shook her hand. "Now that is a very blessed name. Speaks of a very special person. You know who she was?"

"A Biblical character," she shrugged.

"Oh, she was much more than just a character. She was a blessing to the poor of her community, her friends, and all who knew her. So much so that Saint Peter, when he came across her in his travels, brought her back to life after she had died. In other words, God gave her a second chance at life to continue doing so much good. That's quite a namesake you've got yourself there."

The priest's explanation of her name was a pleasant surprise. "I don't think I ever knew that. My grandma told me the name Tabitha was Dorcas in Greek and I never liked the sound of that very much," she giggled.

"Well, Dorcas may not translate so well in English these days," the priest continued, "but both of them mean gazelle or deer. Now that's certainly a lovely name for a charming young lady."

"Oh," she looked down, caught by surprise once more.

"Well, you know this land that you all are looking over…." She stepped over the edge of the road into the higher grass. "It is one of the favorite places to see the deer around here. They are always up here, especially back along the tree line over there. Wild turkeys, too."

"Named after the deer and she knows where they gather. How fascinating!" the priest responded.

"Interesting, yes, well," Bob McCleary interrupted. "I hate to say so, but I need to get back to town, Father. I'll check in with you tomorrow. Did you say you were going to hold Mass here this Saturday, instead of close to the water?"

"Yes, I think so." Father nodded, apparently deep in thought. "What do you think?" He turned to look at Frankie who was still watching Tabitha as she walked through the grass.

"Okay, well then, I'll get a lawnmower out here in the next day or two and cut us a clear space," Frankie answered. "You'll set up the folding table, just like along the spring branch, right?"

The priest nodded as his eyes drifted away toward the back tree line. "Yes, yes, I think so."

"Tabby," Frankie called as he glanced at his uncle's back who was making his way to the pickup truck they'd driven from Lebanon. "I've got to go. It was good to..." he glanced sideways, but then realized that Father Clem's attention was elsewhere. "It was nice walking with you."

She turned and waved, shielding her eyes from the sun with her other hand. "And with you," she called back.

Frankie hopped into the driver's seat, hardly glancing at his uncle who was already tucked comfortably into the truck's passenger side. As he backed up, his uncle spoke up.

"Well, you didn't take long to find a young lady from one of the best known Bennett Spring families, that's for sure."

"Tabby Shine? What do you mean?"

"Tabby Shine. Her mama is Becky Darling, who is married to J.C. Shine, the writer. Those Darlings have lived here a long time, all the way from back when there was still a town of Brice out this way. How did you manage that?"

* * * * *

42

Tabby continued to wander around in the high grass before turning toward home. The truth was she was hesitant to go back. She didn't have any answers for her mother, her grandmother, and, most especially, she had no answers for herself.

"What did you know about it all?" that guy had asked. That guy, that Catholic guy. Oh, my heavens, she realized. She had told him her name when the time for introductions came but she hadn't gotten his. Irish. He looked Irish. Her grandmother, Fionna, her father's mother, was Irish. She would call him Irish, she thought, since she didn't have any other name for him.

Names. The priest gave her a new definition of hers and yet the last time she had officially been asked her name, she had lied. Tabby Darling, she had told the cops that morning in Seeker's apartment. Her thoughts drifted back to California. Seeker had been so good to her at a time when she needed it so badly and yet, once the authorities were there, she got scared.

How did things get so crazy? She wasn't the first one to go to college without a clue as to what she wanted to do with an education once she got it. She knew she didn't want to be like Lizbeth, her older sister. Everyone was so proud of her and her accomplishments, her and her Ph.D husband, Brian. They lived in Columbia where Lizbeth spent her days in a classroom with a bunch of kids. Like her sister, Tabby had studied to become a teacher to a great extent because she really didn't know what else to choose. She didn't want to be a nurse like her Aunt Esther or a social worker like her Aunt Jessica. I may not know what I want, Tabby's random thoughts continued to roam, but I know what I don't!

She also knew she didn't want to stay here, like her brother, Jesse, Lizbeth's twin. He ran the family campground. He had actually started it with a bunch of his buddies, camping down the hill from their farmhouse while he was still in high school and from there, it just kept growing. She couldn't stay here, living under her parents' scrutiny like that. And now she found out her grandmother was selling off the old house. How could she?

It was ridiculous, she knew, but she turned to walk back down the hill that she had just climbed with Irish. Maybe she would feel better if she went down to Grandpa Zeb and Granny Hannah's house herself. She had already been on quite the walk this morning, but it wasn't like she had so many more important things to do. She cruised past the dividing road with its Bennett Spring sign and the spring, turning east up the trail away from the spring.

The familiar path was a true comfort to her feet as well as her soul. The rocky trail was punctuated with tree roots, stone outcroppings, and little cavities, some of them actual openings into animal hiding places, for minks, muskrats, and other river critters as Grandpa always called them. It was enough to keep her eyes constantly glancing at her feet to make certain she didn't take a tumble into the water slipping along just below. The trees in their full greenery now were laced with tangles of brown grapevines, thick and thin, that tied the whole of the woods together somehow. Buttercups, spring beauties, dog-toothed violets, and yellow cinquefoils pushed their tiny heads through the gray and brown forest litter decorating the ground like bright bits of colored confetti.

At first glance upon her arrival at the house, it looked just the same and yet, Zeb should have been on the porch in his favorite oak slat rocker and Granny Hannah should have been inside, cooking up something special on her wood stove. Her mother still complained about how often she and Uncle Ben and even Aunt Esther had tried to replace that stove with a more modern electric or even propane model but her grandmother wouldn't have it. Granny said she knew exactly how all of her best, from cornbread to blackberry or peach cobbler and even gooseberry pie, came out using that wood stove and Zeb's answer was he wasn't about to meddle with perfection! How do you argue with that, she smiled to herself.

Walking up to the porch, she decided at the last minute against going inside. She didn't want to see it, empty and abandoned, lifeless, the exact opposite of how she had always experienced this house filled with love and laughter over the years. She made her way around the outside and stopped briefly at Blue's old dog house. He was Grandpa's last old foxhound who had died a few years ago and this time, for the first time, Zeb had refused to get another. The little dog house where she had played, crawling inside with Blue, right there beside her, was falling in on itself. She turned away sharply, wishing to escape one more unpleasant reminder of the passing of time. She wandered up the way toward the big garden and was surprised at its condition. As she understood it, Granny Hannah had already been at her parents' home for weeks so she couldn't imagine that she had been up here to plant and tend what she saw before her.

The garden was Grandpa Zeb's pride and joy. He spent hours planting, weeding, and tending the tomatoes, beans, corn, melons, potatoes, lettuce, beets, radishes, spinach, parsnips, turnips, squash, zucchini, broccoli, cauliflower, and cucumbers. And there it all was, laid out in perfect symmetry, like it always was, always had been, year after year. Much of it was in raised beds of various sizes because Grandpa said the Ozarks was mostly rock with a little thin layer of soil stretched over the top. The corn, potatoes, and beans were in rows in the back, while the melons were planted in several large tractor tires along the sides, where the wandering vines could meander all about. The strawberry patch took up one whole side. All of it was surrounded by thin wires bearing a rag tag collection of tin pans, bright ribbons, and tiny bags of "secret things" Grandpa Zeb said helped to ward off the deer and other critters.

The corn was a quarter way grown, lush and green, the spinach was begging to be picked and the lettuce had already lost some of its luster due to the growing heat of the late spring sun. The tomatoes were full of bright yellow blossoms, including her personal favorite, the cherry tomatoes. She walked slowly around, touching the wooden stakes, each one beside a thriving tomato plant. She bent over and plucked out a few weeds. The garden was growing but there were a few more weeds than Grandpa had ever allowed. Oh, how she had complained as a child about weeding the garden! It was hot, sweaty work and she always hated it but right now, what she wouldn't give to be back here, weeding this blessed garden with her dear grandfather, standing nearby as he contemplated whether to plant more beans or thin the lettuce or just hoe around what was already growing and let it go at that.

Grandpa Zeb was gone before Christmas and she couldn't imagine that her grandmother had done all this. She came out and helped Grandpa occasionally and she was always there when it was time to pick beans or tomatoes but generally, Tabby didn't associate her with the gardening to any great extent. So who? It certainly wouldn't have been her parents. Her mother knew how to garden, there was no doubt, but she wouldn't have done this nor her father. She sniffed at that notion. Not his way. Ben had pulled him reluctantly into the cattle business but despite living on a farm the last of his growing up years, agricultural pursuits in general were not his strength. She pulled a few more weeds but a sense of being watched was suddenly overwhelming. She all but leaped to her feet, glancing around, hoping to see something, someone, while fearing the same but there was nothing to see. She didn't notice the high grass moving behind her as she began to retrace her steps away from the memories of her grandparents, back toward the state park.

She wondered vaguely why she had even bothered to come back this way. As she approached the spring once again, she noticed the string of tourists on horseback coming up the trail on the far side of the spring. Five horses of various colors, including a majestic-looking white lead horse, trailed single-file along the water's edge, preparing to cross the low water bridge. They were headed toward the little concrete block barn on the privately owned campground, just south of the spring.

"Tabby!" The lead rider suddenly whipped off her cowboy hat, revealing a headful of blond wavy curls, and waved it madly at a very surprised Tabby. "It's so good to see you!"

CHAPTER 4

"Sally Ann?" Tabby waited as the line of horses drew up beside her where she stood on the low water bridge beside the spring. "Sally Ann, how are you?"

"I'm fine. Working at the moment." She smiled and waved at the line of riders behind her in an overly enthusiastic fashion. "Hey, come talk with me over at the resort. Come on over and climb up on one of those rocks up there."

Tabby quickly complied and Sally Ann guided her horse up next to the large rock. She and Tabby clasped arms as a mounted Sally Ann glided past, and Tabby seamlessly slid up behind Sally Ann's saddle, to ride double, her arms locked around Sally Ann's waist.

They both giggled. "I haven't done that in ever so long," Sally Ann laughed. "Nice job!"

"You, too," Tabby answered back as they proceeded on to the resort a short distance past the spring.

"Aunt Willa Jean will be so tickled to see you!" Sally Ann continued to bubble.

Tabby dismounted first, sliding down the horse's left side again holding tight to Tabby's arm until her toes touched solid ground once they reached the corral area. Looping her horse's reins over the nearby corral post, Sally Ann scooted back to help each of the tourists from their mount, making certain all did so without any problems.

"Great ride!" Tabby overheard one exclaim.

"Thank you so much!" Another lady told Sally Ann. "I haven't been on a horse in years. Yours are nice and gentle."

"So glad you had a good time," Sally Ann responded to each one. "Hope you enjoy the rest of your stay here at Bennett Spring. Take care now."

As fast as the last one had walked away, the cowgirl turned to her friend. "How are you?" she squealed. "I heard you were in California. So how was that?"

Tabby shrugged with a smile at her friend's exuberance. "Okay, I guess. Not exactly what I expected."

"Really? I think it would be so exciting to go out there. Geez, I can't imagine!" She continued to chatter as she stepped back to her horse. "Easy, Dancer," she cooed as she took a brush to him and then looked back over her shoulder at Tabby, picking up where she left off. "I mean, the beach. Are there really Hippies everywhere? That would be so cool! How was it?"

"Cold."

"Cold?"

"San Francisco is cold, I'm telling you. It is sunny but not very warm. More like a day in March a lot of the time, sunshine with a cool wind that'll surprise you."

"Really?" Sally Ann stepped back to survey her handiwork before moving on to the next horse. "Well, it's gotta be better than this. I'm telling you. I love the horses, you know, but some days...." She rolled her eyes with as much drama as she could manage. "This bunch was fine but some of these others can be pretty cranky and just plain dumb when it comes to horses. Then of course, you always get the guys who think they know everything about a horse because they watch all those television western shows!"

She laughed suddenly, surprising her friend. "But hey! Every job has its problems, right? So what are you doing, just wandering 'round? Been over to your Grandma's house? How's she's doing with losing your Grandpa and all? I am so sorry, Tabby. I didn't get back here for his funeral. I was up at Kansas City at school and all and you know..." She apparently caught a glimpse of the cloud that passed over Tabby's face at the mention of her grandparents.

The sweet smell of the horses, the creak of the leather and the stamp of their hooves on the dirt to discourage the flies sent a flood of memories washing over Tabby. Even the familiar sound of fresh manure hitting the ground behind her was more pleasant in its familiarity than not. Tabby picked up another brush from the nearby bucket that held brushes and curry combs and proceeded to brush the opposite side of the horse that Sally Ann was working on before answering. Her thoughts harkened back to the overcast afternoon when they buried Zeb, a day she couldn't catch her breath even though they were standing in the open air, in the small family cemetery beyond their house on the farm.

"I'm going back to Kansas City at the end of next week," Sally Ann prattled on. "Aunt Willa Jean isn't too happy with me about that, what with this part-time job and all, but Randy, you know, he's this guy I met up there this last year and he's really pretty special. He wants me to come up for the summer. I can get my old job back at this café across from the college campus. We can just spend a little time together, if you know what I mean, before school starts and we're back in that rat race again. I failed a couple of classes in the fall semester so I spent last semester here but I've signed up for summer classes and once they get going, there just doesn't seem to be any time for anything fun!" She winked coyly at her friend. "Of course, the folks don't know why I'm going back quite so early. I convinced 'em I need the time at the job and to get ready before classes start again.

"There." She stepped back and surveyed the bay's shining coat. "That looks pretty good." She moved on to the next horse, tied to the corral post and began again. "So what are you doing with yourself? You working or just living off your mom and dad for a while?" She flashed her dazzling smile, robbing her words of any offense.

"No, nothing really. I've only been back a few days and I'm actually staying with my Uncle Ben and my Aunt Jessica, closer to town." She hesitated and then quickly added, "My grandma just moved in with the folks so they are trying to get her all settled in. It was just easier to stay with my aunt and uncle." She told the quick lie, hoping to avoid being added to the local gossip circle, which seemed to be a constant here in their small community, she remembered.

"Hey, you were always riding the horses, just like me. Maybe you could take over here for me after I leave and that might get me out of hot water and help you out, too. You want to? There's nothing to it really. Just saddle and bridle the horses and take the folks who are here on a ride. I take 'em down along the far side of the stream there, all the way to the dam and back. Half these people have never been on a horse, I swear, so believe me, that's enough for them. You see some of them get off, actually walking bow-legged for a few minutes after they dismount. No joke!"

Sally Ann performed a hysterically funny pantomime to go along with her apt descriptions which made Tabby laugh despite her mood. "Oh, Sally Ann, I don't know. I haven't been on a horse since last summer and—"

"Are you kidding? This is like riding that bike people are always talking about. You've forgotten more about horses than most of the tourists know or want to know. Don't get me wrong. They're pretty nice folks, all things considered and truthfully, I mostly get the wives and the kids 'cuz the dads are too busy trout fishing, which makes sense. Aunt Willa Jean just takes their names and makes like a schedule so you might have only one ride a day or every other day, and some, none at all. It would be real convenient with you living right up the road there, if you move back home any time soon. She could just call you when she gets some folks scheduled. What do you say? It would sure get me off the hook and it's not like it's a full time job or anything. And if you're not doing anything, anyway—please, Tabby!"

Sally Ann's nonsensical mood was infectious. "Oh, all right, I'll talk to Miz Willa Jean. I guess it wouldn't hurt to take a couple of rides. So what do you do? Come down and saddle up however many you need and then ride 'em around for..."

"Thirty to forty-five minutes," Sally Ann added, "and that's about it. Nothing fancy. Like I said, most of the folks are happy to just have a nice little ride. It's always been a pretty place to ride, I'll give it that. Come on."

She accompanied Sally Ann inside the nearby tiny resort office to talk to Willa Jean, the owner, along with her husband, Ralph. It was good to see someone she knew who didn't ask her about California, she thought as she walked out the same door a half hour later. She meandered on along the spring branch, sticking close to the water's edge, headed toward the dam and its well-known waterfall.

She had heard Grandpa Zeb in his storytelling say that these waters had healing powers. Not the kind of waters that a person soaked in, like the hot springs of Arkansas. No, Zeb Darling claimed that Bennett Spring had the power to heal souls. He said he'd seen the power of Bennett Spring heal her Aunt Jessica when she came here from down along the Arkansas line outside of West Plains and that the same was true of her Aunt Esther, his youngest daughter. Zeb said when she came back home after World War II, she was only a shell of the girl who had run off to join up as a Navy nurse a few years before. Still, a couple months back home here and she was 'right as rain' he liked to say.

Just above the dam, with her toes at the water's edge, she wavered, considering the icy water, with the zany hope that any healing might inch its way up from her toes to her heart to her head. She could only hope that Grandpa Zeb was right.

* * * * *

Three days later, J.C. Shine was tucked snugly into a northbound airplane seat, contemplating the slim, dark-haired teen who slept fitfully in the seat next to him. He couldn't really believe she was here. Jeff Dugan, the state department employee, had called back the next day and said they had cleared her. She appeared to be just what she claimed, a refugee, someone simply fleeing Cuba for a better life and the US government had no problem with her going home with J.C. to the Ozarks, at least for the time being. He was told to keep them advised if there was any change in her status or if she left for any other destination. He spoke with Maria Consuelo briefly and afterwards, assured the official that he was certain neither of those would be an issue. The girl was simply looking for a safe haven, a home free of war, political intrigue, and its accompanying threats. She showed him the photographs she had in the plastic bag that Jeff Dugan had mentioned on the phone.

J.C. studied the two photos now in his hands that she brought with her, one of him and Becky, standing in front of palm trees and her family's home along with Miguelito and his wife, Pilar. The second one showed the two of them again, this time with Miguelito, his wife, his father, Miguel, and various other family members, including Connie and her older brother, Miguel Angel. How bittersweet to see Miguelito and his family again, after all these years, knowing all that had transpired in Cuba! He had worried about his friends, prayed for them but of course, like so many others, never heard a word from them or about them. Now, at least, he knew they were alive and had survived the revolution in Cuba. Perhaps he would soon know exactly how they were. How he would love to find a way to let his old friend know that his daughter was safe with people who would take good care of her. His heart wrenched at what his friend must be going through, wondering where she was now. He shuddered to think what they all must have been through to allow her to undertake the life-threatening journey that she had. He said a silent prayer of thanks that his daughter had only gone as far as California and that she was now back home.

J.C. took a few extra minutes and a handful of dimes to call Becky after their plane landed at Lambert Field Airport in St. Louis.

"Becky?" He still spoke louder into a pay telephone on a long distance call than he would have, had he been sitting in his own living room. "We're in St. Louis and getting ready to go find the car in the parking lot. We should be home in another few hours. Just wanted to let you know. We're fine. She's fine, I think. She's pretty tired, maybe a little confused and she hasn't said much yet but otherwise, she seems to be all right.

"Yes, yes, good. We'll see you in a little while."

Becky hung up the phone and turned around to see her mother watching her closely.

"So who's coming?" Hannah asked after a few seconds. "Who's coming home with J.C.?"

"Anybody home?" Tabby came in the front door, in her blue jeans, plaid button up blouse, cowboy boots and hat to match. "I just stopped in to say 'hi', coming back from running a trail ride in the park and—" She was talking as she walked in until she saw their faces. "What's going on?"

"Well, I'm not completely sure," Becky began, glancing at Tabby, "but I think your father is bringing home a girl from Cuba, a refugee, the daughter of his good friend Miguelito from his school days. Apparently, she was on a fishing boat with several others who managed to make their way across from Cuba to Florida. The authorities picked her up and called us a couple of days ago so your father went down yesterday to pick her up and bring her back here."

"Oh, my gosh, Mom!" Tabby's eyes were wide with surprise. "What is this all about?"

"Well, that's about all I know, really." Becky pushed her once blond, now nearly all white hair back from her forehead. "J.C. called last night from the hotel and said she had been hospitalized briefly because of dehydration and sunburn. Their boat was adrift for about five days after the engine conked out and they didn't have enough food or water for the eight people on board. I guess she didn't really know the others that well. They all have family in Miami but she came with photos and our name and address and that's about it. J.C. said he was going down there to see if he could get her out and bring her back here and I guess he did." She shook her head with a little smile. "I have no idea what happens now but your father probably does. He usually has a plan so I'll just wait and see."

"Mom, does she speak English? Is Dad going to be the only one who can talk to her?" Tabby was full of questions.

"I honestly don't know, Tabby. We'll just have to wait, like I said."

Hannah said nothing, but simply stared at her daughter.

Tabby drifted into the kitchen and plucked a banana from a bowl of mixed fruit sitting on the counter, which she peeled as she went back out the front door, deep in thought. She was starting to feel a bit better about being home on familiar territory and now the very ground seemed to be shifting under her once again. The truth was she had avoided actually moving back home as yet, still staying at Ben and Jessica's house. Amazingly, her mother had not said any more about it the last couple of days and now maybe, she would have something else to occupy her other than Tabby's personal situation.

She glanced across the thick green grass back toward the road and noticed the gathering vehicles on the other side where she had met that guy, the one she now called Irish, a few days before. She gulped down the last of the banana and tossed the peel behind her mother's rose bushes and headed down the drive. Close to the edge of the pavement, she peered across the road, looking for a singular familiar face.

"Tabby!" She jerked in surprise upon hearing her name and

looked further down the road, where she saw a man with auburn curls, waving wildly. "Hey, Tabby. How are you?" He covered the distance between them in short order despite his irregular gait and she crossed the road to meet him.

"So what are you doing?" he asked with a smile.

"Oh!" She looked down at her wrangler's outfit. "I forgot." She giggled. "I've been guiding a couple of trail rides for the resort just above the spring down below. I must look like a real cowgirl." She laughed again.

"You look great, like a real all-American girl. You look just like what a lot of folks overseas expect from us here in the Midwest and western states. They think we are all still cowboys and they want to know if there are Indians living nearby as well."

Her eyes widened in surprise as she continued to laugh. "You're joking?"

"No, I'm serious. They really do. When I was overseas with the Marines, it made me laugh, too. But then I found out they weren't kidding!"

She shook her head, still in disbelief. "So what are you doing here, Irish? Still figuring out where to build what?"

"Oh, no," he said. "Not today. We're getting ready to have Mass, our first one here on the new land. Irish, heh?"

"Well, you never did tell me your name, you know." She dropped her voice to a heavy whisper as she confided, "I couldn't just keep calling you that Catholic guy." She glanced around at the others gathering. "Hey, I should go so you can get ready or do whatever you do beforehand."

"What do you do before a church service?" he asked with a smile.

"What? Well, I guess, we, uh, stand around and visit with our friends." She frowned, thinking about her answer.

"And so do we. Want to come?"

"But I'm not Catholic."

"Does a person have to be a Methodist or Baptist to go to one of your worship services?"

"Church of God. And no, of course not but I'm not exactly dressed for a worship service either!"

"Well, you certainly don't have to be Catholic to come to Mass. And you have to see how these guys come dressed. This is the Bennett Spring Mass so people come in shorts, their waders and their fishing gear. You look great. Come on." He held out a hand which she took to cross over the ditch in front of her.

They climbed the short steep bank that ran along the paved road. True to his promise a few days before, Frankie had managed to cut a wide swath of grass, leaving a cleared area for those gathering. She immediately noticed a group of men tightly circled on the far side of the clearing, dancing and poking at the ground with a couple of sticks.

"Hey, stop it, Jim! Get it!"

"Stop him now. Don't let it get away!"

"I've got a shovel in the truck. I'll get it and we can kill it!" One of the men in the circle broke away to go after the tool as Tabby and Frankie hurried over to see what was causing the excitement.

"Oh, good grief!" Tabby rolled her eyes as she saw what their dance was really all about.

"It's a snake, Frankie!" One of the men cautioned. "Watch out now! Better step back, Miss!"

"What are they going to do?" Tabby shot a look of concern in her new friend's direction.

"Al went to his truck to get a shovel so we can kill it," one of others answered. "We can't have snakes up here during a Mass."

"They can't kill it!" Tabby hissed at her companion. "It's a salt and pepper snake."

"What?" Two of the men stopped to look at her.

"It's a salt and pepper snake," she repeated. "That's what we always called 'em as kids. It's actually a speckled king snake. Here." She stepped into the men's makeshift circle with the squirming two foot long serpent in their midst. She scooped up the reptile, took a few steps over to the uncut grass and tossed it gently into the high growth where it could make its escape.

"He won't hurt you. He's more scared of you than you are of him and besides, he'll run off the more dangerous snakes, like the copperheads, the only ones you really have to be worried about around here." She dusted her hands off against her jeans before stopping to look up at their shocked faces. "What?"

Frankie laughed out loud, watching the situation unfold. "Now, that's a homegrown Bennett Spring girl. Horsewoman trail guide who simply sweeps snakes out of her path."

"For heaven's sakes, it was just a little ol' king snake!" She blushed as the men broke up their circle, walking toward the latest arriving car, driven by Father Clem.

"I heard there are still snake-handlin' Pentecostals in the

Ozarks hills around here," one of the men hoarsely whispered to another as he walked away, casting a furtive peek back over his shoulder at the pair. "Maybe it's true."

Tabby shook her head as she glanced sideways at Frankie. "I'm sorry. I didn't mean to upset them but there just wasn't any reason to kill that poor snake."

"It's not a problem, don't worry about it." He watched her with growing admiration. "You did fine. Believe me, they will remember this day for a long time to come. I love it!"

"Well, they need to remember who invaded whose territory." She sniffed as she straightened her cowboy hat. "After all, the snake was here first!"

"Yes, yes he was," Frankie agreed with a grin. "Come on. Say hello to Father Clem. I always try to see if he needs any help setting up. Not that he brings much with him. He's got a pretty portable set up. I saw my uncle pull up here a minute ago, too."

Within the next few minutes, another half dozen cars arrived and Father Clem was ready to begin.

He said something that Tabby did not quite catch but all the others in the group quickly repeated it back. "It is another beautiful day here in the Ozarks." The priest opened the Mass. "We welcome one and all to our very first Mass on our newly donated land. And so we begin.

"We must always remember God is not Catholic. God is not Protestant." He looked pointedly at Tabby with a smile as he continued. "God is simply God and we know He loves variety. If you have any doubt, simply look at the variety around you, in the trees and flowers, in the animals, from the deer in the nearby woods to those blessed trout, down to the lowly snake. Perhaps God's greatest love of variety, however, can be seen in his most beloved creatures,

His children. We come in all colors and are of many cultures but God only sees the heart of each and every one as He did in the case of King David."

As he spoke, Tabby looked around at the variety in just the small group gathered in this field. Growing up here, she could pick out the visiting fishermen and their families and she recognized a few of the locals who were mixed in. She had even seen a couple of these families at Jesse's campground in recent days. She didn't remember ever having attended a Catholic Mass before. She tried to pay attention and was surprised that it was essentially not that different from her own church's services although she had never seen anyone actually show up there wearing waders. She would certainly not have considered walking down the center aisle of her church in the blue jeans and dusty cowboy boots she wore at the moment. She looked down to hide the smile that came to her, thinking of her mother's reaction if she did!

Afterward, she walked over to thank the priest for the message. "I'm glad you came and that you enjoyed it," he commented. "Frankie, your uncle invited me to have supper with him at the Dining Lodge. You coming with us?"

"Yeah, sure." Frankie was pleased at the additional company. He looked over at Tabby. "Want to come with us?"

"What?" Tabby was caught by surprise.

"Do you want to have some supper with us down at the Bennett Spring Dining Lodge? Of course, you live here. You probably eat there all the time."

"No, not really," she answered, trying to decide how she should answer. "We go there on occasion for pie and coffee mostly, but really, if you live here, you just don't think about it most of the time."

"Uh-huh." He was watching her closely. "So do you want to go now?"

"Yes." She made a decision. "I'll go."

They found a table for four in the far back corner of the cut stone Dining Lodge, built by the Civilian Conservation Corps (CCC) forty years before. The native wood and stone structure, with its massive fireplaces facing one another across the main dining hall, still held the rustic appeal it had from the first day its doors opened. The inimitable one-of-a-kind metal trout sculptured light fixtures graced the diners with light, day and evening. The charm of a bygone era surrounded those who enjoyed breakfast, lunch, and dinner here, and perhaps best of all, that slice of pie or other middle of the day or evening delight. The entire structure seemed to whisper secrets of the beauty that was and is life at Bennett Spring.

They were seated out of the main traffic of the busy restaurant. "So over all, how are you doing, settling in, now that you are back in Missouri?" Father Clem opened a new line of conversation as he perused the menu before him.

Tabby's eyes bore a hole in the table, no longer reading the menu. How did he know? Who told him she'd been away and just come home? She didn't know him well enough for him to ask her such a personal question! The color rose in her cheeks as she glanced his way, only to see the priest wasn't even looking at her.

"Well," Frankie began, with a slightly self-conscious smile, as he toyed with the tines of the fork resting on the plastic place mat. "I think I'm making progress. It's good to be here with Uncle Bob and actually be working again. I spent months in St. Louis looking for work but with almost no luck. I don't really know why, if it was the injury, if employers see it as a handicap or they are just afraid of it or me." A little laugh came out more like a snort. "All I know is I've worked every day since I moved down here. Nobody's paid any attention to the way I walk and that's been a relief. So, I think I'm doing all right." He stopped speaking as the waitress arrived with a tray full of chilled glasses filled with tinkling ice and water.

Tabby was, at once, relieved and overwhelmed, and now more curious than ever to know about Frankie's situation. She was also pleased to have finally heard one of the parishioners and the priest call him by his first name, so now she knew Irish's real name.

"Maybe it was God's providence," the priest replied, as he took a sip of his ice water. "Perhaps that was His plan all along and He knew you needed that little push to get you this far south. Things are a bit different here than life in the big city, are they not?"

"Oh, yeah," Frankie nodded, "a big difference, no doubt, but not bad. Just takes a little getting used to is all." He grinned again.

"So what are we eating tonight?" Father asked them all. "The fried chicken is always excellent as is the trout and the catfish. What's your pleasure?"

It didn't take long for all four to decide that catfish was their best decision all the way around. Tabby was busy trying to decide which of the many questions on her mind she might dare ask first when she spotted a rail thin man, wearing a ratty green Army cap, as he hobbled across the dining room on a pair of wooden crutches. His blue jeans were split along the outside seam, from hip to ankle, revealing a plaster cast of the same length.

As he passed their table, Tabby looked up into a face she hadn't seen in over a year. "Hello, Delbert," she said. "What happened to you?"

"Hey, Tabby." The man stopped, slouching back on his crutches with a lopsided grin that revealed a couple of missing teeth despite the fact that he was as young as the woman before him. "You know, Viet Nam. What can I say?"

"Omigosh, what happened? I heard you were over there. Did you get shot?"

"Not exactly." He looked down, still smiling, and then glanced at the backs of his companions who had continued on. "I, uh...." He shrugged and licked his lips before he confessed. "I flipped over a go-cart on the fire base where I was stationed. Messed up my leg pretty good so they sent me home. Hey, I gotta go. Good to see ya, Tabby. Tell your Uncle Ben I said 'hey'."

"I will," she answered, still smiling as she turned back to the gentlemen at her table. "Only Delbert could go to Viet Nam and get hurt on a go-cart." She shook her head.

"Friend of yours?" Frankie asked with a raised eyebrow.

"Well, a neighbor," she answered. "He's a Kendrix. They've always lived around here and always been in one kind of trouble or another. My Uncle Ben used to be the sheriff here and over the years he's arrested Delbert's dad, his uncles and older brother, even his grandpa. When it got 'round to Delbert, he was pretty young on his first serious arrest for bootleggin'. My uncle convinced the judge to give him a choice, jail or the military, and Delbert chose the army. So whenever Delbert sees me, he likes to remind me that my uncle sent him to the military while the rest of his family went to jail. It's like a joke between us, kind of a sick one, I guess, but just a thing he always mentions when he sees me."

Why did she feel so foolish?

"Well, maybe he's telling you in his own way that he's grateful," Father Clem interjected. "Possible?"

"Uh, I don't know." Tabby tilted her head sideways while looking at the priest, considering the situation anew.

"Maybe he doesn't know how to say it but surely he knows he's better off in the military than locked up somewhere. It must be difficult to look at other men in his family whom he surely cares for and realize that they are hardly model citizens and yet, the man whose job it was to bring them to justice is also the one who made it possible for him to have a better chance at life. That's a heavy burden for any young man to carry but one that should make you rather proud."

"Me?"

"Certainly." Father Clem moved the utensils already on the table as the waitress arrived with plates of fried catfish, heaped high with home-cut french fries, corn bread, and a big, long slice of a Kosher pickle. A plate of butter pats and, even better, small dishes of whipped honey butter completed the overloaded table.

"Of course, you. You should be proud of your uncle. He sounds like a compassionate man, going out of his way like that for a young man in a difficult position. That's all too rare in our world these days. Shall we thank the Lord?" He bowed his head and began the well-known Catholic grace, "Bless us, O Lord, in these thy gifts we are about to receive...."

Tabby bowed hers as well, following the prayer's intent, if not the precise words. "In the name of the Father, Son, and the Holy Ghost." The other three quickly crossed themselves and picked up the dinner conversation, without missing a beat.

"So he flipped a go-kart on a firebase?" Frankie wagged his head, back and forth, preparing to bite into a thick square of steaming cornbread. "He must live under a lucky star."

"He's a Kendrix," Tabby snickered, taking a fork to the crispy whole catfish in front of her. "They often seem to slip through the tight spots with little or no harm." She hesitated and then decided to seize the moment. "So what kind of accident were you talking about that kept you from getting work? Were you hurt on the job in St. Louis?"

"No, I was in the same part of the world as your buddy, Delbert. Outside Saigon. I was on a helicopter that didn't make a very good landing."

"Oh, Irish! That's awful! I'm so sorry," she responded immediately. "I don't even know...."

"What to say," he finished for her. "Nobody does. It's okay. I'm glad it wasn't any worse. It took me quite a while to be able to say that but now I can. But nobody wants to think about over there when we can think about over here instead. Let me tell you, Viet Nam and Bennett Spring are both really green, but Bennett Spring is a lot better." He laughed out loud at the comparison.

"Well, I'm sure that's probably true," Father Clem added. "But that's not quite the whole story. It was a helicopter crash that ended with a bronze star for you, if I'm not mistaken."

"Well, somebody probably was," Frankie shrugged. "I pulled two of my buddies out of that same bird, but that is what you do when they're in trouble and you get thrown clear."

"Uh-huh." Father Clem nodded. "I'll try to remember that if I'm ever in that kind of situation."

"Hmmm." Frankie smiled and picked up a couple of French fries as his way of dismissing the matter.

"Bob, are you all right? You've hardly said a word since we arrived." Father Clem turned his attention elsewhere.

Bob McCleary shook his head slowly. "I don't know, Father. Coming to dinner sounded like a good idea when we were still over at Mass but I'm just not feeling that good." He rubbed his upper abdomen.

"Do you want to go home? We don't have to stay."

"Oh, no." Bob pushed back from the table a bit. "I'm fine, really. Not a problem. You all enjoy your meal. I'll just bag mine up in one of those doggie bags, for the scraps, you know. I'll take my fish with me but my dog's name is Bob!" He smiled without much enthusiasm at his own joke.

"Uncle Bob, are you sure?" Frankie echoed the priest's concern.

"No, no." He smiled again, now more embarrassed than anything else. "Go on and eat. I'll be fine."

"A bronze star? That's like a medal, right?" Tabby returned to the priest's last comment.

"Yeah, that's right." Frankie's reticence returned. "Just a medal."

 She eyed him in silence, unsure of what to say next.

"So what's our next step, up on the hill?" Frankie changed the subject. "Uncle Bob?"

"Oh, I'll send some guys out to take some measurements in the next few days." The man spoke in a slow, deliberate fashion, as if he were choosing his words with great care.

Father Clem gave him a concerned look but only nodded in response.

As the three who were eating each enjoyed a piece of the Dining Lodge's well-known pie, it occurred to Tabby that Frankie might be as confused about his future as she was about hers. The cloud of concern passed from his face as he grinned. "Man, this is really good cherry pie."

It was a short while later that Frankie pulled his truck into the drive leading to the Shine house, where every light in the house appeared to be on in the gathering darkness.

"Oh, my gosh my dad is home! I forgot..." She didn't finish the thought, but instead turned to Frankie and began to climb out of his truck. "Oh, Irish, thanks for dinner and the ride back home. I'd invite you in but I honestly have no idea what's waiting inside so it might not be the best time. If you don't mind—"

"It's okay, Tabby, really. Don't worry. We'll get together another time."

"Oh, thank you," she gushed before whirling back to lean through the window once more. "I won't forget that but I gotta run."

She burst in the front door as he pulled back onto the paved road.

"Tabby, where have you been?" Becky's worried response was immediate. "You went out the front door hours ago when I was talking to Ma and never came back. I do declare—"

"I know. I'm sorry. I just didn't think. I really didn't realize how late it was until I saw the lights were already on and–"

"Tabby." Her father stood up from where he had been sitting on the couch next to a dark-haired young lady whose large ebony eyes, edged with fatigue, seemed to take up nearly her entire face. She also leaped to her feet upon Tabby's unceremonial entrance. "Tabby, I would like you to meet Maria Consuelo Rios, the daughter of a good friend from Cuba. She's going to be staying with us for a while."

"Mucho gusto." The slightly built young woman before her extended her hand in a formal handshake. "Oh, I mean…" She glanced apologetically at J.C. and then back at his daughter. "It is a very nice pleasure to meet you."

CHAPTER 5

Frankie drove on toward Lebanon, deep in thought. She was a funny girl, attractive, intriguing, and yet slightly distant from time to time. He couldn't figure her out but he knew he wanted to know more.

Distracted by pleasant thoughts centered around his female dinner companion, it took him an extra minute to realize the pickup truck meandering across the center line in front of him belonged to his uncle. As it rolled to a stop on the narrow highway's unpaved shoulder, Frankie pulled up behind, gearing down to a sudden stop. He scrambled to the driver's door of his uncle's truck to find him slumped over the steering wheel. He jerked open the door and helped to ease Bob McCleary across the bench seat as he climbed inside.

"Uncle Bob! What's going on?"

The barely conscious driver looked over at the younger man with glassy eyes that veered about helplessly in pain and confusion. "Frankie?" He questioned his nephew's presence as he clutched his chest. "Frankie? Where did you come from?" Bob asked in a weak voice.

"Never mind, Uncle Bob. I'm getting you some help. Sit

back and try to relax. Breathe real slow. Can you do that?" Frankie thought his voice sounded surprisingly calm, despite his own racing heart. "I'm driving you to the hospital in Lebanon," he continued in a most rational manner. "It'll be okay. Just breathe easy now." Frankie tried to collect his conflicting thoughts, harking back to the last time he had used such a soothing tone, attempting to calm his fellow soldiers after the helicopter crash over a year ago. He drove fast, thankful there was little traffic as he sped around the few vehicles he did encounter, his lights flashing while he leaned on his horn in warning.

At the Emergency Room, orderlies helped him to ease his uncle into a wheelchair before he was whisked inside. After what seemed like relentless activity for much more than the few minutes that had actually elapsed, Frankie quickly found himself sitting alone in a sterile waiting room.

*****

"My name is Connie." The young Hispanic girl standing before her managed to stammer. "That is the name my family calls me." Although heavily accented, her English was excellent.

"Wow," Tabby's eyes widened. "That's lots easier than Maria Con-something, huh? Welcome to America! My dad has told us lots about where you live, growing up in Cuba and all. This must be a whole lot different to you!" They walked back to the couch and J.C. was thankful for his daughter's welcoming attitude, putting the visitor instantly at ease.

"Miami, of course, was much the same. It is only ninety miles from the coast of my country, but here is different and no one speaks Spanish, yes? But it is warm and green so that is good."

"Warm now, yeah," Tabby laughed, "but in a few months, it will be all covered in snow and ice!"

"Oh, I want to see that! I have never seen snow. It looks very beautiful in all the pictures I see."

"Beautiful, but cold! Kinda like the inside of the freezer in the refrigerator."

"Oh! *En la refri....*" Connie's eyes grew even larger at the thought.

J.C. watched in contentment, glad to see Connie the most comfortable he had seen her since finding her in Miami two days before. He was anxious to ask her about his good friend, Miguelito, her father and her mother, Pilar as well as her grandfather, Miguel, all the people he remembered so well from his childhood, but he forced himself to wait. Give her time, he told himself once again.

He and Becky slipped off into the kitchen as he heard Tabby ask, "Do you ride horses? That is where I was earlier today, with the horses in the park."

"Horses?" Connie's head snapped around. "I am a full-blooded *cubana*. Of course, I love horses!"

"So what's next?" Becky raised an eyebrow in J.C.'s direction. "Any ideas?"

"No, not really." J.C. grinned as he held out his open arms to her, an invitation she readily accepted. "Just glad to see those two getting along so well already. Let us hope that continues. I talked to Jeff Dugan down there in Miami and he said she could stay with us. He gave me initial processing paperwork they give to all the newly arrived Cubans. I guess now they have it down to a system after so many continue to come across. At least her boat made it, thank heavens. He says there are lots that don't and they drown or worse, meet up with sharks. Pretty gruesome."

Becky shuddered in his arms at the thought. "You know, despite the problems we deal with every day, we have no idea how truly lucky we are."

"You are so right, my pretty girl. Dugan said he will send the appropriate papers for a work permit a little later so that when she is ready for a job she can look for one. In the meantime, if she wants to go to school, she can do that, too. He asked if she would need financial assistance and I told him that wouldn't be a problem. If the situation were reversed, I know I could depend on Miguelito's family to take care of one of ours, no questions asked. I just so wish there was a way to let them know she is here with us and safe. They must be going out of their minds, worrying about her. And how bad is the situation there, if such a perilous journey was their best option? I just can't imagine."

"I know." Becky looked up at her still handsome husband, whose appearance, in her opinion, had changed very little from the first day they had met. "It must be terrible for them right now."

Tabby spent her first night at her parents' home since returning from California, albeit sleeping on their living room couch. Her mother had put the newest arrival in Tabby's room since her grandmother, Hannah, had moved into her brother, Jesse's, old room. Tabby and Connie stayed up for hours that first night, chatting away like long lost friends in the living room. By the time they realized how late it was, Tabby was tired enough to happily stretch out on the long comfortable sofa with a light afghan. Compared to some of the places she had slept on her trek to California, it was pure luxury. Connie was immediately apologetic when she realized she had displaced Tabby, but her hostess was insistent.

"I've been gone for months, Connie. Really, it's no problem. Since I've been back, I've been staying with my aunt and uncle, closer to town. It's a long story but basically, I don't always get along with my mother." She finished with a shrug.

Connie giggled in response. "*Ay, es cierto*. I understand. I have the same problem."

Bright and early the next morning, the Shine household was up and moving on a Sunday. Tabby began poking around in the back of her closet to find something she could wear to church with the rest of her family before getting a shower while her mother was making cornmeal pancakes for one and all.

Jessica and Ben were at the front door as Becky set the pancakes on the table. "Oh, I'm so glad to see you here." Jessica breathed a sigh of relief as she came in and gave Tabby a quick hug. "When you didn't call last night, I figured you just stayed here but I wasn't sure."

"Oh, Jessica, I'm so sorry. I should have called you. I didn't even think!" Becky broke in. "With Connie's arrival, oh, yes, this is Maria Consuelo, Miguelito's daughter I told you about. She got here with J.C. last night and everything has been a bit of a whirlwind since. By the time I realized Tabby was still here..."

"It's no problem," her sister-in-law assured her. "You have plenty to say grace over with more additions to your household." She threw a big smile in Hannah's direction, where she sat sipping her coffee, nibbling on a pancake, seemingly oblivious to all the bustling activity going on around her.

"That makes me think." Becky turned the conversation back to the newest arrival. "Connie, there will be lots of introductions in the next few days, like this morning at church. How do you want to be introduced? I just don't want to say something that would make you feel uncomfortable. Your father and J.C. are lifelong friends so that makes you a friend of the family but there will be questions about where you are from, where the rest of your family is and that sort of thing. What do you think?"

Despite feeling self-conscious, the young girl looked down at her feet for a moment as the color rose in her cheeks. She was also deeply complimented that her new American friends were already so considerate of her feelings.

"I really do not know. I know the Americans hate Castro and his government as so many of us do but I do not want to make a big political talk. Maybe it is best to say only what you said now, that I am the daughter of family friends and I am staying with you for a little while. If they ask more, then it will be your decision to answer the best way at the time. Is that a good plan?"

"Sounds pretty good to me," J.C. agreed with a nod. He looked around at his growing family with a sudden rush of pride, a tender sentiment that stayed with him as they made their way to the Bennett Spring Church of God.

The picturesque stone church set in the valley was the last remaining building of the tiny village of Brice, Missouri. Built in 1917 after a week-long tent revival, the church had been a silent witness to the town's transformation into a state park, the only one to boast a house of God in its midst. Despite the coming and going of the seasons, summer and winter, trout fishing or not, the small congregation arrived faithfully each and every Sunday morning and Wednesday evening for prayer meetings and Bible studies.

The Reverend Jamison Trundle, married to Becky and Ben's younger sister, Esther, had been the church's pastor in the years immediately following World War II in the late 1940s and early 1950s. In more recent years, he had served other churches, including spending several years in Jefferson City but last year, he and Esther and their three boys, Matthew, Mark, and Luke, had returned to the Bennett Spring church.

Connie was at once delighted but also overwhelmed as she was introduced to more family members and many new friends at the morning worship. After a couple of opening hymns, Reverend Trundle welcomed park visitors and members alike before beginning the morning message that centered on a well-known Biblical character.

"How many of us know the story of Jonah?" he began. "Since we were knee-high to a grasshopper, as the old timers like to say, we have all heard about the man swallowed by a great fish and yet, for so many of us, that is all the more we truly know about Jonah. It is one of those Bible stories that people often argue about. Could a man actually be swallowed by a fish and survive? But is that the whole story? How did Jonah get there in the first place? Isn't that what this is really all about?

"God had asked Jonah to carry out a specific task, to go and preach to the people of Nineveh. He didn't ask Jonah to build an ark, lead his people out of slavery and into the desert, challenge the ruling authorities or any of the other tasks various other Biblical people were asked to do. But Jonah refused to go and do as he was asked. He tried to run away from God and that is how he ended up tossed overboard off the ship he was on, after trying to hide from God by going to sea. God allowed him to be swallowed by a fish to have some time to himself to contemplate his situation and eventually change his mind. Once he did, God had the fish to vomit up Jonah on the beach and he went off to do what he was asked to do in the first place."

The preacher paused for a moment before continuing. "You have to hand it to God for coming up with a place unmatched for being quiet, with no interruptions or undue influence from others! Now, of course, Jonah went on to do as he was instructed even though he wasn't particularly happy with the outcome but more importantly, God was. Jonah, once again, needed an adjustment in the way he looked at things. But for our purposes today, the more important lesson is listening to God and doing what he would have us to do in the first place."

For the first time in months, possibly years, Tabby found herself captivated by a pastor's words. She had been in grade school when her Uncle Jamison and Aunt Esther had moved from Bennett Spring and over the years, she had probably heard him preach less than half a dozen times. This morning, however, he was speaking right to her heart.

"Where are we when we hear the voice of God?" Jamison asked the congregation as he paced before them. He used no notes and much to the discomfiture of a few in his congregation, he also made little use of the wooden pulpit, except to hold his Bible which he quoted but never consulted once he began to speak. "We are not comfortably ensconced in the living room in front of the television or tucked snugly into our own beds. More likely, one hears the voice of God when, like the nation of Israel fleeing across the desert, we find ourselves in the wilderness, lost and feeling very much alone. But when we turn ourselves over to God at those times, He will provide whatever it is we need—water from a rock in the desert, manna from Heaven, meat flying into our camp on the wing that we call quail. What is it you need God to provide for you? Food and shelter or a direction in life?

"If you read the newspapers or watch the nightly news, it is pretty obvious a great many of our young people need exactly that last one. But how many of them will look in the right direction and turn back to God? Instead, they chase after drugs, free love, a promised land far away, whether a real place or just one of their own imagination...."

Tabby's concentration drifted away from the little church in the valley as she considered the past year of her own life and wondered if God was looking down on her at this very moment. Her face flushed at the mere notion and yet it was also inexplicably comforting. She bowed her head and squeezed her eyes shut tight, the way she did as a small child to pray. Maybe all of this was not in vain, was her last fleeting thought before the organ began again and the congregation rose to its feet for a final hymn and the passing of the collection plate.

After the service, people filed out the front door, most stopping at the card table set up on the gravel in front of the church where a couple of the ladies of the church were handing out paper cups of coffee and sharing a variety of homemade cookies. Connie found herself surrounded by more folks with questions and from the expression on her face, Tabby decided she could use a little help.

"Connie," she called. "Come have a cookie." Tabby made her way past the curious and caught her new friend by the hand and proceeded to drag her away, with an apologetic wave to those left behind.

"*Muchas gracias,*" Connie muttered under her breath with a sly grin as she selected a butter cookie with a fruit center.

"They mean well but you know how old ladies can be sometimes," Tabby grinned. "If we start now, we can walk back to the house and I can show you some of the park on the way."

Connie answered with a shrug and a smile and with a wave and word in Becky's direction, the two set off.

"Who would have thought?" Becky shook her head, dumbfounded, as she leaned over to speak softly to J.C. They watched as the two young women strolled toward the hatchery. "I worried when you were on your way home with Connie, if Tabby would be angry or upset that we let her stay in her room and I thought about putting her in the other twin bed in Jesse's room, next to Ma. I wasn't sure how Ma would take that though and I didn't want to make Connie feel in any way like she was putting us out. But after all that, Connie's arrival is finally the thing that gets Tabby to come and sleep under her own roof again!"

"Indeed," J.C. replied, seemingly lost in thought as he sipped his coffee.

Tabby reveled in the bright sunshine, thankful for its warmth as her new friend had remarked last night, but also that it was far from the humid heat they would be facing within another couple of weeks. She wore a brightly flowered sleeveless dress she had found in the back of her closet this morning along with a pair of heeled sandals. She had noticed a couple of glares from the older women at church who undoubtedly did not approve of her bare-legged casual look, but she was still trying to adjust to a number of lifestyle shifts between California and the Ozarks and fashions here versus there were the least of her concerns at the moment. She was surprised her mother had said nothing although she thought she noticed a tightening of her lips when Becky first laid eyes on her daughter this morning. Still, Tabby had to give credit where credit was due. Her mother had said nothing.

"This is the hatchery," Tabby began as they walked along the narrow road. "It's where they raise all the trout. And then they put them in the spring branch." She literally sounded like a tour guide, she thought to herself as they walked.

"Why?" Connie asked.

"So the fishermen can catch them."

"But are there not fish in the water already?"

"Yes," Tabby answered with a smile, turning toward her companion, "but not enough of them."

"Not enough?" Connie frowned.

"Not enough trout for all the fishermen who come. This is a very popular park. People come here from St. Louis and Kansas City as well as many other states like Iowa to the north, Kansas to the west, Illinois, Arkansas, and Oklahoma," she explained. "Each fisherman is allowed to take home five trout and then—"

"Only five?" Connie was full of questions. "What if they catch more than that?"

"Well," Tabby laughed as she tried to shed more light on the entire process. "They can only *keep* five. They have to put the ones they want on a stringer. Look!" She motioned to her as they approached the bridge and pointed to the fishermen spread below in front of Bennett Spring's signature waterfall at the dam. "See the fish hanging off that man's belt over there? That's his stringer and he has two fish on it. A fisherman can put four on there and then keep fishing all day long, if he wants. But once he puts that fifth one on, he is done and has to quit for the day. He can come back tomorrow and start again."

Connie nodded but her look of confusion continued as she tried to follow her friend's logic. "The hatchery raises the fish and then the fishermen come and catch them out. Who counts to make sure each one only takes five? Do they do this every day? Who pays for the fish they put in there? Is it a business? How strange this is! There is nothing like this in my country!"

"Really?" Tabby stopped to look directly at her.

"No," Connie laughed at the concept. "We fish in the river or the ocean but no one puts the fish there but God. We catch them out with a pole like these men to take them home to eat but we do not wear big boots like that. Fishermen who make their life from the fish, they use nets just like the *disipulos* in the Bible, the ones who followed Jesus, like Peter, John, and Andrew. They fish with nets and eat some but they sell the rest. Do these people sell the ones they catch here?" She waved her arm toward the fishermen below. "Is that why they can only catch five?"

"No!" Tabby's sudden burst of good-natured laughter startled Connie. "I'm sorry, I'm sorry." She followed with an instant apology. "They are not allowed to sell them. Oh my, there is a lot to explain about park life and how it all works around here. Hey, we can change clothes and come back later or another day to look at the fish in the hatchery and even feed them. Let's go this way for now. We can keep walking along the spring branch, that's what we call this stream because all of the water comes from Bennett Spring up this way." She pointed vaguely to the left. "It runs all the way through and out of the park, over a mile, that way." She made a wave in the opposite direction. "That's where it meets the Niangua River."

Connie nodded silently, trying to take in all the new information. She watched another fisherman for a few moments as they walked.

Tabby stopped to look back behind them.

"What is it?" Connie asked as she noticed the look on her

friend's face.

"I don't know," she answered. "It's weird but it just feels like somebody is watching us. Silly, huh?"

Connie took a slow look around but noticed nothing. It was so much more difficult here, in a foreign country, a completely new place, to even know what to look for. In her own country, she could easily have spotted something out of the ordinary but here, it was simply not possible.

"I do not know." She shrugged. "I do not see anyone but there are people all around, yes? Fishermen, people walking. Are you certain?"

"No, not at all," Tabby laughed nervously. "Just some silly feeling."

They walked on in silence for a short distance before Connie spoke again. "Before the revolution, many tourists came to Cuba from the US and many other countries. Some of them hired boats to take them out to fish with long heavy poles. They call it deep sea fishing. But now…" Her sigh said more than her words. "It is very different, of course."

"I know that there was a revolution, almost ten years ago," Tabby began with some hesitation. "I've heard my dad speak of it but I don't really know much about it, to be honest."

"It is very difficult to explain to someone outside of Cuba." Connie's frown returned. "My father and grandfather owned two of the big hotels in Havana before the revolution. That is how they met your father and his father. Your grandfather came to Cuba many years ago and worked in the hotel business with mine. Our fathers were in school together. It is true that my family made a good life from the hotels but they also worked hard. We had a big house, another smaller one at the beach, and cars. I went to a Catholic school. My parents had many employees at the hotel and at our home. There was a maid and a cook and a gardener, but they were much like part of the family. Most of them had worked for us many years. When Fidel Castro and his government came in, they said all of the people who had property and any money were evil. It is true that President Batista, the one who fled when Castro came in, was corrupt but not everyone in the country was his supporter. Fidel Castro did not see any differences though and my family has suffered greatly, losing everything." She turned her face toward the water as tears blinded her and she stumbled.

"Careful!" Tabby cautioned as she grabbed her friend's arm to steady her. "It's okay. You don't have to explain anything to me. My folks said you needed to stay with us and that's good enough for me."

"There is so much to explain." Connie shook her head as she continued, "but even I do not understand it all. So many things were taken from us. They said it was to make things more fair and give the money to the people who had nothing but they gave our houses to different ones in the government. It is the same with our cars. I have seen them! They sent my father to prison because he would not join their political party. He is home now but he is not the same as he was before and through all of this, my mother says I must not become bitter. But how do I do that when so much has happened?" The anger in her voice threatened to bring back the tears, leaving Tabby at a complete loss.

"Hey, look here." She tried to pull the distraught girl back to Bennett Spring and away from such painful memories. "You said they don't wear big boots to fish in Cuba? We call 'em waders and I bet the water there is not like this." She started down a roughly asphalted wing dam that stretched out into the frigid blue-green waters of the spring branch. They had been initially installed to deepen the channel and improve the quality of the fishing, but fishermen and visitors had found them a convenient way to get closer to the water as well.

"Check this out." Tabby kneeled down gingerly, her bare knees on the bumpy pavement, and dipped her hand in the icy spring water. Connie followed her example.

"Oh!" Connie squealed, pulling her hand back immediately. "It is so cold!"

"Oh, yes," Tabby giggled. "It's spring water. Never gets above sixty degrees and 100,000,000 gallons of it pours out of Bennett Spring each day."

"So much?" Connie's eyes grew wide in disbelief. "That cannot be true!"

"No, really. There is a sign up by the spring. I can show you." They climbed back to their feet.

"It's sure 'nough true." The voice came from behind them, startling them both. In her haste and with her attention focused on Connie's distress, Tabby had not even noticed the young man in the wheelchair at the far end of the wing dam. He pivoted his chair to face in their direction and with some difficulty, directed it over the uneven surface that was little more than a thin layer of asphalt spread unevenly over large rounded rocks.

"I wanted to see if I could do this," he said to no one in particular as he approached them, "before I brought my fishing rod down here." He stopped and pushed his fishing hat back on his forehead, revealing his face and a pair of bright blue eyes. "Hi ya, Tabby! How are ya?"

CHAPTER 6

Father Clem stood without moving before a dozing Frankie O'Donnell in the early hours of Sunday morning. He gently touched the younger man's shoulder but was unprepared for his reaction.

"Wha, what?" Frankie jumped to his feet, his fists up and ready. His eyes swept the room, taking in the quiet emptiness of the hospital waiting area. He dropped his fists. "I'm sorry, Father," he stammered. "Is everything….he's not…"

"He's fine, Frankie, not to worry. Your uncle is doing better. One of the nurses from our parish recognized him and called me. One of the benefits of life in a small town, don't you know," he smiled.

"Oh, Father, thanks be to God." The starch went out of the younger man's knees and he sank back down to the upholstered chair where he had been sleeping. "I'm sorry I came up at you like that. Still happens when I get woke up suddenly. After my time over there…" his voice trailed off.

"Not a problem. I understand. Not an unusual reaction from those who have been in combat. I've been in talking to Bob for a bit now. He's drifted off to sleep and the doctor had an emergency call so I told him I'd talk to you. Your uncle didn't want me to wake you up earlier." The priest grinned again as he took a seat beside Frankie. "Just like him," he continued. "Always thinking of someone else."

"So how is he?" Frankie sat up straight, wiping a hand over his face to banish the last traces of sleep. "It's better than what I thought when I first saw you…"

"I know. I'm sorry. I didn't mean to startle you. He's doing better for the moment." Father Clem, dressed in a characteristic black blouse and white collar over a pair of black slacks, looked down at his feet. He hesitated for a moment before continuing. "They really don't know a lot right now, other than that the doctor wants him to remain here for the next few days so that they can watch him, run a few tests, and make sure he is really all right."

"So what is it? What happened? A heart attack?" Frankie's rapid fire questions gave the priest no time to answer.

"They suspect that was probably it but they don't know yet. It may be a few days before they can determine that for certain. Sorry, I don't have more to tell you."

"No, no it's okay."

"You should have called me sooner. I would have come and sat with you last night."

"Oh, Father. I didn't really know what to think or do. I came in here to wait and I guess I fell asleep. I don't have any idea what time it is or even how long I've been here."

Father Clem glanced at his watch. "About 6 a.m. Why don't you go home and get a shower, something to eat, and some rest. Bob is going to sleep for several hours now, I imagine. We can leave word with the nurses for him to call you when he is awake again."

Frankie slumped forward, resting his elbows on his knees. "Yeah, that's probably a good idea. I mean, I'd really just like to stay here but I don't guess that's going to help much right now." He grinned self-consciously. "I must look like I slept in the bus station."

"Pretty close," the priest agreed as he stood up. "Your uncle and I had a good chat. He's out of pain now, for the most part, thanks to the medication they were able to give him. He's very grateful to you for getting him here so fast. He is overly concerned now about the building project out there at Bennett Spring. I told him we need to let that rest for now but I'm not sure I convinced him."

"Well, I can get out there, get some measurements, and get the process moving a little more quickly, if it will help him rest easier. In the next few days, can you get in touch with Jim and Al and the rest of the Sugar Creek gang and see how soon they can come down to help out?"

"Certainly, whatever you think." Father Clem shook his head, deep in thought. "I wish I could get him to just forget about it for a while but I doubt that will happen, especially if he's going to have time to think while he's supposed to be resting."

"Thank you, Father, for being here, for him and for me. I really appreciate it."

"Of course. You let me know if you think of any other way I can help. Before you go, let me say a blessing over you both." The priest took both of Frankie's hands in his and the two men bowed their heads as Father Clem spoke softly.

* * * * *

"J. Junior!" The name flew out of Tabby's mouth before she could stop it and the color drained from her face.

"What? What are you doing here? Like…like…"

"Like this?" He finished the question for her with a mischievous grin. "Sorry. I've just been back a few days myself and I really did plan on stopping by this afternoon to come see you all. I asked my folks to keep it quiet for a while." He spread his hands wide in front of himself and then out to his sides. "Not exactly an easy thing to talk about, for any of us, but I have to say, I'm getting better at it."

Another man who had been squatting, unnoticed, almost behind where the wheelchair had been, stood up.

"Uncle Joey?" Joey Schultz, J. Junior's father who was married to Grace, her Aunt Jessica's little sister, was not actually Tabby's uncle but she and her siblings had always called him that. "I don't understand. What happened? I heard you were missing…" She looked back at J. Junior.

"Tabby, are you okay? Do you need to sit down or something? You're looking kinda pale." Joey stepped to her side.

"I'm all right," she insisted. "I just didn't expect…"

"Tabby." Connie was at her side and handed her a handkerchief she first dipped in the spring water.

The cool damp cloth felt good against her forehead. "I'm sorry," Tabby tried again.

"No, I'm sorry," J. Junior grinned out of embarrassment now. "It was the Army's foul up at first, telling everyone I was MIA, and then by the time they realized I'd been evac'd out for medical under somebody else's name, I was able to get on the phone and talk to the folks myself. But I also knew I wasn't in the same shape as when I left here and I wanted some time to deal with that. The folks came out and saw me at the V.A. hospital in California but I asked 'em not to tell anybody at first."

"Oh, J., why? We were all so worried and scared. All we could think…Uncle Joey, you know what we thought!"

"I know, I know, Tabby." The wiry man put up his hands in mock defense. "Believe me, we weren't crazy about it either but we talked to your parents so they knew and it was what J. Junior really wanted. I didn't think it was so much to ask, all things considered."

"Oh, my gosh, J.!" Tabby gave up her protests and bent over to throw her arms around his shoulders. "You are as crazy as ever! I am so glad to see you."

He laughed good-naturedly. "So am I forgiven?"

"Hmm, for the moment." She stood up straight. "Oh, my gosh!" she repeated. "J., this is a family friend, Connie. Her dad and my dad went to school together and she is staying with us for a while."

Connie stepped forward although her eyes had hardly left J. Junior from the first moment he'd spoken. "It is very nice to meet you," she said in softly stilted syllables as she extended her hand.

"And where are you from?" J. Junior's smile was wide as he accepted the formal handshake.

"Havana," she answered evenly. "Cuba."

"Cuba?" He gave Tabby a startled look. "You didn't exactly come in on a regular Pam Am flight then, did you?"

"No," she shook her head slightly. "I did not."

"Well, however you got here, it's got to beat being down there with Mr. Fidel these days," he laughed. "Glad you are here with Tabby. Maybe you can keep her out of trouble, like running off to California and becoming some kinda flower child. What were you thinking, girl?" He turned his eyes back on his lifelong friend.

"Oh, probably about the same thing you were thinking when you signed up for the Army!" she shot back. "Just wanting to get out of here for a while and out in the world! Oh, J., what is all this? Are you all right? Are you getting out of that thing soon?" She blurted out exactly what was on her mind but she and J. Junior had always been able to talk to each other about almost anything.

"No." He gave a big sigh but his smile remained strong. "This looks like it may be with me a very long time so that's why I was down here today, kinda checking it out on the rocks. Dad here wasn't too keen about it but agreed as long as he could come with me. Today, I told him. I got to learn how to do this stuff on my own. Lookie here, I even found my ol' fishing hat." He whipped off the canvas style fishing hat he was wearing, revealing his light brown hair, pulled back in a short low ponytail.

"Oh, J." Tabby let out a little moan despite her friend's upbeat approach.

"Now don't go giving me that hang dog look," J. Junior scolded. "This was why I told the folks I had to have some time first to take this all in. I can't be whining about what's done and what can't be undone. All any of us can do is move ahead forward, as my one sergeant used to say. Got him in trouble with some smart mouth English teacher recruit who got drafted in with us. 'Course after he corrected the sergeant's English, the sergeant gave him fifty pushups to do! So, none of that 'pity the poor guy in the wheelchair' stuff, you got it?"

She glanced at her Uncle Joey who nodded with a small grin on his face.

"Yes, sir!" She snapped to attention with a mock salute.

"So you are Tabby's friend from long ago, yes?" Connie spoke up as she glanced back and forth between the two.

"Oh, yeah," J. Junior chortled, "since we were little bittys. Hey, you girls, wanna take a ride? That's what we were really doing out today. Dad's been working on his old Jeep, remember the one he used when he first took over your dad's postal route? Well, the nice thing about them Jeeps is that you can pretty much take 'em apart and put 'em back together, however you need 'em to be. He's been working on this one now, ever since he first saw me in the hospital, and we were test driving it today. The Jeep and the driver!" He laughed suddenly. "Wanna give it a go? I promise I'll be good."

"Sure!" Tabby shrugged and followed the rolling J. Junior, looking over her shoulder to make certain Connie was following, which she was but with considerably less enthusiasm than her companion.

"Here." Joey stepped up as J. Junior reached over his head and grasped a homemade set of straps that Joey had attached to the roll bar passing above and behind the driver's and passenger's seats. J. Junior pulled himself up into the driver's seat that actually swiveled and tilted down somewhat to accommodate his transfer.

"Pretty slick, heh?" J. Junior smiled triumphantly. He leaned back and swung his legs into place using his hands and tucked himself in below the dashboard. He snapped a seat belt across his lap and reached forward to push a shiny new button low on the left side of the dash as the engine roared to life.

"Now, you remember my motorcycle I had the last couple of years in high school?"

"Nellybelle? How could I forget! I got grounded for a whole week the first time I rode on her with you, when my mother found out!" She looked around as if someone was watching her in secret. "After that, I learned to just make sure to be a little more careful and not get caught!"

Connie burst into laughter and Joey simply ducked his head to hide his smile.

"You named her Nellybelle after the Jeep on the ol' Roy Rogers TV show we always liked to watch as kids, but I always thought you named her that just 'cause when you'd pull up to a stop, you liked to say, 'whoa, Nelly!'"

"Well, yeah, there was that, too," he shrugged with a wide smile.

"But I also remember you wrecked that bike after a party on your graduation night." Tabby frowned.

"Yeah, that's true. Pretty good memory, girl."

"Mostly, I remember at the time we were all thrilled that you didn't get killed in a motorcycle wreck!" Tabby glared at him. "You were lucky that night. Nellybelle ended up on one side of the road and you landed on the other in a whole bunch of leaves, brambles, and brush, as I recall. You were a mess, all scratched up, but not dead!"

"Yeah, well…" he shrugged with a cockeyed grin. "Well, the important part now is that my dad, kept all the parts and pieces so—lookie here. He took the linkage from the motorcycle and used it to make me an accelerator and brakes for his old Jeep. I can operate the whole thing with my hands and drive with no feet or legs. I'm telling you…." He shook his head in admiration. "I mean, I always knew my dad was one heck of a mechanic but this is great! I now have two sets of wheels, my chair and my own very special Jeep, and I still got a piece of Nellybelle here with me, too. Now you can't beat that. Here, climb up and I'll show you." He indicated the passenger seat next to him as he looked at Tabby. "Do you mind to sit right back here, behind her?" J. Junior turned his charming smile on Connie.

Joey held out a hand to help the teen into the back of the vehicle and then climbed in across from her, sitting on the opposite wheel well.

Joey collapsed the wheelchair and hung it on a large hook on the side of the Jeep, just behind the driver's seat. "Still working on that part," J. Junior added with a grin. "Here we go," he announced to all and then slowly backed the packed Jeep out of the parking area, onto the park road immediately behind them. He turned toward the hatchery, rolling along at a moderate speed as did all of the traffic in the park on a Sunday afternoon.

"Oh, Lordy, look at that!" J. Junior slowed to look across the green space between the road they were on and the road running slightly above and out of the park. Below that road were a couple of large brick-lined storm water drains, passing like small tunnels under the roads. "Remember playing hide and seek in there? You got so mad at me the first time I hid there because you couldn't find me!" He giggled at the memory and then frowned slightly. "Guess we won't be doing that anymore."

"Oh, J.!" Tabby rolled her eyes but with half a smile, despite the sadness in her voice.

He shook his head but turned away for a moment. "Guess I'll just have to find some other way to bug you from now on," he added under his breath.

"Oh, I'm sure you'll figure out something pretty quick!" Tabby laughed out loud. "Hey, this Jeep is quite a ride.

What a deal, Uncle Joey! I don't know anything about cars and engines but I'm impressed."

"And me," Connie spoke up as she held onto the roll bar overhead. "We have no new American cars in my country. The men there are always finding ways to fix the ones we have but this is something special."

"Yes, it is." J. Junior's voice took on a more somber note as he threw her an appreciative glance over his shoulder. "Very special." He turned the Jeep with ease, as if he had been doing it for years, and headed up the road toward Tabby's home.

He pulled up to the front porch, rolling to a gentle stop. "Everybody out," J. Junior called, more like a train conductor than the driver of a made over Jeep.

"I'm surprised you didn't come to church today," Tabby added as she climbed out of the passenger seat. Connie hopped out of the back and climbed the steps but not without a long look back at the driver of the vehicle.

"Yeah, well, I know. My mother wasn't too happy with me not going this morning and then Dad here felt like he should go with me. Was she there?"

"I didn't see her."

"Hmm, well, I'm just not quite ready for all those folks standing around at church, looking at their feet instead of my face when I roll in, if you know what I mean. I'll get there."

"Yes, you will." Tabby's spirit was finally buoyed by J. Junior's relentless optimism. "You coming in here? You know Mom will have enough food on the table for a small army, like every Sunday after church."

He leaned back in his seat a bit more. "No," he sighed.

"Not today. Soon, I promise. To be honest, I am starting to feel kinda tired at this point. A Sunday afternoon nap is sounding pretty good and pretty normal and I think I like that." He grinned and Tabby could see the weariness around his eyes.

She reached out and patted his hand, resting on the back of the passenger seat. "It's okay. Get some rest. I am glad to see you, even if you did surprise me half to death down there on the spring branch. I'm just glad you are home."

"You ain't the only one, Tabby," Joey chimed in as he climbed into the passenger seat beside his son. "We're headed back to the house. We'll catch up to Grace and maybe we'll see you all next Sunday."

"I'll tell Mama then," Tabby called out as she waved goodbye and turned to find Connie still standing a couple of steps above her, watching the departing Jeep intently.

"What an interesting man!" Connie barely breathed. "He has eyes the color of the sea. Did you not notice?"

"J. Junior?" Tabby's surprise was complete. "Well, yeah, I guess you could say that."

Connie said nothing more, just kept watch on the Jeep until it pulled out of sight, traveling up the highway.

Inside, they found most of the family gathering around Becky's very full table of fried chicken, mashed potatoes and gravy, fresh biscuits, fresh steamed broccoli, canned beets, carrots, and heavily-cinnamoned applesauce.

"Wondered if you two got lost between church and home?" Becky tossed at the two new arrivals as they came into the dining room.

"No, we found J. Junior and Uncle Joey down on the spring branch. I didn't even know he was back and I certainly didn't know he was in a wheelchair! Why didn't anybody tell me?" She scooted a chair in between her brother, Jesse, on her left and her Uncle Ben on the right. Connie slipped into a chair on the opposite side of the table beside J.C. who was at the head of the table.

"Ladies," he admonished gently. "Let us not be cross with one another. Tabby, to be honest, J. Junior asked us as did his parents to say as little as possible about his return and his condition. Maybe it sounds strange to us, but I can't imagine how any of us would handle his situation. Under the circumstances, it seemed the least we could do, to let them handle it in their own way. From what I've seen and heard so far, I think they are doing so with an amazing amount of grace. Let's share the blessing, shall we?" He held out a hand to each side and all quickly joined hands as they bowed their heads.

"Dear Lord, bless us today, all who gather at this table as well as those of ours who are not able to join us today. We come with grateful hearts for all your many blessings, today and every day. Keep us safe and constantly in your service. Bless this food, the hands that prepared it, and may it strengthen us each and every one to further serve you. In the name of your son, Jesus, we pray. Amen." That last word echoed 'round the table as most of those present repeated it.

"Well, J. Junior is pretty amazing, I'll give you that." Tabby picked up the previous conversation right where it left off. She pulled a napkin into her lap. "But then he always was crazy. That's what made running around with him so much fun. Connie thinks so, too!" She shot a glance across the table at her new friend.

"*¿Qué dices?*" Connie's head shot up. "What are you saying?"

"Oh, just that you could not take your eyes off of J. Junior today. He is something else again." Tabby continued to giggle as she looked down at her plate.

"Oh, that is not, not..." Connie stammered as her face flushed.

"Not true?" Tabby challenged.

"Not fair," her friend countered. "I have never seen a man in a chair like that before."

"Really?" Tabby looked up.

"We have people in *sillas con rodillas*, I do not mean that. I do not know how you call them here, but the ones there are old and wooden and not like the one I saw today. It was small and fast, like a race car is to a regular car, yes?"

"Well, now that you say that, it was kinda different. I can't say I really noticed until you mentioned it. Not a surprise, considering."

"Considering?" J.C. raised an eyebrow in his daughter's direction.

"Considering it's J. Junior!" Tabby added with a smile of triumph. "So it was the chair that was so fascinating, not the man." She continued to tease.

Connie rolled her eyes dramatically. *"No seas berraca,"* Connie muttered.

"Whoa, now you've been told, as only a Cuban can tell it," J.C. chortled as he looked down, a smile of amusement and happy memories crossed his face.

"No fair!" Tabby retorted with a huge smile, obviously enjoying the verbal volleyball game. "What does that mean?"

"No seas berraco, don't be a stupid…sorta," J.C. was still shaking his head. "How many times did your father say that to me over the years?"

Esther, the youngest of the Darling siblings, chimed in as well. "Oh, just ignore her, Connie." Tabby's aunt passed the mashed potatoes around the table as she frowned at Tabby and continued in a matter-of-fact tone. "These kids are just awful to one another sometimes with the teasing. I guess the good news for you is that they consider you one of them, if they are already hassling you so." She switched her attention to her youngest, sitting next to her. "Please make use of that napkin, young man, to wipe that face before you eat any more. I'm not sure if you are eating or wearing most of that gravy." Six-year-old Luke gave a gap-toothed grin as he complied and his mother smiled despite her scolding tone.

Connie nodded her appreciation to Esther with a smile which she quickly covered with her hand, since her mouth was full. She squinted her eyes at Tabby, a silent gesture made more in fun than annoyance.

Sitting next to Tabby, her older brother, Jesse, poked a gentle elbow into his sister's ribs. "If you girls don't have anything to do except flirt with local fellas and pester people, you could always come down and help out at the camp store and office," he began, only half in jest.

"You have a store?" Connie frowned.

"Yes, down the way," he drawled. "We run the campground and a little store out of there. Come on down and we'll give you a tour."

"We can do that, yes?" Connie bobbed her head at Tabby.

"Yes, we can do that," Tabby agreed with a smile and a deep sigh as she pretended to glare at her brother. "Hey, I have another question for you. I went up to Granny Hannah's house earlier in the week and the garden is all laid out so nice."

"Oh, yeah, that was me. Guess it is just kinda my way of remembering Grandpa. Besides, if I don't do it, what is this family gonna do for vegetables? Certain people would probably curl up and die if we opened an actual can of veggies from the grocery store, you know?" He raised his eyebrows and nodded his head, first toward his mother and then toward his grandmother.

Tabby burst into laughter in agreement.

"I'll thank you to keep a civil tongue in your head, young man," Becky scolded in mock seriousness.

"Well, it all looks good up there. We ought to have lots of green goodies in short order from what I saw."

"Already got lettuce, spinach, broccoli, and cabbages, of course," Jesse replied.

"Yes, and then if someone can just get some beef on this table," Becky chimed in.

"Beef? Did somebody say beef?" Ben piped up. "I'm telling you, J.C., this Beefmaster breed is the new way to go. It's a three way cross, Brahma, Herefords, and Shorthorns. They are a good-looking cow. I really like the reds myself. They're bigger, taller than most the cows you see around here in the Ozarks, but a really good buy for the money. They are out of Texas originally and—"

"Now see what you've done, Becky?" Jessica turned imploring eyes to her best friend and sister-in-law. "You've opened the Pandora's box of cattle breeding. That is all he will talk about for the rest of the meal, I guarantee."

"No, it's not," J.C. began to laugh. "Because I won't let

him. Ben, my friend, you are a wealth of enthusiasm on the subject there is no doubt, but I really just need a little more time to think about this. You are talking some pretty hefty changes here. Eddie Jackson at church this morning mentioned something about them, too, but he said they had some drawbacks as well."

"Like what? I bet he was talking about their big ears, wasn't he? That's the silliest thing I ever heard. Since when does the size of a cow's ears have anything to do with the quality or quantity of meat, but there are people who believe that!"

"Speaking of church," Becky quickly interjected.

The conversation continued to ricochet around the table, like a rapid fire ping-pong game, for the rest of the meal, centering on the church service, who was there as well as who wasn't, and other bits and pieces about the community at large.

"Jessica," Becky turned the conversation again. "What do you hear of Jesse these days?"

Her son's head popped up and she clarified quickly. "Jesse, her twin brother, *your* namesake uncle." His mother winked at the younger Jesse whose attention returned to his dinner.

"We got a letter last week," Jessica responded. "He and Akira are fine and said the girls, Gina and Hana, are doing well."

"How old are they now?" Becky asked.

"Oh, let's see, Gina is ten and Hana is eight. He said life in Tokyo is incredibly busy, life in any big city, I guess. I can't believe my brother is in the electronics business in Japan, of all things. Not exactly where you expect a boy from the Ozarks to end up, is it?"

"No, I'd say not," J.C. chuckled, "but then a number of us do that. Jesse is Jessica's twin brother," he explained to Connie. "After Jessica came here and met Ben, Jesse came, too, and worked for the CCC as well. He and his co-workers are the ones who built the Dining Lodge in 1937. After the CCC, he said he had gotten pretty accustomed to that kind of life so he joined the military even before the beginning of World War II. He ended up a flier in the Air Force and was in Japan as fast as the war ended. He met a woman there, Akira, and married her. When they came back here toward the end of his military career, they found life was pretty difficult for her. After a couple of situations where his wife was treated unkindly because she was Japanese, Jesse decided they would go back to Japan. He said he was treated better over there than she ever was here." J.C. shrugged.

"At any rate, Jesse retired and found himself an excellent opportunity over there with the Sony company and they've done very well ever since. He has two beautiful American-Japanese daughters. We love the fact that he and Akira found Japanese names for them that also work well in English, Gina and Hana."

"Those are lovely," Connie bobbed her head. "Have you been to Japan to visit them?"

J.C. shook his head.

"Ben and I went a few years ago, just once. I wanted to see where he lived and how it all was," Jessica replied with a wide smile. "It was quite a trip. Everything, of course, is so different than here but when you remember the pictures we saw in *Look* and *Life* magazines years ago of how completely destroyed Japan was after the war, it is really an amazing place. They have rebuilt everything. The main thing I wanted to see though was that my brother was well and happy."

"And is he?" the newest arrival asked.

"Oh yes, I think so," Jessica's face reflected her contentment. "I really think he is. Akira is so sweet. We were pretty worried at first that life would be harder for him with a Japanese wife but he seems to be doing fine. It's pretty funny seeing him over there as he is a tall man, so he doesn't fit in like that, but everyone is very kind to him and he has lots of friends even a few other American friends, so it is good. We had met Akira and seen Gina as a baby over here years before but we also knew they were having troubles being accepted here."

"Well, it was an interesting trip, that's for sure. Seen lots of really different things, but if I never eat rice again, it won't hurt my feelings!" Ben burst out with a laugh. "And to be honest, I don't know what kind of a music and electronics man Jesse really is but I remember he was one heck of a salesman," he added, with a wry grin.

"Really?" Becky frowned.

"Oh yeah, you should have seen him the morning, he and Jessica and I went down to see Captain Wilbur Smith, head of the local CCC, the day after he showed up here. He did some fine convincing that day of why he and Jessica had really done nothing wrong in coming here the way they did. It was really pretty funny. Captain Smith was outgunned that morning from the very beginning and he didn't even know it. I'd say ol' Jesse could convince people to buy Sony products, in English or Japanese either one!"

The conversation hit a lull for a few moments until J.C. spoke up again. "Oh, as we were leaving church this morning, someone said that one of the gents involved in the building across the road for the Catholics is in the hospital."

"What? Who?" Tabby nearly choked on her last bite. "Who was it, Dad?"

"Oh, I'm sorry. That's right, you've met some of them. Let's see. It wasn't a name I recognized. A Bob McCleary, I think they said."

"Bob McCleary? Oh my, that's Irish's uncle. What's wrong with him?"

"Irish, heh?" Her father seemed amused. "I don't know. I'm not sure anyone knows just yet."

"I just had dinner with them last night. I went to Mass with them first and then we went down to the Dining Lodge and—"

"You did what?" Her grandmother, who had been dissecting her chicken as much as eating it, gave her a sharp look. "You went to Mass with them? Where? You went to the Catholic Church in Lebanon?"

"No, Granny." Tabby smiled hesitantly, glancing first at her father and then at her mother, who caught her eye and shook her head ever so slightly.

"They had their Mass, their worship service, across the road on their new land yesterday afternoon. I saw Irish, a guy I met over there a few days ago, and he invited me to join them." She could see her grandmother's expression was not changing for the better but she couldn't seem to stop. "It was fine, Grannny, honest. They didn't do or say anything all that different than what we do at our worship. They were outside and used a guitar to sing some hymns and then the priest prayed and talked a bit, just like Uncle Jamison." She looked at him imploringly and he came to her rescue.

"Miz Hannah, I'm sure it was just fine," Esther's husband spoke up. "It's good that Tabby is getting out and meeting others and welcoming people to our valley, for that matter. Surely Bennett Spring is big enough for more than one church," he added with his charming smile.

"Why does it have to be Catholics?" Hannah muttered to herself as her attention dropped back to her chicken. "I don't see why Tabby has to be over there. She has a perfectly good church right here in her own family."

"Well, of course, she does, Ma," Becky gulped, "but that doesn't mean she can't go visit elsewhere once in a while. She still went to church with us this morning, didn't she?"

"All I know is my father came from the old country, Scotland. He always said the Irish Protestants were a fine lot—"

"Ma!" Becky cut her off. "For the love of heaven, you've got two Irish son-in-laws in J.C. and Jamison. You remember Miz Fiona, don't you? They didn't get more Irish than her and certainly no closer to heaven on this earth either. J.C.'s mother was always so sweet. And Jamison is what? Scotch-Irish." She stopped speaking, her exasperation making it difficult to even put her frustration into words.

"That's what I'm saying. My father said the Irish Protestants were fine but he didn't have no use for them Irish Catholics at all!" She fell silent but the invisible black cloud over her head was no less palpable.

It was times like these, Becky could just strangle her own mother. She dared to steal a glance at Connie, whose eyes had grown wide as she understood what she was hearing. Her face was down now as she concentrated on her plate although there was nothing left there to eat. Becky shifted her gaze to the gray-haired woman who seemed to have no idea how much of an impact her outburst had had on everyone at the table. Hannah was now tearing bits of chicken off the bone and piling them together on the side of her plate.

J.C. tried turning everyone's attention to dessert, a large chocolate cake Becky had made the day before while waiting for J.C. and Connie's initial arrival. "She baked it yesterday as a welcome home gesture for Connie but by the time we got around to it last night, we were all too tired and too full to even cut it," he chuckled.

"Connie? Chocolate cake?" Becky asked cheerily.

"Oh, yes." The shy girl rallied a bit but her eyes remained downcast.

Becky forced her attention back to the cake as she cut even slices and passed them around on cake plates.

It took several tries by different ones to lighten the mood back to something close to the jovial disposition their Sunday dinner had enjoyed before Hannah's commentary. As soon as she finished her cake, Connie excused herself and slipped back to her room. Tabby watched and was about to follow when her Uncle Ben spoke up.

"Tabby, I've been thinking, if it's agreeable with you, I've got that old truck at the house that I thought I might bring down here for you. I mean, Jessica and I aren't using it and that would give you and Connie some transportation. It ain't fancy, mind you, but it will get you back and forth to town or around here. If you are interested…"

"Oh, Ben, you don't have to do that," Becky interrupted.

"Well, I know I don't have to, Sis, but I figure with another person or two here to run for, you could use the extra transport and—"

"Uncle Benji, that would be so super groovy!" Tabby jumped up and threw her arms around her uncle's neck and kissed him on the cheek. "Thank you so much! Do you need me to do anything for you, come with you, now or later, to get it or something?"

"No, Jessica and I can bring it down here later today. You still remember how to drive a stick shift, don't you?"

"Of course, Uncle Benji. I can do that. Listen, I've got to go check on something, if you don't need me." She glanced at her mother who gave her a small nod as she scampered off toward her bedroom.

She could hear Ben's comment to his wife as she headed down the hall. "Groovy, huh? Exactly what is groovy again?"

"Connie, Connie." Tabby sat down on the bed, beside the girl sobbing into her pillow. "Please don't let my grandmother's ridiculous words upset you. She is an old lady and you know sometimes they just say stupid things. It doesn't mean anything."

The young woman pulled her tear-streaked face out of the pillow. "It is not just what she said," she barely whispered with a soft sniffle. "It is everything. Nothing is the same. You are trying, I know this and I am grateful as is my whole family. I feel so ashamed, crying like this. I did not want to do it but all at once, I could not stop." She dropped her face back into the pillow for a moment.

"Oh, you are homesick," Tabby all but squealed. "That's all."

"Homesick?"

"Yes, when you are so lonesome for home, your family, things you are used to there. How long since you left home? I know you were on a boat and then in Florida but how long?"

"Oh, I do not know. Let me think." Concentrating on the details stopped the flow of tears as Connie flipped onto her back, facing the ceiling, and began to count on her fingers.

"I think we were on the boat maybe five days, I am not sure but long enough to be very sick. Then two days in the hospital in Florida and then another two days before the government people let me see your father. And another day to fly to Missouri and drive from the airport. Your country is so big. As far as we went on the airplane and your father said we only crossed half the country!"

"Well, yes, that's true. From Florida to Missouri. I was in the other half, Missouri to California. But let me see, you've been gone from home almost two weeks. That's long enough. Ever been away from home before? Like to camp or vacation or anything like that?" Tabby continued her questions.

Connie smiled with an expression on her face fit for a child who understands little about the real world. "We do not take vacations in Cuba. No one has any money for that sort of thing now. We once had a house at the beach and we could go there but Castro and his people took both of our houses and now we live in a small apartment on the second floor, behind some stores. It is very hard for my grandfather to go up and down the steps which are not very good so he almost never leaves. There were five of us there, with my parents, my grandfather, my brother, and me, but now my brother is gone. Like my father before, we think maybe he is in prison."

She sniffled again as the tears threatened a return. "It is

better to say we hope he is in prison and not worse. I think my father was afraid for a time that he had joined Castro's army but I told him I do not believe he would ever do that. He may have joined rebels in the hills but if he did, he would not want us to know, to keep us safe. After he was gone, my father decided I should leave, too, and that is how he made the plan for me to come on the boat with some others he knew. I think he is afraid neither of his children will survive."

"Oh, Connie, I am so sorry. I can't imagine. So you never have really left home before?"

Connie's eyes grew wide with tears as she shook her head slightly.

"Then," Tabby slapped her leg playfully, "you are just homesick. I know it's miserable. I was that way the first time I went to church camp for a week as a kid. And today, of course, my grandma didn't help. Sorry. You can't just lay here. Let's go do something."

"Do something? What do you mean?"

"Well, honestly, most Sundays I have to go help Mom wash dishes right after dinner but today Aunt Jessica and Aunt Esther are both here so with her sister and her sister-in-law to help, if we play our cards just right, we can slip out and go walking again. My mom keeps talking about putting in a dishwasher and I can't wait but until then..." She shrugged with a grin. "Come on."

Connie sat up on the bed. "Is it all right? If we leave?"

Out the front door, they noticed the men heading out the back door to look at the cattle, across the wooden back fence, with Jamison and Esther's three boys scampering along behind. Tabby caught snippets of their conversation as they continued their earlier discussion about the advantages and disadvantages of different cattle breeds. The two girls headed down the drive instead.

"I'll show you where they are going to build this great Catholic Church that has my grandmother all upset."

"But how do you think about Catholics? Truly?" Connie put her fear into words.

A giggle escaped Tabby. "You know, I don't really think I ever thought about Catholics one way or the other until recently when my grandmother started her fussing." A crooked smile crossed her face. "I embarrassed myself so badly with this really cute guy a few days ago over the whole business. But I can tell you about that later. You are Catholic, right?"

Connie nodded silently, still holding her breath, awaiting an answer to her question.

"Well, like I said at dinner, I went to Mass yesterday with this fella, Irish. That's not his real name, of course, because I didn't know his name at first and he knew mine, so I had to call him *something,* you know," she chattered on, spilling out the brief history between herself and Frankie until she achieved her goal which was coaxing a genuine smile out of the homesick girl.

"Oh my gosh!" Tabby stopped at the end of the drive. "There he is! Come on!"

She led the way across the asphalt highway where they found Frankie, walking about once again in the grass, small wooden stakes in his hands, a hammer and a roll of twine suspended from the tool belt around his waist and a half dozen thin nails protruding from his lips which made it hard for him to return Tabby's robust greeting.

"What are you doing here? I just heard about your Uncle

Bob! How is he?" Her thoughts ran one into another in her excitement.

"Man, it was quite a night." Frankie straightened up and spit the nails into his hand as he stalled for answers. "Uncle Bob is okay for now. I found him on the road last night after I dropped you off, just barely driving his truck. I got him to the hospital and he's been there ever since. They think it's his heart." He pulled his wrist across his forehead. "The doctor said they are going to keep him a few days. I spent the night there in a chair and that's where Father Clem found me early this morning. I went home after that and tried to sleep a little more but..." He shrugged. "All Uncle Bob was worried about was this project out here so I thought I'd come out and get started. Maybe if he feels like it's moving along at least close on schedule, he can relax a little and pay more attention to getting better."

"That makes sense," Tabby agreed. "Irish, this is a family friend, Connie, from Cuba. Our dads went to school together."

"Welcome to Missouri." Frankie started to offer a dirty hand still holding damp nails and then thought better of it. Both girls giggled at his predicament. "Little different than Cuba, I imagine?"

"Yes," she nodded but then cast an eye in Tabby's direction. "Different but good."

"Well, that's nice to hear. What are you two doing out on a Sunday afternoon?"

"Just wandering," Tabby answered honestly. "Trying to stay out of Granny Hannah's way and out of the kitchen so we don't have to wash dishes and uh....that's about all, I guess."

"Hmm, sounds like enough." Frankie looked back down at

the stakes and twine, now at his feet. "Just trying to get some things lined out here."

"Hey, have you had anything to eat?" Tabby gave him a sharp look. "It's way past dinner. How long you been out here?"

"Oh, not that long, probably. I dunno." His attention was not focused on what she was saying. "Not really been that hungry today."

"Well, you should probably have something. Here, wait a minute." She walked over to the far edge of the high grass where the lush thickness of it thinned again, going across a layer of mixed rocks, right where she had been exploring a few days before. She bent over and then came back to the other two, cupping something in her hands.

"Here." She gave him a handful of bright red berries. "Wild strawberries. Not everybody gets those for breakfast, you know."

"You're kidding!" He looked them over gingerly. "Wild strawberries?" He tried one and then popped the next few in his mouth after separating off the tiny green tops. "Kinda tart but not bad. How did you know where to find them anyway?"

"I saw the blossoms the other day when we were up here with Father Clem and your uncle. I knew it wouldn't be long after that there would be berries."

"Quite the little nature girl, aren't you? Salt and pepper snakes and wild strawberries."

Tabby snorted her answer. "That's nothing. Just life here in the Ozarks."

He shook his head with a sideways grin. "Here, hold this, will you?" He handed her one end of a measuring tape and walked backwards away from the two girls, silently counting his steps.

They helped him measure, scribbled down a few notes, set out stakes and the accompanying twine for a time, and then Tabby made an excuse that she had forgotten to check on something before they left the house. When they returned a short time later, she was carrying a brown paper sack that held left over fried chicken, biscuits, potato chips, an apple, a large piece of chocolate cake in a sandwich carton, and a cold bottle of pop.

"Hey, this is like a regular picnic!" Frankie chirped as he hoisted himself up onto the tailgate of his pickup. The girls scrambled up into the back of the truck as well and sat there, each of them sipping a cold soft drink that they had snagged before leaving the house.

"Thanks!" The word came out a bit muffled through a mouthful of chicken. "Hungrier than I thought," he added softly with a sheepish grin.

The three continued their visit, punctuated by much laughter as Frankie enjoyed his late lunch. They were oblivious to the fact that they were all under observation from a distant vehicle, parked higher up the road, whose driver sat without moving, binoculars fixed on the three of them.

CHAPTER 7

The next few days flew by as Tabby and Connie alternated their time between keeping their promise to Jesse, helping out at the store as well as seeing more of the park. Tabby still found the general daily minutia of storekeeping tedious even on its best days. Connie, on the other hand, seemed to thrive on the business of selling sundries, stocking shelves, greeting visitors, assigning camping sites, and solving various minor problems for everyone involved from Jesse to the latest arrival. Tabby was not unhappy to escape on more than one occasion to lead a trail ride when called. She asked Connie if she wanted to come along and she smiled each time and said yes, but maybe another day.

Tabby was about to climb into the passenger seat of her uncle's pickup truck after finishing up another afternoon ride, when a pickup pulled in beside her with a spew of gravel and a dramatic tromp on the brakes.

"Hey, Beautiful," the driver drawled as he stepped out of his truck. "I heard you were back in town."

She looked over her shoulder and then immediately glanced down at her hand already on the door handle and wished she had the fortitude to just open it and drive away. Instead, she turned around with a forced smile and leaned against her own truck door.

"Hello, Tommy." She made a genuine effort to be pleasant.

Dressed in an old T-shirt, worn blue jeans, sweat-stained ball cap, and cowboy boots, he looked to Tabby as if he had just gotten off his job at the Stave Mill in town. He and she had gone to school together most of their lives and at one time, been quite close. The big man sauntered toward her in what he undoubtedly considered to be a flirtatious manner. "When were you gonna call me, Baby?"

"Well, Tommy, you know, it's been real busy since I got home, what with my family and all. And I've been working here doing trail rides and at the campground helping Jesse..."

He slid up beside her and she could smell the beer on his breath. "Well, you still could have called." His drawl was thick with a syrupy sweetness. "You don't work every night of the week, do you?"

"No, I don't, Tommy," she sighed, "but I didn't see any point in calling either, to be honest."

"Why not, Baby? Can't we just pick up where we left off? I know you got mad the last time we went out but come on. Let's let bygones be bygones, as they say. We can—"

"No we can't." She gave up the effort to be amiable. "Look, I know you are just a good ol' boy looking for a good time and that's all fine for you, but I'm not your good time girl, Tommy. Not any more, anyway. So let's just leave it at that and go on. No harm done. It just didn't work out."

"We were good together." He reached for her upper arm with a grip that was way too tight for comfort. "There ain't no reason to mess that up. You've come home now and everything can go right back to the way it was before. You and me and—"

"You take your hand off of me before I scream loud enough to bring half this valley down on your neck!" she spit out as she pulled away and jerked open the door of her truck.

"I told you, no harm done. Don't make it worse and while you are at it, sober up. No girl likes a drunk."

She goosed the engine to a roar and slammed the truck into reverse, leaving Tommy Burton scrambling to stay on his feet.

Back at the house, she tried to put the confrontation with Tommy out of her thoughts. She ducked into her bedroom to change, but took a moment first to look around her room. How much had changed in such a short time! It wasn't that long ago that she was dreading coming back to Missouri from California and yet, things were not going so badly. At least, nothing like she had feared when she left California. Late this past Sunday afternoon, barely twenty-four hours after they met, Connie had invited her to move back into her own room.

"If you want to…" Connie began shyly. "We could share. I feel bad that I took your room and now you live at the house of your aunt and uncle. We can stay here together."

Tabby had laughed out loud at her new friend's hesitancy. "We can try it out," she answered. "If we don't like it, I can go back."

And fortunately, it was working well. The truth was they were both so busy during the day, the two were only there in the evening, long enough to get a bath and fall into bed. She still had no clear idea of what she was going to do for the long-term but certainly for now, she had plenty to keep her busy. Still, what would happen when the summer was over? When the tourists left, others went back to college, or even some, like the guy supervising the park pool and its lifeguards, went back to a full-time job of teaching school? She had no idea what Connie would do either. While she was a few years younger than Tabby, if she was going to stay in the United States, she, too, would soon have to make some important decisions.

Tabby slipped into a matching blouse and shorts set and swapped her cowboy boots for a pair of sandals before wandering back down the way to the campground's combination store and office, where she found Connie sorting out Jesse's latest round of invoices to be paid.

"Oh, good grief!" Tabby shook her head with a grin. "Did he talk you into doing those, too? He's always been terrible at the bookkeeping. Until Marcia started doing it, he was about to end up in debtor's prison!"

"What is that?"

"Nothing," Tabby laughed, realizing the comment would be lost on the Cuban girl. "Or rather something that doesn't really exist. In the United States, there is no such thing. They used to have them in England before America was its own country. If you owed a lot of money to business people, they could have you put in prison for not paying. Now people declare bankruptcy, which means you go to court and tell a judge you don't have enough money to pay your bills. Either way it is a nasty business and my brother is not the best at paying his bills on time." She dropped her voice to a conspiratorial whisper before continuing. "It is not even that he doesn't have the money most of the time. He just doesn't like the paperwork involved!" Tabby put a hand to her mouth in a futile attempt to hide her laughter.

"Jesse said Marcia did not have time because their baby,

Adam, had been sick and that if I wanted to look at them and see what needed paid right now, that would be good," Connie shared by way of explanation. "That is all right, yes?"

"Oh sure, if he asked you to, no problem," Tabby nodded.

"Just be careful or he will have you doing all of them."

"I do not mind," Connie continued in a solemn tone as opposed to Tabby's more jovial attitude. She pushed a lock of dark hair out of her eyes. "It is good to be busy and useful. I do not want to simply sit here and do nothing. You have all done so much for me already. Helping in any way is a good thing for me. I know it is what my parents would expect also." The mention of her family cast a momentary shadow across her face. She frowned at the papers in her hand, trying to decipher the hand scrawled notes on the next invoice.

"You are quite the serious little piece of work, aren't you?" Tabby contemplated her new friend over a cold bottle of Coca-Cola she had just pulled from a nearby home-style refrigerator with a large hand written sign on its door, lining out the flavors and prices of the bottles inside.

"This is a bad thing?" Connie looked up for a moment.

"No, not at all," Tabby replied. "It's fine, especially in business. So tomorrow is Friday. What do you want to do?"

"What do you mean?" Connie dropped the papers to squint at her friend. "What do you do different on Friday?"

"Oh, nothing. Actually, we will probably be pretty busy here as campers come in for the weekend on Friday afternoon and evening, but Saturday night, the Cat Hollow Dance Barn, just up the highway, is always fun. They have a live band and dancing, cold drinks and snacks. It's just a good time to get out, have a little fun. What do you think?"

"I think I love to dance. That would be wonderful!" Connie's eyes were shining.

* * * * *

Saturday afternoon the girls found their way across the road to another outdoor Mass. Tabby silently marveled at how much had happened in just the past week. Looking around it was obvious that Frankie had made good on his plans to get the construction project rolling. A stack of two by fours was left over from the pieces used to build concrete forms for the floor. Frankie said the concrete truck would be arriving early next week to deliver the floor in liquid form. He had come out to the site each evening after leaving the construction site at the end of the day. With his Uncle Bob out of commission, he had double the work to oversee.

Bob McCleary left the hospital late Friday afternoon and Frankie stayed with him that night as he was under doctor's orders to comply with complete bed rest at home. Frankie made arrangements for a nurse to come and spend the afternoon and evening with him on Saturday so he could spend more time at the building site.

"This is exciting that you can make a Mass wherever you want to in your country," Connie confided to both Frankie and Tabby as the priest made preparations to begin. "In my country, the church is all but outlawed now. The truth is Fidel and his people are afraid of the church. Most government leaders in Latin America are. They know the church has more power with the people than they do and it makes them angry and more than a little nervous. It is true at times the church has been on the rich people's side, but not always. Many times the priests fight right beside the people. Either way, the people should have the right to choose if they want to follow the church, yes?"

"Yes!" Frankie agreed as Father Clem began.

Tabby observed Connie as much as possible without her notice. It warmed her heart to see her friend's face relax as she participated in parts of the Mass that she clearly recognized, despite the fact that they were in English rather than Spanish. Once again, Tabby listened and watched closely, determined to keep pace better this week than last. She discovered things she had missed her first time, like the responsive "Lord, hear our prayer" as the participants recited after the priest's recitation of various concerns.

"Oh, that was wonderful!" Connie's eyes shone as the worshippers began to scatter at the end of the Mass. "I am not sure when I last went to Mass. We have to do so in secret at home and we do not go often. It is dangerous and my grandfather does not leave the apartment much because my parents do not like to leave him alone."

"Oh, Connie, I cannot imagine." Tabby's angst could be seen on her face and heard in her voice. "We take so much for granted," she added, almost in a whisper.

Connie shrugged with a smile, trying to will away the tears that were forming, unbidden.

"Come on," Frankie told them both. "Let me introduce you to Father Clem, Connie."

"Oh yes, please." She pressed both of her palms against the corners of her eyes.

"Father Clem," he began. "This is a friend of ours, Connie Rios, who arrived last week from Cuba."

"*¿De Cuba?*" The priest surprised all three of them with his response. "*Bienvenidos a los Estados Unidos.*"

"*¿Habla usted español? ¡Qué maravillosa!*" Connie replied with a delighted giggle.

"No, not really," Father laughed, putting up his hands in defense. "Just a little I remember from my days back in seminary. Truly though, it is a pleasure to meet you. I hope your journey here was not too difficult."

"Oh!" Now it was Connie's turn to be slightly taken aback. "Yes, it was not so good, ending in the hospital. Too much ocean, but since then, being here at Bennett Spring, it is very good."

"Yes, it certainly is, isn't it?" The priest agreed. "Did you enjoy the Mass?"

"Oh yes, thank you so much. It has been so long…"

"I would imagine that is true. Señor Fidel Castro is not exactly a friend of the Church, is he?"

"No, he is not." Connie was overjoyed to find someone who apparently understood a great deal about her country's situation without additional explanation. "Do you know Cuba? You have been there?"

"No, I never have but maybe someday yet. I had a Cuban roommate at seminary so I learned a lot then and, of course, all of us have watched very closely these last many years."

"It has been very difficult," Connie nodded. "I wish…"

"What?" Tabby jumped in.

"Oh, I wish there was a way to tell my family I am here and I am well." She smiled through her tears again. "I am sorry. I do not mean to cry."

"It's okay." Tabby reached an arm around her to give her shoulders a quick embrace. "I think we can all understand."

"Well," Father Clem spoke thoughtfully. "There may be a way to get a message through."

"Really? You know people in Cuba?" Frankie was impressed.

"It is probably better to say, I know someone who knows someone who can pass along a message. Here, write down your full name, your parents' names, and how you would contact them if you were in Cuba. Do they still have a telephone? It may be someone could give them a call and let them know that you reached your destination and you are safe and well."

With her eyes closed reverently, Connie made the sign of the cross. "That would be a miracle, Padre. A miracle *de Dios*."

"This is the place for that," the priest replied with a wide smile, his hands uplifted.

"Yes, it is," Connie agreed. Frankie pulled a small notebook from his back pocket and handed it to Connie who immediately began to scribble.

"So where are you going from here?" Tabby looked up at Frankie.

"I dunno. I guess I hadn't thought about it much. Why?"

"Oh, like you, we have been working hard all week and we thought we'd get out a little tonight. Going back across the road to the house to grab something to eat and then going up to the Cat Hollow Dance Barn. Wondered if you wanted to tag along?"

"Sure." He shrugged with a smile but was more than pleased that they were inviting him along. Since moving to Lebanon, he had spent almost all of his time working and helping his uncle any way he could. Uncle Bob's wife, June, had died the year before of cancer and Frankie, like his mother, Bob's sister, had worried about him living all alone.

After Connie gave Father Clem her information, he bid them good evening as he left for dinner with some of his other parishioners. As the three walked up the drive together, Tabby explained that her parents had gone to a Chamber of Commerce dinner and meeting for the evening. Granny Hannah had gone to spend the night at Ben and Jessica's home outside Lebanon.

"Mom told me she would cook some burgers and leave them for us," Tabby said, "but I think I'm going to wash my hair first, real quick before we go."

"Really?" Frankie seemed surprised.

"Sure, it won't take long. I don't mind to go with it wet afterward."

"Okay," he shrugged as he stood on the porch a moment. She walked in the house and came out immediately with a large glass pitcher. She walked over to the corner of the porch and filled the pitcher from the rain barrel at the corner. "No running water in the house?" He asked with half a smile.

"Of course, but this is rainwater. That's what you want to wash hair."

"Rainwater?"

"Sure, it makes your hair really soft. Just a second. We got this new thing and it heats up the water fast. Come on. I'll show you."

In the kitchen, she popped the entire pitcher inside a modern-looking appliance sitting on the counter.

"It's called a microwave oven and Daddy just got it from one of his businessman friends at the Chamber of

Commerce last week."

"A micro-what?"

"A microwave oven. One of the gents bought it for his wife because it's the latest thing, kinda fancy, huh? but somebody told her it might give off radiation or something and she got scared and said she didn't want it in her house. The man was telling Daddy about it and told him to take it home and try it so here it is. It is really different." She bent down to peak in the glass window as it hummed along. "You can only heat things in glass or some plastics, but no metal or it makes sparks and smokes which is pretty scary. But it heats stuff up hot and quick. You can even heat things on a paper plate. Can you imagine? I guess the salesman who sold it to the guy who gave it to Daddy said, before long there would be one in every house in America but Mama said that's ridiculous. I guess to buy one, they actually cost about $500 and Mama says nobody is gonna pay that just to heat water quick or make a hot dog in thirty seconds!"

"Hmpf!" Frankie looked at the thing as it beeped and stopped humming. "A microwave oven, huh?"

"Yeah, to think when Granny Hannah left her house a few months ago, she was still cooking on a wood stove and Mama loves her electric range. Maybe I'll be the first one in the family to do all my cooking in a microwave oven!"

"Maybe so," Frankie shook his head at the wonders of the modern world.

"Here, come help for a second." Tabby led him back out to the porch, where she wet her hair with a little of the now-warmed rainwater and added a small amount of shampoo to quickly lather it up. "Nice thing about rainwater, too, is it is soft water and you don't need much shampoo." She stood at the far side of the porch and leaned over the railing. "Here, pour a little of that water over my hair, real slow to rinse."

Frankie did as he was told and in short order, she had wrapped her long blond tresses up in a towel as she took the now empty pitcher from him. "Thank you." She gave him a dazzling smile and he followed her into the house, still marveling at the new discoveries he made every time he encountered this girl.

An hour later, the three walked back to where they had celebrated Mass earlier to pile into Frankie's pickup for the short drive to the dance barn. They could hear the music pulsing as fast as they pulled into the gravel parking lot. Inside, the place had the basics, a concrete floor, aging wooden walls, a makeshift box of a stage, and was already nearly filled with locals and a few tourists, enjoying the music, dancing, and visiting with one another.

"Hey, girls. Good to see you!" A voice from behind made them both turn as fast as they made their way inside.

"J. Junior!" Tabby greeted. "You are getting out some now, aren't you?"

"Yeah, finally biting the bullet, I guess you could say."

"You come to a dance house?" Connie blurted out and then clapped her hand over her mouth in embarrassment.

J. Junior laughed out loud. "Yeah, must seem kinda silly but Tabby can tell you, even before this..." He flipped his hands across the handrails of his chair. "I was like so many of these boys, often came to listen to the music but you couldn't get me out there to dance. Some things don't change."

Connie nodded solemnly.

"But the music is still good," he grinned. "These boys can play."

"And so can you, as I remember," Tabby added.

He simply smiled.

"J., this is a friend, Frankie, who is working across the road from our house, putting up a little church building over there."

"Oh, yeah, the Catholics." J. Junior flashed a cockeyed smile, robbing his words of any possible offense. "I heard about that. How's it going? The building project?"

"Just getting started really." Frankie appreciated the other man's straightforward approach. "Got the concrete forms up but that's about it."

"Well, I don't envy you building on this rock we call ground here at Bennett Spring. Where you from, Frankie?"

"St. Louis, but I came here a few months ago by way of Saigon."

"You, too, huh? Well, you can see the souvenir I brought back from Da Nang." J. Junior gave a back-handed flip of his hands across his wheelchair's arm rests.

"Tough break," Frankie replied evenly.

"Life is full of those, ain't it?" J. Junior grinned up at him.

"Yeah," Frankie smiled in return. "It is."

The country band kicked in and for whatever they may have lacked in quality they made up for with sheer volume. Tabby cast an eye over the band members as they played, recognizing a couple from days gone by.

"You girls want something to drink?" Frankie offered, all

but shouting as he angled his head toward the concession counter. Both nodded and he turned back to J. Junior. "Want something?"

"No, thanks." J. Junior gave a friendly wave and rolled toward the small stage.

The girls found a couple of wooden folding chairs at a nearby table and prepared to settle in.

"Be careful of the chairs," Tabby warned as they sat down.

"Why?" Connie looked hers over cautiously. "Do they fall down?" She hesitated to put her weight on it.

"No," Tabby grinned. "They pinch if you are not careful how you sit on them."

"Oh." Connie pretended to understand but simply perched on the front edge of hers, prepared for the thing to collapse underneath her at any moment.

Frankie joined them with three paper cups and a basket of popcorn. In short order, he and Tabby tried out the dance floor.

"I haven't done this in a while," he cautioned as they started with a slower number, allowing them to dance closer than many of the songs of the day. "Not since...." He glanced down at his leg.

"Me, either," she smiled up at him. "Not to worry. We'll just see how it goes." And it went exceedingly well. She would never have known there was a problem by the way he swayed with her so gently, in perfect rhythm to the music.

The next song began with a long pull on a harmonica and Tabby reluctantly stepped away from the warm comfort of Frankie's arms and looked toward the stage. "He's still got it!" she cried out loud as she pointed toward the band. "Look!"

Just below the stage, J. Junior could be seen, seated in his wheelchair with a microphone on a heavy stand parked in front of him, his hands cupped around a harmonica up close to his face. The other musicians on stage followed his lead and the whole place was soon jumping to a well-known old time favorite. Another musician's fingers held the bow that flew over the strings of his country fiddle and the steel guitar, bass, and drums followed, the electrified music, filling the place. As the music cranked higher and faster, many like Tabby and Frankie, who had drifted back to the table to join Connie, simply stopped to watch and appreciate the lively music and those producing it.

"Whew!" Frankie enthusiastically joined the whole hall as they hooted their approval with whistles and cat calls as well as applause. Connie was on her feet, clapping as fast as her hands could move. Another song began and J. Junior rolled toward his friends as they welcomed him to their table. Frankie didn't ask this time but simply plunked a large Coke down in front of J. Junior.

"Thanks, Man!" He lifted the cup in Frankie's direction and gulped half of it.

"That was wonderful!" Connie's enthusiasm was contagious. "I have never heard something like that before!"

"Yeah?" J. Junior grinned. "Harmonicas came from Europe but us Americans have sure made 'em our own since."

The new friends passed their time visiting, laughing, and enjoying the music. Tabby and Frankie returned to the dance floor a few times. After yet another dance, Frankie escorted her back to the table and then whispered in her ear that he was off to the little soldier's room. Tabby grinned her understanding over the blaring music but did not return immediately to her seat. Instead, she stood off a short distance, in cheerful observance of her friends, J. Junior and Connie, and the animated conversation they were sharing. It occurred to her that a photograph of the two would be a nice touch when she remembered Seeker's little camera was still in her bag that was stuffed under the seat of Frankie's pickup.

Out in the parking lot, the music could still be heard clearly as she walked out of the glare of the lights attached to the outside of the dance barn. She looked up at the brightness of the quarter moon and the many stars dotting the inky blue sky above. In San Francisco, only the brightest stars had ever been visible with so many city lights flooding the skies with their artificially produced illumination. Her words to Connie from earlier in the day echoed back in her head…we take so much for granted.

It took a few more steps before she became aware of the fact that there were several persons standing about in the shadows, apparently savoring the music without paying for the privilege. She thought little more about it as she reached for the truck door. That's when she heard a slurred voice behind her.

"So this is where you spending your Saturday nights?" She whirled at the unexpected closeness of the voice and the familiar sickeningly sweet smell of his boozy breath. She chided herself for not paying closer attention as her heart leaped.

"Tommy! Geez, you scared me half to death! I didn't hear you behind me!"

A small chuckle escaped him but it held no warmth. "You wasn't supposed to," was all he said. He drew close, pinning the door shut with his bulk, and leaned in to cup her face closer to his, an arm engulfing her shoulders.

"No!" She pushed hard away from him, both hands on his shoulders, but he took no notice, sliding his face down the side of her neck which he nibbled sharply, causing her to wince in pain. "Stop it, Tommy! Stop it! I swear…" She hit him with balled up fists but his only response was to move his mouth up her neck this time to cover her lips with his and squeeze her painfully tight. The fear that welled up in her and the acrid smell of him made her feel as if she might throw up at any moment. The frightening weakness in her knees was not the response she needed from her own body at this moment and she twisted her face away in an effort to scream. The pathetically strangled cry that emerged further alarmed her.

"Tommy, please!" she begged. "Don't do this!" He flattened her against the truck beneath him and pulled at her new shirt, bursting the buttons to throw it open.

Suddenly, Tommy rolled to one side as if suddenly thrown off balance.

"I think she said pretty clear to cut it out." Delbert Kendrix's voice was unmistakable behind her, despite his own slurred words.

"Ain't your business, Kendrix. Move on!" The threat in Tommy's low guttural response was undeniable.

"That's your opinion, Tommy." Delbert kept his voice even if somewhat muffled. A flash of reflected light told Tabby he was holding something in his hand she couldn't quite make out. "But I don't like nobody messing with my neighbors and that includes her."

"Well, I don't care much about what you like." Tommy gave his head a shake to clear it while he leaned against the truck next to Tabby, still holding on to her wrist. He dropped her hand and lunged at Delbert, who, despite the heavy cast on his leg, still managed to dodge out of the bigger man's way.

"Better knock it off," Delbert warned Tommy with a grin as Tommy spun around like a bull in the ring to make another charge at the smaller man.

The second attempt went completely awry for Tommy as Delbert hit him hard on the side of the head with the unseen object. Tabby heard the sound of shards of glass hitting the ground as Tommy bashed his head into the side of the truck and then also fell to the gravel with a heavy thud.

"Tabby!" Frankie moved across the parking lot at what she considered lightning speed at that point. "What the…are you all right?"

"Yeah," she answered breathlessly, her heart still beating faster than she would ever have thought possible. "I think so." Despite her answer, she still leaned heavily against his shoulder as he swept a protective arm around her.

"Delbert, are you okay?" She looked up immediately.

"Oh, yeah." She heard him laughing in the dark and then he stepped closer to the couple, where they could see him more clearly. "Ma will probably be mad that I broke one of her Mason jars. Dang, Tommy! That boy doesn't know when to quit."

The big man stirred at their feet and sat up, holding his head. Two other men also moved into the light, one on each side of him. "What's going on?" one of them asked in a menacing tone.

"Nothing you really wanna know about unless you want a piece of what he got," Delbert replied while kicking at the remains of his shattered Mason jar. "Waste of good 'shine," he muttered.

"Oh hey, Delbert," the questioning companion shot back. "Didn't see it was you. Tommy giving you trouble?"

"Not me as much as Miz Tabby Shine here. Just no need for it, is all," he continued as if discussing nothing more innocuous than the weather forecast.

"Uh-huh. Well, hey." The latest arrival tipped his shabby cowboy hat toward her as she continued to stand in the safety of close proximity to Frankie. "Tommy, come on. Get up! We gotta go."

"No, no way," Tommy mumbled as he got to his feet. "I gotta take care of this, I'm telling you—"

"Tommy!" The cowboy hat hissed. "It's took care of. It's Delbert, for cryin' out loud. Come on, let's go." He and the other silent companion helped the big man to his feet and the three stumbled off into the darkness.

"Thanks, Delbert." Tabby's words were still a bit shaky but she was feeling much better now that Tommy had moved on and Frankie and Delbert were both standing in her corner.

"Yeah, thanks a lot." Frankie offered a hearty handshake which Delbert readily accepted.

"No problem," he answered. "We take care of our own out here, don't we?" He tipped his Army cap toward Tabby. "Bunch of us come up here most Saturday nights and listen outside." He shrugged. "Can't drink inside, legal or 'shine, so we stay outside. Ain't like we're dancers. We ain't missing much out here," he added with a laugh. "As long as we don't bother nobody, it don't seem to matter. Have to make sure Tommy don't get into no more shenanigans or they might come down on all of us and that wouldn't be no good. See ya, Tabby. Tell your uncle 'hey'."

"I will." She smiled quietly as he walked away. She stepped away from the safety of Frankie's arms but not before he noticed her long hair was incredibly soft and fragrant, lending an extra measure of interest to the evening ambiance.

Still, with his head in the clouds, all he could manage to ask was, "What were you thinking coming out here all alone?" They walked back toward the open door where the music was still flowing freely.

"Nothing," Tabby shrugged. "It's no big deal really. I live down the road, for Pete's sake. This ain't like the big city. It's my own backyard. I was just going to get a camera to take a picture of Connie and J. Junior together. They were so cute, sitting there chatting away. Hey!" She stopped suddenly and took hold of his arm. "Don't say anything to them, please? I don't want them upset or worried. Tommy and I dated a long time ago in high school, that's all."

Frankie gave her a dubious look.

"Hey, everybody changes after high school, don't they? He was a much nicer guy then, honest and about fifty pounds lighter, too. Too much beer hasn't been good for him in a lot of ways!"

"I'll take your word for it," Frankie murmured.

"Well, I just don't want to say anything to them, okay?"

He nodded. He reached out to open the door for her but just as quick she shot past him and hooted at a cat, just beyond the corner of the building where it crept along the edge of the woods with something in its mouth.

"Drop that!" She hissed at the gray creeping feline which

stopped, seemingly confused by the sudden attack. "You heard me!" She continued her rant, stomping toward the cat. "Let him go! Let him go right now!"

The cat had had enough. He dropped the small mound of brown fur and scurried off into the nearby weeds.

"What the heck are you doing?" Frankie struggled to catch up to her. She turned around toward him, her hands cupped around a tiny chipmunk she held close to her chest and neck. "Tabby, are you crazy? Those things bite!" He stopped square in front of her.

"He's fine." She cooed to him in the same honeyed voice she was using to comfort the shaken chippie. "He's just scared. Wouldn't you be if you were caught in some big cat's choppers just a moment before?

"You'll be fine, baby," she continued, running a gentle finger over the cuddly rodent's distinctive coat of five dark brown stripes. She ambled over to the broken stone foundation of a nearby storage building of weathered gray wood. She bent over to release her tiny new friend who scampered off into the recesses of the aging stone wall.

"What?" She looked Frankie straight in the eye as he tried to decide if he should fuss, congratulate, or just hug this most enigmatic young woman.

"I don't even know where to begin." He shook his head but his smile was wide and his dark eyes were dancing.

Tabby was content to spend the rest of the evening seated at the table, sipping Cokes and nibbling popcorn. She encouraged Frankie to ask Connie to dance which he did but she declined shyly and stayed seated until J. Junior played one more song with the band. At the end of the evening, J. Junior offered Connie a ride home in his Jeep and she accepted, leaving Frankie and Tabby to make their way home the very short drive down Highway 64 to the turn off to the park.

Both couples sat in the driveway in their respective vehicles, discussing the night and moving toward the inevitable awkward end of the evening, when bright headlights flashed behind them as J.C. and Becky pulled in behind the two other vehicles in the circle drive in front of the house. Both girls quickly exited the cars, bidding the fellows a quick if inelegant good night.

They waited on the porch for the two adults to join them as all entered the house together, talking and laughing about their very enjoyable but different evenings. Connie kicked off her shoes and picked them up to carry them down the hall to the bedroom.

Her startled scream brought all conversation to an immediate halt as the other three scrambled down the hall to her aid.

CHAPTER 8

"I can't imagine my mother could even find a key to her front door." Becky stood in the hallway outside the girls' bedroom a half hour later, still surveying what looked like the aftermath of a tornado. The double bed mattress had been flipped and slit open, with part of its stuffing dragged from the split. The contents of the closet and the large dresser were all over the floor. The pictures had been flipped from the walls and tossed onto the floor and the lamp and the bedside table that supported it had been turned over. "I'm not sure I could for this house, either." She continued to shake her head. "I don't know that any of us here at Bennett Spring have ever locked our doors. What is happening to our world?" Her voice cracked with her last words.

"Becky, come on. I think your brother just pulled into the drive." J.C. took her hand and pulled her away from the bedroom door, toward the kitchen where Tabby was making herself and Connie each a cup of hot chocolate as her way of coping with the stress of the situation.

While none of them had been in the house for hours during the evening, it was obvious that someone else had. Former Sheriff Ben Darling came in, greeted his brother-in-law, and immediately went to work, flipping open a small spiral notebook as he began to ask questions.

Becky sat on the living room couch, seemingly almost in shock. "Sis, you gonna be all right?" was Ben's first question as he cupped her shoulder. "It'll be okay, I promise."

"Mama, I'm making us some hot cocoa. You want some?" her daughter called from the kitchen.

"Yes," J.C. answered for her. "Bring her a cup. It can't hurt."

"All right," Ben proceeded. "I called Sheriff Murphy's office and like I figured, they asked if they could send somebody out here tomorrow in the daylight. Since nobody is in any danger tonight, that's a better idea over all. They can look for footprints and other evidence outside when the light is better. J.C., you told me in looking around, you didn't find anything disturbed in any part of the house except the girls' room, right?"

J.C. nodded silently.

"Okay, I want to look at that in a minute but let me get a few details down first. Nobody was here tonight, right? What time did the last person leave and what time did you all come back in?"

J.C. looked at the girls as they came in with a tray of coffee mugs fragrant with homemade hot cocoa. "Oh, I'm sorry, Uncle Benji," Tabby said as she set her mother's cup down on the coffee table in front of her. "I didn't ask if you wanted any."

"No, it's fine." He waved his left hand as if chasing a fly from his face, going back to his note-taking.

"What time did you two leave for the dance?" J.C. repeated Ben's question.

"Oh, I dunno." Tabby glanced at Connie. "Maybe six or six-thirty?"

Connie nodded in silence.

"Any idea who might be after what?" Ben asked the next question in the basic straight forward custom of most cops.

They all shook their heads in unison.

"Let's have a look at this room." He stood up unexpectedly, as J.C. and Tabby scrambled to follow. Becky and Connie stayed in the living room and Connie reached over to lay her hand over Becky's. Becky grabbed the trembling hand that covered hers.

"Child, you're shakin'!" Becky exclaimed in surprise.

"It...it is so frightening," Connie whispered, as Becky pulled the girl from the nearby chair to sit next to her on the sofa. She flipped the throw on the back of the sofa around the teen's shoulders and slipped an arm around her. "It is just like home," Connie barely breathed, "when they decide to come after you or your people."

"Oh, this is not like that," Becky tried to assure her. "This is just some local idiot, I'm sure. Can't imagine what he's after but it's somebody looking for something to steal, most likely. Nothing more. Like my brother said, it'll be okay. I feel better just having him here." Her laughter still held an edge of nervousness despite her words.

Ben took his time, surveying the damage, touching little except with the top of his ball point pen to move an occasional object or look beneath a larger one.

"Hmphf!" he finally huffed when he stepped out of the bedroom. "Whoever he was he was thorough, I'll give him that. Sheriff Murphy's boys can come out and try to get some fingerprints tomorrow. Maybe he was foolish enough to leave some on the mirror over the dresser. Did you notice the window was broken, too? Kinda strange he could have walked in the unlocked front door but looks like he went through the window instead. Makes me wonder...."

"About what?" J.C. finally put forth a question of his own as the two men stood in the hallway.

"Well, a whole lot of things, to be honest. Whatever he was looking for, he was definitely only interested in this room, right? Didn't bother your room or Jesse's ol' room? If he was looking for jewelry or valuables, it's the master bedroom they go for. Nothing was bothered in the rest of the house either?" He stopped speaking and looked past J.C. at Tabby, crouching behind her father.

J.C. turned around and gently put his hands on his daughter's shoulders. "Go check on your mother for me, will you? I think she's the one most rattled by this whole thing right now."

She obediently complied but the silent glare she gave both of them said she wasn't particularly happy about it.

"Let me just ask this straight out." Ben closed his notebook as he looked his old friend in the eye. "How much do you really know about this Cuban girl? Do you think somebody could be after her or something she's got? I'm telling you right now that is the first thing Murphy's deputies are going to be looking for, with her coming from Castro-land. Those Communist types still make most of us pretty nervous around here."

J.C. sighed heavily. "You are not the first one to have that thought but honestly, Ben, I just can't make it work. She's a seventeen year old kid who just barely arrived in Miami alive after spending days on what was little more than a large inflatable raft. I wouldn't have gone to sea on it, I can tell you that, let alone tried to cross the shark-infested ninety miles between here and Cuba on such a flimsy thing! What could she possibly have? The State Department said all she had on her was a plastic bag with a couple of pictures which she showed them and me. She had one little bag of personal belongings which those state department guys went through, I can guarantee you. I can ask her and I'm sure she'll show it to you or the deputies if you like. Becky, Tabby, and I bought or gave her the rest of her clothes, shoes, and few other personal items she now has." He stopped speaking and rubbed his temples before continuing.

"Jeff Dugan, the state department man who called me, seemed convinced she was legitimate. I've known her father and grandfather since I was in junior high and that's all I can tell you, really. Except that I feel as protective of her as I do of Tabby about now and I want whoever did this and I want him now, just for scaring my girls so!"

* * * * *

A sheriff's deputy arrived the next morning and asked many of the same questions Ben had the night before. All of them sat down in the living room once again, this time without the comfort of hot cocoa, and did their best to answer his many questions, some of which were not as considerate as those posed by the former sheriff.

"I've gone over that room now, pretty good," Deputy Ed Franklin began as he nestled down in an overstuffed chair beside the couch. "You know he broke the window coming in or out, which don't make much sense if the front door was unlocked as you said, Miz Shine. Even looks like there's some blood on the pieces of window glass I found on the ground outside, along with a couple of good-sized shoe prints. We'll see what we can make of those."

"The blood on the glass or the shoe prints?" J.C. asked quietly, seated across from the deputy.

"Both, sir," came the answer as he made a few more scribbles in his flip note book. "I also took a bunch of pictures with the department camera so we can look them over later. Now like I was saying—"

"Excuse me, Deputy Franklin, is it? My thought was that if this man went to the trouble to break in through the window rather than just stroll through the front door, that might be a strong indication that he is not from around here. Most locals, especially thieves, would be inclined, it would seem, to at least try the door first whereas those from a bigger city would break in through a window, just assuming that the front door would be locked if no one was home."

"Well, now, that's a good point, Mr. Shine." The uniformed officer nodded as he made even more notes. "I'll add that to my report. Now, girls, I need you to think very hard." He turned to face Tabby and Connie as they perched, side by side, on the nearby sofa. "Is there anyone you have had some kind of fight or argument with lately? Got a boyfriend mad at you? Maybe he gave you something he wants back now?"

Tabby shook her head, frowning at his words. Yes, there was an obnoxious boyfriend in the past but she didn't have anything he had given her that he might want returned. "I can't think of anything or anyone like that," she began slowly, deep in thought. "And Connie hasn't been here long enough to meet anyone or have anybody upset with her. She's only been here a little over a week."

"Yes, well, speaking of just that," he continued, "Connie Rios, is it? I understand that you are from Cuba. Not exactly a country that is friendly with America right now.

Did you leave there with people upset with you, looking for you? Should we be on the lookout for some Cuban fellers up here, searching for you?"

Connie's eyes widened in horror. "I do not know for certain but I cannot imagine that would be true. My father sent me out of the country to protect me after my brother disappeared but not so much because of any certain threat against me. It is a threat right now in Cuba to be young if you do not follow everything that Castro and his political party says. If your family, like mine, has fought against him and refused to follow the Communist party, then everyone is always at risk, but I am a very little fish. I cannot believe they would send anyone after me. I have not been involved in any kind of politics. I went to school until they closed my Catholic high school and I tried to take care of my family, nothing more." Once again, silent tears coursed down her cheeks.

"Hey, it's okay. I didn't mean to make you cry." The deputy immediately apologized and Becky handed the teen a couple of tissues from a nearby box on the coffee table.

"I know it is hard to fathom," J.C. spoke up once more, "but honestly, I've spent much of the night awake, analyzing all of this, Deputy. And the truth is none of it makes any sense. Someone breaks in, destroys the girls' room, takes nothing from there nor the rest of the house and then scampers out of here before any of us comes home. I am, to be quite honest, at a total loss."

"Well, sir," Deputy Franklin stood up, "I'll be taking my leave now. If you think of anything else, just give our office a call. I know Sheriff Murphy is well aware of this and wants to be kept up-to-date on anything we find. He would have been out here this morning himself but a cattle truck turned over out on Route 66 this morning. He had to be out there, helping with the traffic and rounding up cows.

I heard some of it on the car radio and it sounded like a real circus. I imagine he would have rather been out here!"

J.C. acknowledged that fact with a sideways smile. "I'm certain that is true."

"I'm going to try and take a few fingerprints off of the mirror in that room and of course, we'll see what we get off the pieces of window glass. Maybe we'll get lucky. I take it nobody slept in that room last night?"

"No," J.C. shook his head. "I'm not convinced anybody slept in this house much at all but the girls stayed in the other bedroom, my son's former room. My mother-in-law has been staying in there but as luck would have it, she went to spend last night at her son's house, Ben Darling, the former sheriff.

"Oh, yeah, Sheriff Darling, good man."

"Yes, he came out last night right after we all came home and first discovered this. He said he had notified your office and just came by to advise us on what was to come next and kind of calm our nerves, if you will."

"I can appreciate that," the deputy concluded. "Well, after I leave here today, you folks can go ahead and clean up that mess, save what you can, and go back to using the room as soon as you want."

"Well, thank you, Deputy. We appreciate your time. If you think of any more questions or find anything more, by all means, give me a call."

"I'll do it, sir." He shook J.C.'s hand and headed out the door.

* * * * *

Late in the day as the sun set low above the ridges,

spreading its yellow-orange glow across the valley, Tabby made her way back up the hill from the park after yet another trail ride. She noticed Frankie's pickup at the church building site. She pulled her truck up behind his and smiled to herself at the fact that her uncle's old truck was even more beat up than Frankie's 'working man's truck'.

"Hey, stranger," she called as she stepped out of her vehicle.

"Oh, hi." He gave her half a wave as he concentrated on the concrete forms at his feet. "Just checking 'em one more time before the concrete truck comes in the morning. I'm a little worried is all. Want to make sure we've got these right. Sure hate for this floor to come out wrong, be uneven, have low spots that hold the water, that sort of thing."

She solemnly contemplated the planks setting on a layer of white gravel, but understanding little of what he said, except for the part about low spots holding water. "Uh-huh," she muttered.

He walked over and sat on the front bumper of his truck, his eyes still fastened on the forms. "I guess I'm just worried about tomorrow," he sighed. "I want so much to get this right, partly for the church and all, but mostly, for my Uncle Bob. He's only been out of the hospital a couple of days and he's already getting restless. He's supposed to be on total bed rest and he's all the time up and around in the house. If he gets the idea that this project isn't going perfect, I swear, he'll be out here, trying to direct things!"

Tabby giggled at his frustration. "Ever been in charge of a full project like this before?" She perched on the truck bumper beside him.

He shook his head. "No, not really."

"Well, see? You're just nervous but it'll be fine."

"Ya think?"

"Sure." She stared at her cuffed blue jeans and dusty cowboy boots, surrounded by green grass.

"Something's bothering you?" He reversed the conversation on her.

She shrugged. "Well, a lot has happened since you boys dropped us off last night."

"Oh yeah? Like what? You went to church this morning, right?"

"Uh, no. We didn't get there. When we got home last night, you remember we walked into the house with my mom and dad?"

"Yeah. I'm not likely to forget that for a while. I haven't felt that dumb since I was in high school." He hung his head with a sheepish grin.

"Well, that ain't the half of it. We walked in the house and Connie went back to our bedroom and let out such a scream. She scared us half to death. We went running back there and found out somebody broke into our house and absolutely destroyed our room. They went through everything, like threw all our clothes out of the closet and the dresser. Even took a knife to our mattress!" Her voice broke as the reality of the situation came back to haunt her once again.

"Hey, hey, it's okay." Frankie pulled her close, reminding her of his protective arms last night after Tommy's appearance in the parking lot. "Your folks were there, right?"

She nodded as she wiped her tears. "Oh, yes and of course,

my dad called my Uncle Benji, who was the sheriff here for years. He came out and told us to stay out of the room and asked us a bunch of questions. He said the deputies would come out today and a Deputy Franklin did this morning so we all stayed home from church. He asked us more questions and he asked Connie who might be after her from Cuba. And of course, that really upset her. She and I slept in Jesse's room last night. The good thing is my Granny Hannah was already at Uncle Benji's and Aunt Jessica's house so hopefully she still doesn't know anything about it. If'n she got so upset about a little ol' Catholic chapel across the road from our house, imagine what she'll be like when she finds out about this!"

Frankie couldn't contain his laughter as that thought took hold. "Oh, Tabby. She will be beside herself, won't she?"

"Yes, I'm afraid so." She agreed with a weak laugh. "At any rate, nobody seems to know anything about who or what or why. The deputy asked me if I had anybody mad at me, if any former boyfriend had given me anything he might want back and I told him there was nobody like that. I mean, part of me was thinking of Tommy but while he's mad at me, there isn't anything he gave me he could want back. And then I thought about this guy in California..."

She fell silent as she began to shake. He hugged her tight beside him. "It's okay, Tabby. You are not in California anymore. You're safe right here in your very own Bennett Spring. What's going on?"

She took a deep breath. "I didn't say anything to the deputy this morning and it feels like somehow I lied by not telling him."

"I think the church calls it lying by omission," Frankie added quietly. "It's considered a lie because you didn't say it. What do they call it in court? The whole truth."

She sat a moment longer and then with a deep breath, she began. "His name was Diablo, or at least that's the name he gave to all of us, but half the people in San Francisco, I swear, make up a new name when they get there. I went to California with my friend from college, Margie. She's actually from Marshfield, just down the highway, but we met in the dorm in Springfield. She fell hard for this Diablo. The next thing I knew we were living in an apartment with him. He and she were tight from the beginning, always together. I couldn't hardly talk to her anymore without him around. I put up with it 'cause there wasn't anywhere else to go, you know? I had my own room, not big but they weren't buggin' me, so I thought I could manage. You know what that name means in Spanish? Diablo? It means the devil and that is exactly what he turned out to be." She took a deep breath before continuing.

"Early one morning, I woke up and he was in my room, and then, *in my bed,* talking to me, tellin' me how beautiful I am, how much he likes blond hair." Her voice went flat. "Margie's a brunette. He tells me not to scream or anything but the truth is I was so scared, I don't think I could have if I'd tried. Anyway, he heard a noise or something, maybe he thought Margie was coming, I don't know. All I know is then he rolled out of the bed and was gone. I caught up to Margie and tried to tell her 'cause I wanted us both to get out of there. But instead, as fast as I started talking, I could see she was losing it. I mean, you could just see it all over her! She walks out of my room and I could tell by the look on his face, he knew. He knew I told her and he knew she didn't believe me. So they went waltzing out the front door together and him with a little smirk on his face. I knew the next time with him would be lots worse so I got out. I packed my bag and ran out of there before they came back."

She stopped talking long enough to take a couple of ragged breaths. "I ended up sitting on a curb on the street a few blocks away. I didn't have anywhere to go and I didn't know what to do. By noon, I was just sitting there, crying. And then this man came along. He told me his name was Seeker and he was so sweet to me. He told me I could come to his place of peace. That's what he called it and that's exactly what it was, Irish. A large apartment really with a bunch of people but they were all so kind and peaceful. They smoked a lot of grass and did some other stuff that wasn't too good for them, I'm sure, but they were so gentle. I kept worrying that Diablo would come find me and although I watched out for him the next couple of months, the whole time I was there, I never did see him. But sometimes, I know I could feel him there, watching me, you know?" She heaved a huge sigh.

"Anyway, I can't believe I didn't say a word about any of that this morning or even last night with Uncle Benji. I mean, I don't know that Diablo came back here. That would be pretty crazy, wouldn't it? But I just couldn't make myself say anything in front of my dad. He thinks I'm still his little girl of sweet sixteen, not nearly twenty-four. I can't tell him I was spending the night in San Francisco with some guy named Seeker. So instead, I sat there with my mouth shut this morning and let Connie take the heat." She shifted, leaning forward, resting her elbows on her knees, dropping her face into her hands.

"Hey, hey." He reached out a hand to comfort her. "It's like you said, that would be pretty crazy for him to follow you all the way back here from California. Where's your friend Margie now? Do you know?"

She shook her head in a negative fashion.

"Well, maybe they are still together but until you see him standing here in Bennett Spring, I wouldn't spend a lot of time worrying about him. I'd be thinking more about that nitwit Tommy from last night. Don't know what he'd be looking for. Maybe just to shake you up."

"Well, if that was anybody's purpose, they sure did a bang up job of it!"

They both laughed at that as they sat together. He gently slid his hand up beside her face, tilted it up toward him, and gently kissed the tears away on both of her cheeks before kissing her lips softly. They spent the next few minutes in tender exploration of each other's lips before standing up in a passionate embrace.

"Oh, Tabby, we gotta hold up here." He pulled back slowly. "We both got a lot going on right now and we don't need to complicate it, do we?"

A genuine smile crossed her face. "Come on." She took his hand and pulled him along behind her. "We can't think here. Too close to your work and my house!"

He followed willingly, climbing into the passenger seat of her truck as she headed back into the park. She stopped in the parking lot in front of the trout hatchery and scurried toward the concrete pools holding thousands of trout of various sizes. She cast a fetching glimpse over her shoulder to make certain her companion followed.

"So what are we doing here?"

"Nothing. Just walking. Everybody loves to come look at the fish. Don't you?"

"Uh, I don't think I ever have but if you say so." He followed a step or two behind her.

She knelt down beside one of the pools and quickly collected a handful of tiny pellets she found along the concrete ledge. "Watch this." She tossed several of them into the water at their feet which produced a sudden swishing of the water as the fish lunged for the bits of trout feed.

"Whoa!" He jumped at the unexpected intensity of their feeding frenzy. "Like sharks or piranha or something!"

She laughed. "No, just trout. You're safe. They sell the food up there in little machines but people spill it and so do the hatchery boys who feed them regularly so as kids we always just learned to pick up the leftovers and toss it in. Here, just the little brown ones. Don't get any pieces of gravel. Those can kill the fish if they eat them by mistake."

"Interesting." He bent over and retrieved a few bits of his own and tossed them in, one by one as they strolled along.

"Better?" she inquired after a few moments of silence.

He grinned back at her. "Yeah. I guess, most of all, I'm just worried about Uncle Bob. The doctors still haven't said a lot except that he has to give his heart time to rest and heal. But then as one of them explained, your heart never really does rest as it has to keep pumping all the time, day and night. He said there is all kinds of new research on hearts and heart disease, coming out of places like Europe and even South Africa but it's all new. Not sure it's anything that's going to help Uncle Bob right now. He's still pretty weak but he doesn't realize it or maybe he just doesn't want to admit it." He hesitated and then added, "Just have to keep going and hope for the best."

"And pray." She touched his arm, sending a wave of warmth coursing through him despite his effort to suppress their earlier fervor. "I'll be praying for him…and for you."

He patted her hand where it remained on his forearm and then he jumped a bit again. "What is that? A weasel?"

They were close to the far end of the pools and a tiny shadow stood tall, stretching its full length, balancing on two back legs to take a long view of the two longer-legged individuals coming his way.

"No," she giggled freely as she shook her head. "You really are a city boy! Look at those pointy little ears. That's a raccoon and he's got a fish. Whew! A dead one from the smell of it, too!" She pinched her nose in a comic fashion as the small marauder turned and scampered out of sight.

"A dead fish with all these live ones?"

"Uh-huh. The hatchery boys drop one occasionally and you've seen 'em jumping, too as we walk along. Sometimes, they jump right out onto the drive and then they can't get back to the water so it's easier for the beasties to pick up one of those than to get down to the faster moving water in those hatchery pools. No nice gentle banks there like along the spring branch. Those concrete walls don't make for such easy pickin's."

"Yeah, I was wondering about those dead fish, if that's a concern."

She smiled broadly. "Yes, all the tourists are always worried about that. One of the boys working here explained it to me like this. There are probably 300,000 trout spread out here in front of you in all of these pools. Think of it as a city of 300,000 people. You gonna have a couple of dead or dying people around in a city that size?"

He nodded.

"Exactly. That's what he said so they don't worry about a couple dead ones, here or there. Just goes with the territory."

"Makes sense."

"Yes, but the kids never get it. They are always the first to be telling a hatchery worker, 'Hey, Mister, there's a dead fish over here!'"

"They really are pretty fish, aren't they?" He bent over to examine the swarming masses more closely.

"Yes, they are." They moved on, stepping up to the small wooden bridge floor, with the hatchery outflow roaring beneath their feet back into the spring branch below. Like thousands of others who stopped at this point, they watched for several moments, fascinated by the force of the white water as it powered past. She turned back toward the pools behind them.

"Right here," she motioned to her left, "is where the last mill was located. It burned to the ground over twenty years ago while two different groups were arguing whether it should be torn down to make room for more trout pools or preserved for historical purposes. In the middle of that, it mysteriously burned one night."

"Really?"

"Yeah, imagine that." She took a few steps over toward the banks of the outermost hatchery pool. "This one was actually the old mill race, built to protect the mill so it didn't sit right on the bank of the spring branch. It protected the mill from floods that way when the water comes up."

"Oh, I never thought of that."

"Floods and fire, two biggest enemies of the mills. There might have been as many as half a dozen mills built along this stream in the hundred plus years since the first settlers came to this valley. Nobody is sure exactly how many because nobody kept records of such things in the beginning. Today, we look on it as history and want to know more about it but to those folks, it was just like making an improvement on your business or adding a garage to your house. Nobody thought much about it."

She continued, "This one was the last one, built in 1900. See those scars up there on the sycamores right there? Sorry, they are kinda hard to see now that it's nearly dark but that's from the fire that got the mill. I was just a baby but my Aunt Esther still gets mad when she talks about it." She smiled. "She was one of the preservationists as you can guess."

"I could see that."

"This right here," she leaned over the dirt-sided hatchery pool in front of them, "was the old mill race. It was built, a little channel off the main part of the spring branch for the mill, again to protect it from flood. If you look real close down there in the water, see that big square stone down there? The turbine rested on that and then the rest of the mill set this way. See? Here's part of the concrete footing that supported the whole building."

He took a step closer and suddenly, a whoosh of flapping wings and a raucous cry came up from beneath a bush at the edge of the water as a startled blue heron took wing, flying up right in front of them. Frankie scrambled backwards so quickly, he landed on all fours, face up, crab walking up the bank.

"What the heck was that?" he bellowed as Tabby dissolved into a fit of giggles.

"It was just a blue heron, looking for his dinner. I'm sure you scared him as bad as he scared you. Oh, Irish, you are too funny! Are you okay? I'm sorry. I didn't mean to laugh but—"

"Yeah, well, I guess it probably did look pretty funny," he conceded as he dusted the dirt off of his palms. "So it was one of those big birds with the long legs? What the heck was he doing down there?"

"Just getting a fish or two. The hatchery guys hate them because they can down a bunch of these little trout in nothing flat. Lot of work down the gullet of a big bird," she smiled.

"I guess so." He shook his head as he continued to back away from the water, keeping a sharp look out for any other unseen surprises. He stepped back to the safety of the wooden floor over the hatchery outflow. She followed, still smirking.

"Look right up there." She pointed to the skies overhead, where a blue heron arced gracefully in the darkening sky, silhouetted against the white clouds that still held onto the last of the fading light.

He watched for a moment before turning back to her. "You know a great deal about the history and the nature of this area. Do you realize that? Your whole family is pretty attached to Bennett Spring and rightly so. It is so special, Tabby. You are very blessed to have grown up in such a place and still live here. I'm sure you are used to it and, like so many of us in so many things, just take it for granted but you really shouldn't. People like Connie and even me, the places we've always known keep changing and not necessarily for the better."

She sighed heavily. "You are right. I know you are. Still, when you grow up in a kind of a backwater place like this, you can't help but feel like the world is passing you by. I think that's a big part of why I took off to California but when you tell people that, they look at you like you are crazy. I mean, you watch the news and can't help but wonder what you're missing. But then San Francisco didn't turn out like I thought. I swear I'd never really been hungry or cold 'til I was out there!"

"Then maybe you learned something important on your trip."

She smiled at him in a way that made his heart leap. "Maybe I did."

CHAPTER 9

The darkening skies and growing intensity of the wind brought Connie to the front door of the house late one afternoon a week and a day later. Like so many early summer days in the Ozarks, the last few had been sprinkled liberally with rain showers and cloud-filled skies. This morning had dawned with light rain that had continued throughout the day but now it seemed to be changing once again. As the dark approached that of night and the rain came down in sheets, she could just barely make out the brand new wooden frame of the Catholic chapel across the road.

"Oh, Tabby!" Connie's concern could be clearly heard in her voice. "I never saw the sky that color before." Her eyes were riveted on the heavens that were streaked with shades of angry purple and gold, even patches of green, as if the artist's pallet had been dropped, smearing the colors in some sort of strange cosmic error. The colors above bore no resemblance to Bennett Spring's normally bright blue skies, trimmed in angelic white fluffy clouds.

Tabby stepped up behind her friend to peer out the glass storm door, a bowl of oatmeal cookie dough in her hands as she prepared to bake more cookies, her answer to combatting the gloom of the day.

"Oh, my stars," she muttered under her breath and turned back to drop the bowl on the kitchen counter. "Stand here and listen. If you hear anything like a super big wind, a roar, an extra noise other than just the rain, you let me know quick, ya hear?"

Connie nodded, her anxiety written across her face.

Tabby scurried toward the bathroom located in the middle of the old house that her parents had worked to restore over the years. She grabbed some pillows off of her bed and tossed them into the bathtub.

"Tabby, look!"

Tabby ran back to the front door, surprised to see J. Junior's Jeep tearing up the front drive. He opened the canvas driver's side door and the wind immediately whipped it out of his hand.

"Hey, girls!" he yelled from the driver's seat over the roar of the storm. "Not the best weather for fishing, huh? Thought I better get off the spring branch and find me a little bit better shelter. Got room for me?"

"You goofy thing!" Tabby swung open the front door to holler back. "You know we do! Get in here!" She moved outside despite the rain and then looked forlornly down at the steps at her feet, wondering how she and Connie would ever get him and his wheelchair up the porch steps.

"J. Junior!" she called back. "Pull your Jeep around to the side door." She pointed frantically around the house. "No steps there!"

He nodded in agreement and started the engine again.

She and Connie scrambled to move a side decorative table

that normally sat across the unused door in the hall. Funny, how old houses were constructed, Tabby mused senselessly, with doors in odd places, like hallways. She whipped a long runner rug out of the way and threw open the door as J. Junior struggled to get his wheelchair up to the doorway. Despite the fact that there were no actual steps, there was still a hefty threshold to cross.

"Here, turn your chair around backwards and we'll pull you in," Tabby commanded, but J. Junior laughed in response.

"Nah, watch this!" He cranked back, lifting the smaller front wheels off the ground and giving a quick push on the back wheels that moved him forward enough to drop the front wheels over the threshold. "Now!" he called out, sticking out both of his hands. The girls each grabbed a hand and tugged him and the chair inside. Wet and laughing, they all tumbled into the hallway.

"Hey, it smells good in here!" J. Junior announced as Tabby closed the door behind them and moved the rug to soak up the rainwater on the floor.

"What are you doing out in this weather!" Tabby exclaimed.

"Just a little fishing," J. Junior grinned. "Wasn't raining all that hard earlier but when I seen how ugly that sky was a-gettin', I decided to hightail it outta there. And you know, they say a vehicle of any kind is a terrible dangerous place to be during a tornado."

"Tornado?!" Connie gave voice to her worst fear. "This is a tornado?"

"Come on." Tabby encouraged her friends to move. She swung past the front door, noting that the weather outside was not improving. "Here!" She snatched a bowl full of warm, fragrant cookies from the kitchen counter and shoved them into J. Junior's lap. "Everybody into the bathroom!" She gave Connie a push down the hall in the right direction and pushed the wheelchair to follow close on her heels. Inside the bathroom, Connie turned, perplexed, to look at her friends.

The wheelchair promptly jammed in the bathroom doorway, refusing to clear the door jamb which brought gales of laughter from J. Junior. "Yeah, well, welcome to the world I live in these days," he chortled. "Here." He backed out into the hallway and ushered Tabby in beside her friend where the two perched on the edge of the bathtub, each with a pillow in their lap.

He rolled back into the doorway as far as the recalcitrant chair would allow. "Close enough," he pronounced the arrangement. "Now to the important stuff." He wiped the last of the rainwater off of his brow with the crook of his elbow and stuffed half a freshly-baked cookie into his mouth.

"This," he continued, spewing crumbs as he did, "is the way to sit out a tornado."

Connie's alarm at the word was clearly seen on her face. "Oh, Tabby." She leaned heavily against her friend in apparent near panic.

"It's okay." Tabby patted her friend's shoulder. "No big deal. Tornadoes are a rite of spring and summer in the Ozarks. Right, J.?"

"Huh? Oh yeah. Just a big thunderstorm, most of the time. Man, you girls make great cookies! I forgot what a good cook your mama is, Tabby. She done taught you good, huh?"

"But the tornado?" Connie looked from one to the other of her friends, still confused.

Something crashed against the outside of the house with the escalating wind which made her jump violently.

"I have seen that movie. We know about tornadoes in Cuba."

"What movie?" J. Junior managed to ask despite his mouthful.

"The one about the girl from Kansas and her little dog and—"

"*The Wizard of Oz?!*" Tabby squealed in delight. "That's what's got you so worried? Connie, we are not going to Oz to battle witches and flying monkey monsters!" Tabby couldn't control her laughter but another crash outside even made her flinch this time. "It'll be okay. It's pretty noisy sometimes, but we'll be fine. I promise."

The look the Cuban girl gave her said she wasn't convinced but she said nothing more.

"So where's the rest of the family?" J. Junior managed to ask after another moment or two. He offered the girls each a cookie and Tabby took one but Connie just shook her head.

"Mama and Daddy took Granny Hannah to town for a doctor's appointment. They were going to do some grocery shopping and have lunch, I think. I sure hope they are somewhere dry and safe about now."

"Oh, they'll be fine," J. Junior grinned. "You know your dad. He was probably all settled in somewheres safe, as fast as the first dark clouds showed up."

"You're probably right." She wished she felt as secure in that knowledge as he sounded.

The wind continued to strengthen, rattling all the windows

in the house and apparently thrashing the house with tree branches or other debris that continued to hammer the exterior walls. When the front storm door shattered, the splintering glass hitting the floor could clearly be heard, even in their interior hideaway. Connie buried her face in the pillow in her lap, whimpering softly.

Even J. Junior's cheerful banter had stopped and he and Tabby exchanged a glance, the grave expression in both their eyes saying more than any words could. He leaned forward in his chair and gave the back of Connie's head a clumsy pat. And just as quickly, the noise outside the house ceased and was replaced by the simple patter of a steady rain.

"Well, that was real interesting." J. breathed a sigh of obvious relief. Carefully, he maneuvered his chair back into the hallway and rolled out into the living room where he turned to face the girls as they followed him.

Tabby made straight for the front door, where rain blew through the remaining shards of glass, dangling from the shattered storm door. She cautiously opened the door frame and looked out across the front lawn of the house, which was littered with chunks of lumber.

"What in the world..." She slipped out onto the front porch for a better look, wondering just exactly what she was looking at. Pieces of new wood lay strewn about the house, apparently the source of much of the crashing they had heard earlier while hunkered down in the bathroom.

"Oh, no!" Tabby jumped off the porch and grabbed a piece of broken two by four from the grass and then looked across the road to where the new chapel frame had been taking shape. There was nothing left standing on the building site.

"Tabby?" Connie followed but stopped on the porch. "Why are you in the rain?"

"Look!" Tabby pointed across the highway.

"What?" She followed her friend's direction, uncomprehending at first and then suddenly, the truth hit her.

"*Por el amor de Díos*," she said softly as she made the sign of the cross."*Pobre Frankie*."

"Frankie?" J. Junior approached the door, making the broken glass crunch beneath the wheels of his chair. "Is Frankie here?"

"No." Connie turned around and pulled open the damaged door, careful to cling to the aluminum frame. "The new chapel is gone, all broken to pieces."

"May the saints have mercy!" He muttered under his breath. "That ain't good."

"No, it isn't." Tabby came inside, stepping gingerly around J. Junior and his chair.

"Here." He rolled backwards in an effort to get out of the way as Connie followed her inside.

"I'll get a broom." Tabby headed toward the far side of the kitchen. She busied herself sweeping up the broken glass as Connie took the dust pan and held it for her. Together, they cleaned up the wet, shattered mess. "Watch out," she warned the other two as she reached up with the broom handle and knocked down the last pieces of window glass still clinging to the metal door.

They swept up those pieces as well and then Tabby reached out with the broom to gently dust off the rubberized wheels of J. Junior's chair.

"You don't need any glass splinters on those wheels now, do you?"

"No," he grinned. "Don't need those, ma'am!" He shook his head. "What a lousy break for Frankie and his folks over there. They just barely got that frame up and now it's all torn down again. Probably scattered across half the county by now. Guess that was some of what we heard hitting the house earlier."

"I suppose." Tabby leaned lightly on the broom. "He was so worried about this project before they even started and now he is going to be so upset."

The crunch of tires on the gravel caught all their attention as J.C., Becky, and Hannah returned from their trip to town.

"Are you all all right?" Becky hurried inside, oblivious to the broken door.

"We're fine, Mama," Tabby assured her with a quick hug. "And you all? I can't believe you were driving in all this!"

"Just a lot of hard rain, really," Becky replied. "Of course, Ma wasn't too happy driving in it but you know, she'll go along with anything J.C. says." She smiled in appreciation of her mother's admiration of her husband. "Your father was pretty worried about you all out here. In town, we heard reports of a tornado at Bennett. We saw a lot of things along the highway, branches down, damaged porches and carports, that sort of thing, but didn't see anything too terrible until we got here and saw what happened to the church over there. What a shame! J. Junior, I'm surprised to see you out on an afternoon like this."

"Well, I can't say this was my plan but I sure was happier than a pig in slop to have a safe place to weather a storm like that one!"

"Glad you were here, then."

J.C. and Hannah made their way inside and everyone continued to reflect on the storm, the current damages, and those of past storms. Hannah even shared a story about a tornado that hit the area years before and flipped over campers and tore up the tents of the day. Fortunately, like this one would turn out, no serious injuries were reported.

After a short visit with all, J. Junior decided it was time for him to make his way home. Since his Jeep was still parked outside the side door toward the back, it was easier for him to leave the same way he had entered. Connie tarried in the hallway and then followed J. Junior outside. He maneuvered himself into his driver's seat and then sat and chatted for several more minutes with Connie. He reached over and gently cupped her face as she leaned in to rest her head briefly on his shoulder. More storm aftermath, Tabby thought with a smile as she watched them from a nearby window.

"We haven't used that door in years," Becky commented, as J.C. re-locked the door and helped Tabby move the table back into its usual place after J. Junior was gone and Connie had come back inside. "We had even talked about taking it out and replacing it with a window but now I'm so glad we never got around to that!"

"Yes, I'd say we might be using it a bit more often now." J.C. kissed his wife on the cheek as he walked past her on his way back through to the living room to survey the damage of what was left of the front storm door. "Think I'll take a walk around the house and see if there is any other damage," he called out before heading out the front door for a walk through the wet grass.

J.C.'s explorations found nothing more other than a plethora of twigs, branches, and leaves scattered all around the house and of course, many more pieces of fresh lumber scattered throughout.

Becky made fresh biscuits to add to the leftovers from the week's after-church dinner the day before. This evening's meal consisted of re-heated roast beef, mashed potatoes and gravy, and as was often their custom, fresh green salad from Jesse's garden.

"Where did those come from?" J.C.'s attention focused on a vase full of fresh picked ox-eye daises as they sat down to eat. "You've been busy," he grinned at his daughter, remembering her fascination with the wild daisies they found sprinkled along the roadsides and throughout every patch of green grass and pasture at this time of year.

"Oh, I picked those before the storm," Tabby smiled. "They've always been my favorite."

"I remember," her father replied.

"I never knew anything of a tornado before today," Connie spoke up as she buttered a biscuit. "I only knew the movie about Dorothy and I thought that was the way they were. I am glad the houses don't really fly away!"

"No," J.C. laughed softly. "They don't. Once in a while, they do fly apart and are completely destroyed. It is terribly sad and often people are killed when that happens. Looks like we were all very fortunate today. We heard in town about high winds out here but nothing in reference to any serious destruction or injuries. Certainly hope that continues to be the case."

"Oh, don't we all?" Becky added.

"Well, it was pretty funny out here, I have to admit," Tabby added. "I mean, J. Junior is busy stuffing his face with warm cookies and Connie is about to come apart at the seams. I hear the front door glass breaking and just keep thinking, oh great! What next?"

J.C. smiled. "Tornadoes are usually pretty nerve-wracking, there's no doubt. But Connie, as I remember, Cuba, like all of Central America and many of the other island nations of the Caribbean, is prone to earthquakes and those aren't exactly a picnic either."

"Earthquakes?" Her eyebrows shot up. "Oh, *Don J.C.,* they happen all the time. They are nothing."

"Connie, is it a characteristic of all younger people to ignore history? The Cuban earthquake of 1932, which happened after my family left there, killed over a thousand people."

She frowned as she studied and pushed at the meat on her plate. "I imagine that is true. I remember the stories of my grandfather...." She cast a quick glance at Hannah who did not seem to be following the conversation. "I guess earthquakes kill people, too. But they are not so frightening as your tornadoes!"

Tabby chortled. "Says you! I cannot imagine an earthquake!" She shuddered visibly at the thought. "All the ground shaking underneath you and buildings falling all around you. That sounds terrible!"

"I think that would be terrible," Connie continued, "but I have lived all my life in Cuba and I have never seen an earthquake that is really bad. The ground shakes a little, sometimes things fall out of the cabinets or off of shelves but it is quick and then it is finished. Maybe..." she shrugged with a smile, "and maybe we are just accustomed to them. Like you and your tornadoes."

"Maybe so," Tabby agreed.

The rest of the evening passed relatively peacefully. Tabby announced that she was going to telephone Frankie and let him know about the damage across the road.

"Oh, Tabby," Becky protested. "It is so unseemly for girls to call young men. Surely someone will tell him about it. It's not as if he can do anything about it this evening anyway. Just let it be."

"But, Mama!" Becky was aghast at her mother's old-fashioned thinking and when she decided to apply it. "He needs to know so he can make plans to re-build and—"

"Whatever he decides to do," Becky stiffened her back at her daughter's tone, "it really is not your business, now is it? I appreciate that you all have become fast friends but truly, he is little more than a visitor here. I understand he works for his uncle's construction company but you know most of those city folks go back to St. Louis after a short while. I cannot imagine that he'll be any different." She turned back to the counters she was wiping down.

Tabby huffed down onto the couch, a pillow hugged tightly to her chest.

J.C. gave his daughter a sympathetic look and pat on the knee and turned on the television to catch the late news, turning the channel selector back and forth, tuning in to the two stations they received, both of which were broadcast out of Springfield. From all that he saw, apparently much of southwest Missouri had suffered various types of damage from high winds and suspected small tornados but nothing more.

Tabby drifted back to the window at the edge of the living room, just before the hallway and door that J. Junior had used earlier. Outside, the rain had finally stopped and the clouds had parted enough to allow the illumination of the partial moon to be seen. With the reflection of the moonlight from millions of tiny raindrops clinging to every twig and blade of grass, it made everything outside seem even brighter. Her attention was captivated by a snaggle-toothed dead tree, towering at the front of the wet woods which began just behind the house. She wondered that she had not noticed it before because it had certainly been there for a couple of years, perhaps struck by lightning in a previous storm. She remembered Frankie's words earlier in the week about how beautiful and special Bennett Spring truly is.

Just as suddenly, her focus shifted. Despite the beauty of the moonlight and reflections, she could clearly see a man standing beneath that same dead tree. He wore blue jeans and lace-up boots like any other local but with a checkered long-sleeved flannel-looking shirt. Her thoughts wandered, why would he be wearing a winter shirt in the summertime? Why did he make her think of a lumberjack? Why? Her heart skipped the next beat as he turned, his face clearly seen in the moonlight. How could she believe her very own eyes? Why was Seeker dressed like that, standing out in *her* woods at Bennett Spring?! And then he was gone.

CHAPTER 10

After a fitful night of less sleep than not, Tabby was up early the next morning. She thought about the fact that she slept worse after seeing Seeker in her own backyard than she had the night they had discovered the break-in. What did it all mean and who could she tell? The answer to that last was obvious and she hurried through breakfast before Connie was even awake.

"What's got into you?" Her mother inquired, taking in her serious manner and uncharacteristic lack of chatter.

Tabby shrugged, feigning ignorance and hoping her mother would assume she was still irritated about the refusal to allow her to call Frankie the night before. "Just couldn't sleep anymore," she answered curtly between bites of cold cereal.

She was out the front door before her mother could question her more, headed down the drive and across the road to survey the damage at the chapel for herself. The early morning mists, so familiar to those along the stream, still shrouded the nearby trees and wisps of the same still clung lightly to the tops of the high grasses. Purple coneflowers stood high above the rest of the turbulent green growth. Like delicate hula dancers, hemmed in on all sides by delicately woven doilies of Queen Anne's lace, they stood ready to sway in the slightest breeze on their long stems.

She was gratified to recognize Frankie's truck already at the building site.

He was bent over, picking up more pieces of scrap lumber and firing them angrily into a pile at the far end of the concrete slab.

"Irish?"

He jumped, straightening up, obviously startled by her presence. "Oh, hi," he greeted her with apparent embarrassment.

"Shhh!" she cautioned with a finger to her pursed lips. "Turn around very slowly."

He did as she asked in time to see a dozen wild turkeys, running through the tall grass off to the east, along the edge of the tree line. "Oh, my!" he breathed. "I don't think I've ever seen that many of them before."

They both stood transfixed for several moments until the wild birds were almost out of sight. The last one seemed to be hanging back at the very end of the pack. "Look close behind that last one, where the grass is moving behind that last hen. Do you see them?" Trailing along behind her were half a dozen baby chicks, running after the others.

"Did you know that Ben Franklin wanted the wild turkey to be our national bird when they were picking out such things when America began?" She spoke again, once the turkeys had disappeared.

"The turkey instead of the bald eagle?" He wrinkled up his nose.

"He said the eagle was a coward and a thief and that the turkey was a bird of courage and deserving of our respect as a symbol of the new country. It didn't turn out that way in the end but I've always thought it was interesting. How would we feel if our national bird was a turkey?"

"I'm thinking not so hot." Frankie shook his head as he turned back to the wood scraps. "Always the nature girl. You sure know how to take the spite out of a good mad."

"Pardon?" Now it was her turn to give him a quizzical look.

"You and your turkeys. I'm up here, feeling so mad about this mess and pretty dang sorry for myself with all our hard work torn up by last night's storm and you come along and ruin it all by showing me something as beautiful as those turkeys on the run. And especially those little cute ones at the end." He gave her his best smile which she returned. He stepped past her to pick up a couple more scraps but kissed her on the forehead as he went by. "It's real hard to stay in a bad mood after seeing something like that."

"Well, I wanted to call you last night and tell you about this. I mean, it was practically the first thing I saw when I went out the front door after the storm had blown itself out. Of course, the fact that there were pieces of your new wood all over our front yard, too, made me look over here."

"Oh, man, you got chunks of this all over your place, too? I'm sorry. I'll get down there and pick 'em up as soon as I finish here. Geez, what a mess!"

"No, it's not a big deal. We'll get them later. I just meant, well, I wanted to call last night but my mother wouldn't let me. Something about her conventional ideas that girls can't call boys unless it's a true emergency. I don't know. I just know it really aggravated me last night."

He grinned. "Just as well. I was so tired after getting home from work, I ate a few bites and fell into bed to the sound of heavy rain. If you had told me, I'm sure I'd have tried to come out and look then or, at least, laid awake all night, worrying about it. Somebody told me this morning on the job site so once I had all the guys working, I came out to see for myself."

Tabby joined him in collecting the last of the scraps. "So now what?" she asked.

"I honestly don't know." He shoved his ball cap back further on his head. "We spent so much of the money we'd collected on materials so far and now, it's all gone." The heavy sigh that escaped him tugged at her heart.

She was quiet for a moment before changing the subject. "You know, last week you told me I shouldn't worry about Diablo unless I saw him standing here at Bennett Spring. And, uh…"

Frankie stopped what he was doing to look straight at her. "You didn't, did you?"

"No, no, not him."

"Then who?"

"Well, that's the weird and scary part. Last night, after the storm, I was looking out the window at the trees just behind our house and I saw, or I thought I saw, Seeker standing there under this dead tree. It was pretty creepy and it scared me so, I didn't even think about being happy that…" she swallowed hard and finished in a whisper, "that he was alive."

"Tabby." His voice was heavy with concern as he walked over to take her hand. "Are you sure? He was the one you said was so good to you, right? But you said he died of an overdose and now you saw him in your own backyard?"

"I know, I know!" She pulled away in frustration. "It makes me sound like I'm totally crazy! I saw his body wheeled out by the ambulance guys with the cops there in the apartment in California. He was dead but last night, I thought I saw…"

"Saw what?"

"Oh, I'm not sure! I noticed him first because of where he was and then, that he looked like some kind of lumberjack. Seeker never dressed like that out there in San Francisco. He wore blue jeans but with big, full shirts, like from Africa or something. Nothing like what this guy was wearing but it was his face. It was Seeker's face." Her voice rose in alarm.

"Okay, okay." He hugged her in an attempt to chase away the demons.

"I mean, I can't talk to anybody else about this. I haven't even told anyone else about Seeker or Diablo or any of it."

"Well, maybe it's time you did."

She shook her head. "I just don't know."

He said nothing more, just embraced her, running his hand down the long mane of blond hair cascading down her back.

While they were still standing there, a light blue sedan pulled into the drive behind Frankie's truck. A gentleman in a conservative gray suit with a blue-striped tie stepped out of the driver's door and made his way over to the two of them.

"Why, hello, Tabby." He greeted her with a tip of his gray fedora.

"Hello, Mr. Elwood," she returned, glancing at her

companion whose face held a slight frown of confusion.

"Charles Elwood." He extended his hand. "You must be Frankie?"

Frankie nodded, his frown deepening. "I'm the local agent for American Contracting Insurance and I just wanted to stop by and let you know that all your damage here will be covered by our company."

"What?" Frankie stammered, glancing at Tabby, as a small smile began to grow. "I don't understand."

"We cover all of Bob McCleary's construction projects, this one included. I've been out since early this morning and so far, this one and one other are the only ones of his that have any significant damage. I had a house under construction by another client, on the county line, the other side of Bennett Spring. Like here, they suffered considerable damage but fortunately, no one was hurt. Same here, I take it?"

Frankie nodded in silence, his eyes brightening.

"You know, Bob has been a good client for years and we insure all his workers, the building itself, and so on." He paced around, surveying the chapel site or what was left of it. "A real shame in that it looks like you were just getting a good running start. Well, no matter. Give us a list. You've got your original invoices for the lumber, joists, and such?" He raised his eyebrows in Frankie's direction and Frankie nodded.

"All right then. Hey, I've got to get back to the office in Lebanon but just bring your papers by and we'll figure out all the costs, replacement, what it will cost to haul off this damaged stuff, and then you can get started again. How does that sound?"

"Wonderful!" Frankie finally found his voice. "Unbelievable!" He reached out to pump Charles Elwood's hand before he turned back to his car. "Thank you so much, Mr. Elwood! You have no idea how wonderful this is!"

Now it was Tabby's turn to share a kiss with Frankie as Charles Elwood backed his car out of the drive. She rose up on her tiptoes to kiss his cheek but he grabbed her by the shoulders and planted a full, heartfelt kiss on her lips instead!

* * * * *

Days went by, turning into weeks as the summer progressed. Frankie's building project moved forward with the help of the volunteers, known as the Sugar Creek gang, with no further major impediments. Both Tabby and Connie continued their work for Jesse with several trail rides sprinkled liberally across Tabby's schedule.

The pungent smell of freshly cut grass greeted Tabby as she stepped out onto her front porch late one morning. She had slept in, feeling no particular urgency to join Connie this morning at the camp store. Mid-week and not much was going on and Jesse had decided it was a good time to take inventory, an endeavor she found even more boring than the rest of the store and office work. Connie, on the other hand, seemed happy with it and Tabby was more than pleased to leave it with her.

She glanced down the way and saw Jesse out on the brilliant green stretch of the grass he had apparently just mowed, followed by a couple of gentlemen. Each of them had a fly rod in his hand. She recognized the brothers as a pair she had checked into the campground over the weekend. She stood there, coffee cup in hand, watching as he cast his fly out with all the grace of a professional dancer, the line arcing out in front of him. She heard snatches of their conversation, Jesse instructing them exactly how to achieve the same results. They both observed for several minutes before stepping forward and attempting to imitate what they had seen with their own fishing rods. The results were hardly similar.

A wistful smile crossed her face as she sat down on the nearby porch swing, her eyes still fastened on the fisherman. Jesse, like the rest of her family, was a dyed-in-the-wool fisherman. Born at Bennett Spring, it was as if the fishing was in their blood from the beginning. In all of them, except her. For whatever reason, the fishing had never greatly appealed to her, leaving her feeling as some sort of misfit, even within the loving confines of her own family.

Her father, J.C. Shine, came to Bennett Spring already a trout fisherman and her uncle, Ben, just a young teen at the time, immediately bonded with the newcomer, first over the fishing and then as J.C. became a new member of the family. Her mother, Becky, was less of a trout enthusiast and a real river fisherman, as she put it. Raised at a time when fishing was more about putting food on the table than a celebrated sport, at least for local residents, she had grown up fishing the Niangua River and Zeb, her father, had guided more than one group of tourists up the river over the years. Jesse, Lizabeth, Esther, they all loved to fish. And while Tabby enjoyed most other aspects of life at Bennett Spring, the fishing had never grabbed her fancy. Still, even she could appreciate the artistry of the fly fisherman and enjoyed watching her older brother demonstrate it in a lesson for the uninitiated.

After a time, she went back inside for more coffee. "Mama, what is today?" she asked, squinting at the kitchen calendar.

"June 30th, Tabby," Becky answered as she sorted laundry

in the back hallway. "Why?"

"Froggin' season starts tonight," Tabby announced with a happy grin. "I nearly forgot. I have to go remind Jesse. I bet he forgot, too. We got things to do to get ready." She might not care about fishing but frogging was a whole different kettle of fish.

Becky shook her head with a smile as Tabby darted out the front door.

As the sun set at the end of that same day, Jesse, Tabby, Connie, and Frankie could be found combing the weeds along the edge of the Niangua River a couple of miles upriver from Bennett Spring State Park.

"Tell me again," Connie asked as they trailed along. "We are hunting for frogs?"

"Yeah, frogs," Jesse tossed over his shoulder. He and Tabby each carried a long pole with a fish gig on the end. Unlike the traditional frog gig which was the basic trident the Devil himself carried with sharp points used to pierce the unfortunate frog or fish, the fish gig consisted of two sets of rounded prongs with a snap hinge in the middle. Jesse had filed the prongs down even more to round off the points, so that once cranked open, the gig was used to grab the frog without piercing it. The fisherman could then examine the frog, decide if it was big enough to keep, and even toss it back unharmed if it didn't suit his needs. And while a frog caught by either method still kicked and struggled, those caught on the end of Jesse's gigs did so without throwing blood all about.

They both carried a gunny sack tied to a rough belt so they could carry their catch easily and as Jesse pointed out, any night they only caught one or two, they could easily toss them back if they didn't want to fuss with cleaning such a small take.

"And then you eat the frogs?" Connie wrinkled up her nose at the thought as she glanced back at Frankie who was also a new convert to this odd sport.

"Oh, they are great! You'll see. You've eaten frog legs before, haven't you?" Tabby's enthusiasm was unmistakable as she peered around Connie, directing her question at Frankie, who brought up their single file line of four.

"Well, no, I can't say I ever have. I've heard of it. Something about them being a French delicacy is the way I always heard about them, but I've never actually eaten them."

"I came to watch and learn," Connie continued in a dubious manner, "but I do not know about eating a frog!" She finished with a small shudder.

Frankie grinned at the thought and how unusual such a practice seemed to him and Connie and yet how much a part of their normal lives each summer frogging was for Jesse and Tabby.

"There's one." Jesse stopped abruptly as his flashlight picked up a tiny shining yellow diamond several feet ahead of him, squatting on the bank at the river's edge.

"That is a frog?" Connie was incredulous.

"Shhh," Jesse cautioned. "Don't move." He crept forward, his gig pole suddenly lowered to the frog's level. He extended the pole smoothly, never letting the light waver from his target. "Come to Papa," he murmured. At the last moment, he jammed the gig forward and suddenly the end of it was alive with approximately half a pound of kicking bullfrog.

He pulled it back, holding the flailing amphibian high so that all the others could get a good look.

"It is so big!" Connie shrieked. "In Cuba, frogs are little things like toads. I am thinking it will take so many of those to make a meal!"

Tabby was overcome with the giggles. "Toads? Oh, my stars! Now that does sound nasty! These are bullfrogs, big 'uns! We'll make a good meal of 'em, you'll see. Toads…." She continued to giggle.

They moved down river and after another good catch and another frog sighted, Jesse turned back to Connie and Frankie. "Want to try?"

Connie hung back but Frankie stepped up to the challenge.

"Okay," Jesse instructed. "Keep the light fixed on his eye. See it? Don't let that move or he'll jump into the water and be gone. Now move slow so he doesn't see you coming." Jesse continued his instructions while he moved along the stream, walking in the water, slightly behind Frankie. Frankie leaned forward to grab the frog with the gig as he had seen Jesse do, but just as he struck at his quarry, Jesse stepped into a hole and stumbled face first into the water.

Frankie shot forward, trying not to encumber Jesse any further and Tabby broke into such a fit of giggles, she had to make her way to the shore and sit down on the dry sand. Connie's gaze flitted from one to the next, trying to determine exactly what had happened.

"I got him! I got him!" Frankie crowed with excitement. He whirled around, almost smacking Connie in the face with the squirming frog which brought a shriek from her as she ducked, covering her face.

Tabby's gales of laughter continued, watching the farce

unfold in front of her. Her brother emerged from the river, shaking the water off like a dog.

"Oh, my—" Tabby couldn't even catch her breath, she was laughing so hard. "Jesse! You are all wet!"

"Yes, Little Sister, and you are gonna be, too, if you keep laughing! What do you think, Frankie?" He made to scoop her up and toss her into the water as well.

"Okay, wait, wait." She put up her hands in serious defense. "I'm sorry. It was just so funny, watching you all. Connie, are you all right?" She looked at the newest frogger who nodded with a wide smile on her face.

"Congratulations, Irish!" she continued. "What did you get?"

"A frog, I think," he laughed and passed the end of the gig toward her, "but I honestly don't have any idea how to get it off of there!"

She cranked open the gig once she had a firm grip on the struggling frog. "Nice one," she complimented him as she slipped the wriggling amphibian into the gunny sack at her waist.

Jesse continued trying to rid himself of river water without the benefit of a towel or dry clothing. "Hey, good reason not to throw you in the water," he said to his sister as he seized her from behind by the shoulders and wiped his face on the back of her T-shirt.

"Hey!" Her mild protest dissolved into laughter at her brother's antics.

"Come on!" He grabbed up the fish gig, leading the expedition once more.

Half a dozen frogs later the novices were ready to call it a night. Connie had begun to shiver and Frankie said his wet feet were turning to prunes in his tennis shoes. Reluctantly, Jesse and Tabby agreed to take them back to their vehicles, waiting up in the open field above the river bank.

Back at the Shine house, all shucked their wet shoes and gathered around the dining room table with hot coffee and homemade brownies that Becky had baked in anticipation of their return.

They repeated their stories of the river, the hilarious introduction of the sport of frogging to the novices and tales of past exploits involving various family members over the years.

"Well, let's see what you all got tonight." Becky brought the conversation down to brass tacks. She joined Jesse and the rest on the front porch as they examined the night's catch under the yellow porch light.

"Jesse, you clean 'em in the morning and we can fry 'em up tomorrow night. You all ready to try your first frog legs?" She cast an amused glance at Connie and Frankie.

"Sure!" He answered with enthusiasm but she wrinkled her nose and smiled as she silently nodded.

"Tomorrow night then!" Becky announced as she stepped back inside.

"Well," J.C. came out briefly to take a long gaze at the wriggling amphibians. "Looks like a nice mess of frogs but we will need a bit more to feed everyone. What do you think, Jesse? Looks like you and I will need to go fishing tomorrow to add a few trout to the evening repast." With that, J.C. ducked back into the house.

The others sat on the porch for a short time more, enjoying the cool evening breeze as they chatted a bit more before

Frankie and Jesse headed to their respective homes.

* * * * *

The next evening found the same group gathered around the table, now laden with fried frog legs, fresh caught fried trout, cornbread still in the cast iron skillet, a large green salad, and home canned peaches Becky and Hannah had put up from the summer before. J. Junior had been at the camp store as Jesse, Connie, and Tabby prepared to close up for the evening and they invited him to join them for dinner. Since it was Friday, Jesse planned to be back a little later to check in more campers for the weekend.

"It all smells so good." Frankie's mouth was already watering with the various delicious aromas.

"You don't have to make kissie-kissie to my mama over her cooking," Tabby teased.

"I'm not," Frankie protested. "It's the absolute truth."

"Yes, well, I appreciate the kindness." Becky gave a nod in his direction.

As fast as J.C. finished the blessing, the feasting began as dishes were passed.

"Now really, frogs taste a little like a cross between fish and chicken." J.C. opened the conversation.

"Oh, you all have never eaten frog legs before?" J. Junior had not realized this was an initiation dinner. He watched with amusement as Connie closed her eyes and took a tiny tentative bite of her first frog leg. Frankie had no such reservations and dug right in.

"Wow, those are pretty darn good," Frankie pronounced almost immediately. "They taste as good as they smell."

"That is," Connie hesitated as if searching for the right words. "That is very good." She added a beautiful smile which was followed by a round of applause and much laughter.

Hannah, who had been sitting quietly at one end of the table, smiled and added, "Frogs are always good."

"Well, important as the frogs are to the meal, let us not forget the generous contribution of fresh trout as well," J.C. added to the light-hearted banter.

"Hear, hear," Jesse joined in. "I mean, me and Dad really had to get out there in the hot afternoon sun and work at putting dinner on the table."

"So we are supposed to feel sorry for you because you *had* to go trout fishing today?" Tabby tried to make the silly question sound legitimate.

"Yeah," Jesse drawled, "I think so. You know, hot sun and all that."

"You think so?" Tabby tossed a crumpled up ball of a napkin at her brother.

"Hey, whoever caught what," Frankie interjected, "it all tastes great! After a bachelor's cooking on a regular basis, you have no idea how much I appreciate this! Oh and today is Friday so it's perfect. We always eat fish on Fridays. I'm not sure about frogs but they look a lot closer to fish than any red meat I've ever seen. I'm hoping the good Lord looks on them that way, too." He chuckled.

"Oh, you are right," Connie suddenly caught the essence of his conversation. "*Es viernes*, it is Friday. "But fish? They are the same as frogs?" She made a quick sign of the cross.

"I'm thinking so," Frankie winked at her. "Say a prayer and don't worry about it, okay?"

She nodded slowly and glanced at Tabby who did a poor job of concealing her amusement over the whole matter.

"Well, anytime you boys need help putting a few extra trout on the table, you just give me a call," J. Junior chimed in. "Don't expect much help from me when it comes to catching them frogs but when it comes to those trout…"

"No." Connie shook her head slowly as she looked at the wheels of J. Junior's chair with a grave expression. "Those would not work where we went to catch the frogs."

"No, they wouldn't," he grinned. "But truth be told, even before, I wasn't much for catching frogs." He gave a little shiver. "Just something about frogs and frog slime. Now fish slime, that's okay but not frog. Besides, you have to walk around in all that water."

"Walk in the water? This is a bad thing?" Connie asked with her nose wrinkled up as if she smelled something unpleasant.

J. Junior continued. "And then there is that business of 'em leaping right out of the skillet once you go to frying 'em."

"What?" Connie's startled look stopped everyone's conversation. "The dead frog hops out of the skillet?" Her earlier distaste for the fried creature on her plate instantly returned.

"Only if some fool forgot to cut the leaders in their legs, for which his mother is sure to box his ears a good one! And rightly so," Jesse commented with his mouth full.

Connie shook her head. "I do not understand."

Frankie's expression said her confusion had nothing to do with any language incompatibilities but he said nothing.

"Oh, there are nerves in the legs," Tabby began to explain

with a dismissive wave of her hand. "When you clean the frog, you need to clip them. Otherwise, they tend to contract when the fresh frog hits the hot grease. Mostly, it just makes them twitch which, of course, is pretty weird already, but they can leap clear out of the skillet. Either way, it tends to fling hot oil everywhere which in turn, tends to upset the cook."

"Hear, hear," Becky added.

"Well, as good as all of this is," Frankie was now following the strange explanation, "don't do that!"

Becky's answer was a smile.

"All I know is eatin' these frogs is real fine," J. Junior put in his two cents worth. "Nothin' wrong with that at all. I'd just rather go fishing than to go catchin' frogs."

"Makes sense," Jesse nodded. "Some folks fish, some folks frog."

"And some of us just appreciate the ones who do so we can eat 'em all," Becky added, glancing at over at her mother.

"Amen!" J.C. added.

"Now, who would like some fresh strawberries that Jesse brought in from the garden this afternoon? I made homemade shortcakes to go with them and of course, there's whipped cream to go on top."

"Now that's the perfect ending to any meal," J. Junior shared with a satisfied smile.

Dinner ended with Connie and Tabby helping Becky clear the table while Jesse decided to go on home to the mobile home he and Marcia shared at the back of the campground. She had declined the dinner invitation tonight, pleading an upset stomach that wouldn't have enjoyed fried food of any kind. Frankie excused himself to go across the road to the building site and Tabby whispered to him that she would join him shortly after she finished helping with dishes. J.C. took up his newspaper to sit in the living room as was his nightly custom after dinner.

J. Junior rolled out onto the back deck to "take a look at the back forty," as he put it, where Connie joined him as soon as the last dish was dried.

Tabby headed out the front door and down the drive as dusk moved in. Once she crossed the road and approached the chapel, she felt the presence of eyes watching her once again. Despite a quick glance around, she didn't see Frankie. Instead, she turned in slow motion to survey her surroundings and it was then she noticed a small fox, sitting at the far end of the site, perched on a pile of gravel, taking in her every move.

"Well, hello," she chirped to the four-footed observer. "And how are you?"

The fox cocked his head to one side as if carefully considering her words. He watched her watching him until she heard footsteps on the gravel. She whirled to see Frankie walking up behind her.

"Look at this!" She giggled with relief. "Remember how I've told you I sometimes feel like someone is watching me? Well, look who was watching tonight!" She turned back to point out the fox but there was nothing there but an empty gravel pile.

"Who was here?" Frankie looked past her, a growing look of alarm on his face.

"No, it's nothing. No one was here," she told him. "Not to worry. There was a little fox, sitting right up there on the gravel and he was watching. That's all. It was just funny because I thought someone was watching and someone was. Just a cute little fox, that's all."

"Oh." He breathed an obvious sigh of relief. "I swear, Tabby, I think the wild creatures themselves watch over you as much as you watch over them."

She grinned and followed him over to his pickup as he dropped the tailgate to unload a few last items to help finish out the major work on the chapel. She sat on the tailgate, swinging her legs like a small child, looking off toward the woods.

"What's wrong?" he asked after finishing the task at hand. "You haven't seen any more of Seeker or anyone else from California, have you?"

She shook her head. "No, nothing like that." She hesitated a moment before adding, "it's just that the summer is already almost half over and I honestly don't know...." She stopped, heaved a sigh and then tried again. "My mother was talking today about me going back to college this fall but I just don't see why. What am I going to do there? I know now I really don't want to be a school teacher but I have no idea what I do want to do!" She all but spit out the last words.

"My Aunt Esther was a nurse in World War II and has been a county health nurse for years. My Aunt Jessica has been a social worker and my mom used to be a midwife. I bet you didn't know that, did you?"

"No, I can't say I did."

"She did that for years until things finally changed and the roads got better and now all the ladies go to the hospital in Lebanon to have their babies. The main thing is they all knew what they wanted to do, what they were meant to do. But I don't!"

He stood there, watching her, his heart twisting with her angst and yet somehow amused by the whole situation. "I can't believe you can't figure this out." They had discussed this before in the most general of terms but he had thought it best to let her work it out on her own.

"What do you mean?" She looked up in confusion.

"Tabby, you love Bennett Spring, even if you don't like to admit it. You can spout off facts and figures about this place from how much water comes out of the spring to when the last mill burned down to where the deer like to play, the way most people list their family members. Why don't you figure out a way to make a living at that? Look at your brother, Jesse. What does he do? He's carved a living out of camping, teaching people how to fly fish, putting them on the river in canoes, and making a business out of it."

"Yes, but that's Jesse, not me. Just like the rest of my family, he loves to fish and I can't say that I do. That is what Bennett Spring is all about and besides, I don't have a head for that kind of business."

"I know. Your knowledge about here is different but it is still things you've known all your life, things you know by heart, and I just don't think you appreciate how valuable that is to others coming here from the outside."

His enthusiasm was lighting a spark within her and yet, she still couldn't quite follow his logic.

"What if," he tried a different approach, "what if you could try that out for a while and see if it is something you might really enjoy?"

She squinted those lovely green eyes at him in an unspoken question.

"Do you know that guy, Richard who is directing the nature program here? The park people who tore down the old museum and are getting ready to build a new one, he's like the one in charge."

"Sure," she nodded. "Richard Campbell. I've met him down at the park store and I've seen him around."

"I sorta had lunch with him the other day at Vern's Malt Shop in Lebanon. You know where that is, right?"

"Everybody in town knows where Vern's is," she returned.

"Well, I was in there with another one of the construction guys and he knew Richard, so he joined us and he was talking about these student naturalists he has working for him here this summer. They are organizing stuff, getting ready for the opening of this big new Nature Center, he called it. This summer they are doing nature walks, teaching visitors, especially kids, about the park and the natural stuff here as well as the history of the park, how it all came to be and so on. Anyway, Richard was complaining because like everybody else, he's got too much to do and not enough people to do it with and now one of the girl naturalists quit to go back to her home town and help take care of her father who is really sick. Richard was saying he needs to replace her but he didn't know how he was going to do that because he needs somebody who knows all the stuff about this place already. He said he didn't have time to educate someone about all that they need to know and put that person to work, too. So I was thinking, what if you went to talk to him and you took over for her for the rest of the summer? That would tell you pretty quick if this was the line of work for you, don't you think?"

"Oh, my gosh! That's brilliant, Irish! I could do that!" She jumped off the tailgate in her excitement and Frankie made certain he was right there to scoop her up in a celebratory embrace. He swung her feet off the ground and kissed her once again but this time, she made certain the return was long and slow.

"Oh, my gosh, indeed!" He let a long, soft sigh as he set her feet back on the ground.

CHAPTER 11

—◈—

The next morning found Miss Tabby Darling Shine in her best jeans and blouse down at the Bennett Spring State Park office in search of Richard Campbell. A bustling man of boundless energy, he was impressed with the typed resume this new applicant presented to him. She failed to mention she was up until the wee hours of the morning, making certain she had every detail perfect. After a brief conversation with her, Richard was quite relieved to have discovered the answer to one of the many problems he faced, bringing this new Bennett Spring Nature Center from a dream to a reality.

"I guess my next question is, how soon can you start?" Richard stood up from his makeshift desk in the back corner of the park office.

"Is tomorrow too soon?"

Richard let out a belly laugh. "Maybe. But this weekend would be great! That's when we do most of our walks because that's when we have the most visitors, although our numbers keep growing and I suspect that will continue. Summer in general is a very busy season. Let me get your shirt size and we'll get you some uniform shirts. How about nine o'clock Saturday morning?"

"I'll be here," she said as she shook his hand.

Outside, she wasn't sure who she should tell first. It wouldn't break her heart to tell Jesse she had a regular job and couldn't work for him much anymore but she did feel bad leaving Connie with all the work. Jesse's wife, Marcia, was pregnant again, which was exciting but she was also fighting morning sickness so she wasn't much help in the store these days. Still, Connie didn't seem to mind the work there so Tabby wasn't too worried about it. She couldn't wait to tell Irish, of course, and then she hoped her parents would be pleased. It would be good to be able to feel like she had made the right decision in their eyes, for a change. She was so busy thinking about all of that she nearly collided with a couple of others coming in the large front door of what had actually been an older house, now converted into the park office years before.

"Oh, excuse me," she began and then stopped.

"Oh, Tabby!" The dark-haired girl in front of her stammered. "I'm so sorry...I mean, I'm so glad to see you. Oh, my heavens, girl!" Her old suite mate, Margie, whom she'd last seen as she departed an apartment in San Francisco, grabbed her in a bear hug and squeezed her tight. When she let go, Tabby was surprised to see tears in her old friend's eyes.

"Margie, are you okay? What are you doing here?"

"Oh my, Tabby, there is so much to tell you! What are you doing? Do you have a few minutes? Hey, Debbie, Carol!" Margie called out to the other two girls who had gone ahead of her into the office. "You two go ahead. You are getting that information for your dad, right? I'll catch up to you later, at the canoe rental down by your dad's cabin. Thanks!"

They nodded and she waved as she turned back to Tabby. "You wanna get some coffee somewhere?"

A few minutes later, they were settled at a table in the Dining Lodge, just across the road, after ordering coffee and the restaurant's celebrated cinnamon rolls.

Margie stared down into her coffee as she lazily stirred in cream and sugar. "I wouldn't blame you if you never wanted to speak to me again," she began in an extra soft voice. "I treated you terribly in California and there really is no excuse for it. I knew you lived here at Bennett Spring somewhere and I swear sometime this weekend, my plan was to ask around and try to find you to apologize. But I also had to keep trying to build up my courage to make myself do it." She finished in a whisper.

"Oh, Margie, it's all right, really. At the time, I was pretty upset, I'll admit, but I've been home now for a couple of months and I'm doing fine. As a matter of fact, I just this minute got hired into a new job so no worries. How are you? I was really surprised to see you here. I figured you were still out there in San Francisco. The place is really hopping these days, according to what I see on the news. I know my dad said the other night he's really glad I'm not out there anymore and I would never tell him, but he's kinda right."

"Tabby, after you left, things just kept getting crazier. Diablo became like this other person altogether. He was so demanding and possessive, like he owned me or something. He was hanging out with all these really weird people. I mean, I like lots of different people and new ideas and I didn't mind smoking a little grass like everybody else, but he was getting into the drugs so heavy. It got really scary and he kept finding more and more creepy types. There was this one guy, Charles, Charlie, they called him. Charlie M-something. The way he looked at me..." She shivered at the memory. "He had just got out of prison in upstate California and I tell you he was the scariest man I have ever met in my life," she finished quietly. She fell silent for a moment as the waitress arrived at their table with warm cinnamon rolls.

"He's in jail, you know," Margie spoke again, without looking up.

"Who is?"

"Diablo. The cops showed up at our apartment about a month ago out there and busted him for major drug dealing. Said he was going by some other name. They called him The Unicorn and said that he was mixing other stuff, even poison, with some of the drugs in some sort of deadly game. Sort of a drug version of Russian roulette. Can you believe it?"

"Oh, Margie, I am so sorry." Tabby reached over and laid a hand on her friend's forearm as that name echoed through her memories of California. The Unicorn.

Tabby took a couple of deep breaths before she said anything more. "You know, after I left you all, I ended up in a good place with a bunch of really good people. Sometimes though, I felt like someone was watching me and I wondered if it was Diablo, if he came looking for me."

Margie almost choked on the bite of roll in her mouth. "Oh, my great Aunt Sadie, Tabby! That was me!"

"You?"

"Yes, after you left like that, I felt bad. Diablo kept asking where you'd gone and I told him the truth, at least at first, and that was I had no idea. But then I started to worry and I went looking for you. I asked some people on the street and they told me they'd seen you with this guy and after a bit of looking, I found you but by then, I was so ashamed of the way I'd behaved and even about the way Diablo was acting. I watched for a little while, several days, just to make sure you were okay and not with anybody dangerous or anything." She let out an amused snort. "The truth is my situation turned into a disaster but you looked like you were doing all right. I had to sneak away and tell Diablo I was off doing some 'girl' things so he didn't catch on. Tabby, I never told him where you were or even that I'd found you. I asked some other people about the guy you were with and they all said he was a decent guy."

"Oh, he was," Tabby added quickly. "He really was. He was good to me."

"Was?" Margie looked up.

Tabby took a deep breath. "He died of an overdose. Somebody in the apartment the morning the cops came and took his body said he got the acid that day from somebody named The Unicorn. The one who told us that even said he told Seeker not to buy from him anymore because he was 'crazy'." She sniffed as her tears welled up and she finished hoarsely. "If only he'd listened…"

"I am so sorry, Tabby. If only we'd known as much as we thought we did when we left for San Francisco, huh?"

"Yeah." Tabby dabbed at her eyes with her napkin. "If only…."

They sat in silence for a few moments, both trying for very different reasons to put the past behind them. "So what are you doing here today?" Tabby finally asked.

"I came down with some friends from Marshfield. Their dad likes to fish here at Bennett Spring and gets a cabin once a summer. They swim and sunbathe. I've been pretty depressed since I got back, feeling like I screwed up so bad. Debbie and Carol are sisters, neighbors. Debbie and I were in the same class in high school. She never went to college, just went to work for her dad in his grocery store there in Marshfield. They invited me along to cheer me up, I think, but I really appreciate it. Just taking a weekend and then have to figure out, what's next? Guess I'm going back to Springfield and the college in the fall but mostly because my folks are making me. There just isn't a lot that interests me there anymore, you know? My major was in business administration before I went to California but I got pretty bored with it even before I left and now..." She let out a heavy sigh.

"Margie, I did some reading after I got back in the magazines about some of the stuff we were doing out there and..."

"What do you mean?"

Tabby dropped her voice to a bare whisper. "The drugs. I didn't do much, to be honest, but they say sometimes the depression afterwards is pretty bad and if that's part of what's bothering you..." Tabby turned back to concentrate on the last of her cinnamon roll. "I'm just saying, maybe it's something you should be aware of. I've struggled with it some, especially in the beginning. I cried all the way back here on the bus feeling like such a failure after running off out there. My family has been really good to me. I know I've been so lucky in that and I've been able to work some at my brother's campground and even down with the horses."

"I saw that they have horses here. What do you know about them?"

"Just about everything," Tabby giggled. "I'm the guide who takes the people on the trail rides!"

"You're pulling my leg!" Margie squealed with delight. "Debbie and Carol were both saying they like to ride here because the horses are so gentle and well-cared for. I've only been on a horse once before so I wasn't so sure."

"Oh, it'll be great! You'll see, just go see Willa Jean down there at the resort with the little barn and she'll get you all set up. Then she'll call me and we'll go on a great ride together!"

"Oh, Tabby." Her old friend leaned back in her chair a smile of real contentment on her face. "I'm so glad we found each other again."

"Me, too, Margie." Tabby leaned over and gave her half an embrace. "Me, too!"

* * * * *

"Come on, you've been promising to go with me for days and weeks now. Let's go. Jesse said he's going to be here around the office and the store for the morning, so it's you and me off for a trail ride," Tabby cajoled as she pushed her friend out the front door, toward the farmhouse. "Go find some blue jeans and solid shoes and we'll go."

Connie laughed at her friend's enthusiasm as she trotted off toward the house. Tabby followed and sat in the truck, waiting. It didn't take Connie long to change.

"Okay," Tabby said as they stood outside the corral. "The white horse Dancer is mine. Which one would you like today?" Tabby had told Willa Jean they were taking two of the horses out this morning and she started to saddle Dancer as Connie walked past each of the others, patting a velvety nose, running her hand across a neck or the withers of each one.

"This one." Connie settled on the last in the line, a red

freckled Appaloosa. "What's his name?"

"That would be Lucky," Tabby answered as she looked up from pulling her horse's cinch tight. "You picked a dandy one, I'll give you that. Wait 'til you see him move under saddle. He arches that neck and looks for all the world like he's marching in a parade somewhere. He's quite the show off."

"I know," Connie smiled as she patted his nose again and came over to retrieve his saddle. "We had ones just like this in Cuba when I was younger. They are very special horses."

"Yes, they are," Tabby grinned. "Need any help?"

"No, I do not believe so," Connie tossed back over her shoulder and she hefted the saddle onto her chosen horse. "We are good."

And they were. The two girls rode along the trail where Tabby had taken so many of her charges over recent weeks but when they reached the hatchery, Tabby and Dancer quickly led Connie and Lucky on past the pools close by the hatchery building and turned down the road toward the Dining Lodge. At the road that heads up the hill, they turned again and climbed up to the steep grade to the first gravel drive on the left.

"Where are we going?" Connie asked at one point.

"Oh, just touring around," Tabby called back over her shoulder. "Do you mind?"

"No, no problem," Connie answered. "This is wonderful."

As they turned off the main road, Connie guided Lucky to walk alongside her friend. Dancer laid back his ears momentarily and gave his head a menacing shake to make certain Lucky still understood who was lead horse and surprisingly, Lucky complied, hanging back ever so slightly.

Tabby smiled, watching their antics and shared a glance with Connie who had also noticed the horse communication. "They are the same everywhere," Connie commented as the horses walked down the road.

"This little house up here," Tabby pointed up the road to the left, "is where my mother and father lived when they first were married."

"Here?" Connie asked. "It is so cute, hidden in the forest, like Snow White. It is only missing the seven *duendes*. How do you call them in English? The little men who lived with Snow White."

"The seven dwarves," Tabby giggled. "Well, I can't say I ever thought of them living up here. My folks moved to the farm after Lizbeth and Jesse were born but I never lived up here. Still, it's kinda fun to just come up here and wander around. If you go that way, you can follow a foot trail all the way back down to the park. It comes out just this side of the hatchery. Pretty steep though, too much for the horses. And if you go up this way...." She guided Dancer off to the right as they walked slowly past the little brown house tucked in amongst the trees. "Come on, I'll show you."

"Wait. Can we stop here for one minute?" Connie asked as she slipped off of her horse, still holding the reins.

"Sure. What?" Tabby turned to watch her friend as she took a few steps to stop beneath a large catalpa tree.

"I keep seeing these and they look like..." Connie scooped up a couple of the blossoms that littered the ground below the trees wide-spread branches, heavy-laden with flowers and saucer-sized heart-shaped leaves. "Now I see," she muttered as she studied the blossoms in her hand for a moment before tossing them back to the ground.

"What was that all about?" Tabby's nose wrinkled in a slight frown blended with a smile of confusion.

Connie climbed back onto Lucky and turned to face her friend. "When I see these trees like this one, I have seen the flowers on the ground now and they looked to me like *palomitas de maiz,* what you call popcorn. Our name for them really means little doves of corn. I told that to J. Junior the other day when we drove past one and he laughed so hard, I think if he had not had that strap on him, he might have fallen right out of the Jeep. We were going somewhere and we were late so we did not stop but I have wanted to look at the flowers or popcorn on the ground so today, I did!"

"A popcorn tree, huh? Well, that's different. We always called them lady cigar trees."

"Cigar trees?"

"Yes, the long seed pods. They always told us those were lady cigars when we were growing up. J. Junior and I tried smoking a couple of them once we were little."

"No!" Connie giggled. "And how was it?"

"Awful, of course," Tabby laughed. "We turned as green as the pods before it was done!"

Oh no!" Connie howled. "How funny!"

"It is now, but at the time," Tabby added, "we just figured we were doing something wrong or maybe we needed to dry the pods out first or something. We never messed with 'em again after that, though."

"I imagine not," Connie nodded.

Tabby shifted in her saddle and looked back at the little brown house again as she guided their horses up the secondary trail, leading away from the house. "You know, I've heard the story more than once although I wasn't around at the time. Lizbeth and Jesse were both born in that house and my Aunt Jessica was here to help when they were."

"Oh, your Aunt Jessica was already married to your Uncle Ben then?"

"No, it was kind of a weird coincidence all the way 'round but Aunt Jessica had really stopped in that day just to say 'hello' to Mama. Mama had fallen down the stairs that go to the basement in there. She helped Mama back up the stairs to her bed and the twins were born not too long after that. Aunt Jessica was still pretty young herself, away from home for the first time but she stayed that day and helped Mama bring those two into the world."

"Oh, my, what a blessing she must have been to your mother but how frightening for her," Connie commented.

"I imagine it was," Tabby agreed, "but I think that is why Mama and Jessica are still so close, as close as real sisters, instead of like regular sister-in-laws."

"That would explain it, yes," Connie nodded.

Their current trail came out above where they had turned off of the road earlier and they proceeded to follow the main road back down to the park. They strolled past the Dining Lodge, down on by the little tourist cabins built by the CCC thirty years before on their right, all the way to the river.

"Connie, I have a favor to ask." Tabby finally admitted to her ulterior motive for bringing her friend on such a long leisurely horseback ride.

"Si? You know whatever it is, if I can possibly do it, I will."

"I hope so. I am starting this new job working at the park and I won't have time to do the horseback rides anymore. I hate to tell Miz Willa Jean that since I was already a replacement for her niece, Sally Ann, but I thought if maybe you would do them. I know you are already working for Jesse but the truth is, he can do more of what needs to be done up there, if you need to do something else. He just takes advantage because he's a man and he knows he can."

"Oh, you are terrible to talk about him that way!" Connie laughed out loud. "He is very kind to me."

"Well, of course, you think so. He's always nice to you. It's different when it's your own brother."

"I suppose that is true," she replied. "My brother and I did not always get along so well although once he was gone, I think my heart broke," she ended wistfully.

"I imagine I would feel the same way," Tabby relented a bit, "if my brother was gone. It's just hard to imagine sometimes."

"If you think it would be all right and not cause any problem with your family and the work, I would not mind to do the horses for you. Is it acceptable with the horse owner? The lady with two names?"

"Willa Jean? I haven't asked her yet but if you can get them saddled and bridled and brushed, and it sure looked to me like you knew what you were doing earlier there at the corral, I'm sure Willa Jean'll be happy she doesn't have to hunt up somebody else. She knows you are living with us so I think it should be fine."

And it was and so guided trail rides continued for a bit

longer in Bennett Spring Park but this time with a Cuban young lady as the guide.

* * * * *

Days later, the Shine family once again gathered at J.C. and Becky's farmhouse, this time on the back deck, around a couple of big rectangular picnic tables.

"So you were born on July 4th?" Ben was busy getting the particulars straight. "Well, I'd say that means you really are meant to be an American girl. So how old today?"

"Eighteen," Connie answered shyly.

"Woo-hoo, I remember eighteen."

"Never mind," his wife, Jessica spoke up, bumping him with her hip as she walked past with a large tray of sliced tomatoes in her hands. "I'm not sure those memories are fit for mixed company."

"Oh, baby," he rolled his eyes as if she had truly wounded him. "You have no idea."

"And nobody else wants to, either!" She laughed as she walked on to set the tomatoes on the far table, already loaded with grilled burgers and a wealth of home grown treasures from Jesse's garden, from sliced tomatoes and onions, lettuce and all the other necessary condiments as well as ears of corn, also grilled, fresh cucumber salad, and roasted potatoes. A single blackberry cobbler sat at the end of the long procession of food.

"Not to sound too much like Grandpa Zeb," Jesse leaned over to inspect the cobbler, "but did you really only make one pie, Mama? I mean, I'm not complaining but…"

"Not complaining?" Becky raised an eyebrow in his direction. "Exactly what would you call it? And you're right, you sound just like Pa."

"Well, I mean, it does seem…"

"Just wait and see, boy," she answered with a small smile.

They stood together, holding hands, gathered around the tables where they would soon sit down together as J.C. said the blessing for them all, including a special thanks for the gift of freedom and God's continued blessings on America.

"Oh yes," Connie breathed out softly, as she opened her eyes.

Each one began to load a paper plate as they moved past the Independence Day buffet. "All looks good, folks," Jesse commented to no one in particular and everyone in general. "Sure hope Esther and Jamison are enjoying the fireworks show in town with their boys. I guarantee the hot dogs they get there won't compare to this. Hope those boys appreciate what their folks are giving up for them tonight," he giggled at his sister's loss.

"Oh, for heaven's sakes, Jesse!" his mother replied. "They took the boys in so they could watch the fireworks with some of their friends. We did the same for you all when you were in school."

"Oh, yeah, I remember the year we did that and it rained on us," Tabby laughed. "It got all their fireworks so wet that most of them didn't go off when they tried to light 'em. We sat outside and got wet and then we got cold. It was a mess!"

"Thanks for the stroll down memory lane, Sis," Jesse moaned as he loaded his plate almost to its meager limits and then quickly moved it over a table before it collapsed on him.

"Just remembering. Tonight will be lots better, right?"

"We hope so," J. Junior piped up as he rolled his chair through the sliding glass back door, coming through the house.

"Hey, J.!" Connie scooted over to him. Joey and Grace walked in behind him, having followed him through his own special 'J' door as Tabby had started to call it. "We brought these." Grace offered two full plates of beautifully made up deviled eggs, artfully sprinkled with paprika.

"Oh, man, got to make room for some of those!" Ben ogled the eggs as they passed by him.

As the different ones loaded plates and found seats, Tabby regaled them with tales of her new job working with the park naturalists. "There is so much to do, getting ready for the new museum, oh, I mean, the new Nature Center. Mr. C., the director, Richard Campbell is his name but all of us that work for him, call him Mr. C. He said not to call it a museum because while it will have history in it, there will be so much more than that. They have pictures of the town of Brice but there will be natural history as well and displays of the animals. They even have plans for this monster water drop and—"

"A monster what drop?" J. Junior was tucked snugly at the end of one of the tables, with a deck railing at his back and a plate piled high with Connie's help. "Now what does anybody need with a monster water drop?"

"Oh, well, it's like magnified," Tabby explained, "and that way you can see all the microbes and other invisible things that live in the water. It's all scientifically-based, of course."

"Not sure I want to know about all them extra critters living in the water I'm drinking." He shook his head with a sly grin. "They can sure think of some different sort of things to study, that's for sure."

"Well, it's important to know," Tabby prattled on, "to help sort out clean water from that that isn't fit to drink and that sort of thing."

"I suppose there's some truth in that." He gave up grudgingly as Connie, sitting by his side, jabbed a gentle elbow in his ribs.

"It also sounds very interesting," his father encouraged.

"I gave my first walk yesterday, a history walk."

"A history walk?" Becky raised an eyebrow in her direction.

"Yes, a walk around, pointing out the hotel, which is, of course, the old CCC officers' barracks, as well as the park store and the Dining Lodge, all built by the CCC. I talked about the town of Brice and even about Grandpa Zeb. It feels so strange to talk about him as part of history but he really is, isn't he?" Her eyes shone bright with tears as she continued. "It made me feel better about him and about his passing and it felt good to share him with others. After I told them about the mill, the town of Brice, and Zeb Darling, and how he first did his mail route on a mustang named Betsy before moving on to a motorized vehicle, then I was able to say, he was my grandfather."

"I bet the tourists loved that!" J.C. chuckled.

"They did!" Tabby's reply was laced with laughter. "They really did!"

"Oh, Tabby." Her mother's eyes were also wet but her smile was genuine. Even Hannah, who said nothing, was smiling as she quietly ate her burger.

"We are also preparing files for the new place as well as

lots of cards identifying plants, for instance."

"Files?" Jesse shot her a look. "I can't get you to file bills down at the store office but now if they are plants, that's different, huh?"

"Oh, Jesse," Connie laughed as she came to her friend's defense. "Of course they are different!"

"Thank you, Connie," Tabby gave her a mock nod of appreciation. "How is it down there at the store now? Is the slave driver working you half to death?"

"No, it is fine. Marcia is coming back in the mornings and she has showed me how to do more things so that helps. She brings Adam with her and he is so cute!" She turned to make a friendly face at the tow-headed toddler who sat across from her.

"Yeah, cute," Jesse snorted, "as he runs down the aisles tearing things off the shelves. That boy…"

"I'm glad you are feeling better." Tabby turned to her freckle-faced sister-in-law. "Good enough to get out a little, anyway."

Marcia nodded, her mouth full.

"Sounds like Adam is a little too much like his father," Becky chirped. "And by the way, don't you talk bad about my grandson now!"

Marcia giggled at that. "I'd say that is probably true," she said. "I am always feeling a little better by evening. The morning sickness seems to hit worst when it's time to actually cook something."

"Sounds like a good excuse to me." Jesse shot her a look with a smile. "Hey, not to change the subject but I was talking to one of the conservation boys down at the spring branch today and he said they found some paw prints up by Granny Hannah's old house."

"Paw prints?" Becky asked as Hannah stared at her grandson.

"Big ones and of all things, they think they belong to a big cat, like a mountain lion from out west in the Rockies."

"Oh, for heaven's sakes, one more reason I'm glad we got you moved down here, Ma." Becky reached over and patted the back of her mother's hand. "That's all you need to meet up with some early morning or dark night."

Her mother nodded with a solemn expression on her face. "I knew he was there. I heard him."

"What?" Her daughter gave her an incredulous look.

"I heard him out there, his cry. Just once before I moved. It was strange but now I understand."

"Understand what, Ma?" Becky shot J.C. a dubious sideways look.

"Understand what I heard," she said in a dismissive manner. "It's not the first time, you know."

"First time?" Becky was growing more concerned.

"The first time a big cat has come through. We used to see bears once in a while, too, years ago. They were here first, the bears, the mountain lions. They were all here first." She fell silent again, turning her attention back to the ear of corn on her plate.

Another invited guest, Frankie, who had remained mute until now, spoke up. "Just be careful telling this girl about a wildcat in the neighborhood, will you? The next thing you know she'll be bringing it home like a new kitten." He teased as he rubbed her arm where she sat next to him.

"Well, that ain't nothing new," J. Junior laughed out loud. "She's always been that a-way. She loves and takes care of the critters and they love her right back."

"Why does that not surprise me?" Frankie asked.

"Scout's honor!" J. Junior's eyes were round and wide as he held up a three finger salute. "Tell him, J.C." J. Junior looked to their host for confirmation. "You're her daddy. You know it's true."

J.C. grinned, often tickled by J. Junior's straightforward approach. "I can't say he's wrong." J.C. looked at Frankie. "She does seem to have a certain touch, a gift, if you will."

"All right, then." Frankie shot a look at Tabby. "Just kidding, hon'. It does sound like you are really enjoying the new job."

"Oh, I am!" Her face was still aglow with her enthusiasm but doubts were already assailing her, although she did an admirable job of disguising them. Someone watching me, she remembered the eerie feeling the last time she was up at her grandparents' old house. Could it be, she wondered, but she voiced an alternate concern.

"There is one little problem." She winced as she looked at her mother. "Mr. C. gave me permission to attend church on Sunday. You know, the weekends are our busiest time but I have to get to work immediately after that so I won't be here for Sunday dinner for a while. Sorry, Mama."

Becky nodded, saying nothing but J.C. spoke up. "That is the way of it, working for the park and essentially, for the tourists who come here. Your new responsibility is to show them all there is here and I have no doubt you will do an excellent job of it. It is a generous thing that Richard is giving you the morning worship time with your family. That says something about his character, too."

"Yes, it does," Becky added with a small smile as she stood up to go back into the house. "So J.C., did you boys finish up that homemade ice cream so we can have it with the cobbler in another few minutes?"

"Of course, it's ready. You doubt our abilities?" He acted as if he had been hurt by her words.

"No, but I don't see it here either," she commented drily.

"Well, we can take care of that." He pulled the ice cream churn up onto the deck from where it had been tucked under the steps and began to extract the paddles from the thick frozen creamy dessert.

"I'll get some spoons. Wait for me." She gave him a direct look and he gave her a small nod in return.

A few moments later, his wife called his name and J.C. stood up and opened the door for Becky as she carried out a large cake, with decorative dollops of white whipped cream, sliced strawberries, and blueberries. It read *Happy Birthday* and Feliz Cumpleaños, *Connie!* around the edges and sported eighteen lit candles.

"Happy Birthday to you…" Becky began the song and the rest quickly joined in.

The birthday girl's face flushed as her eyes disappeared behind her cheeks with a smile so wide it nearly split her face. "It is a red, white, and blue cake!" Connie squealed with delight.

"Well, the trickiest part," J.C. grinned, "was the *Feliz Cumpleaños*. We had to buy the entire alphabet to get the right letters."

"Oh, yes," Esther laughed. "Mickey, Cletus' wife, told me she has the same problem when she tries to write it in French for her daughter. Not a lot of call for that around here, I guess."

"Now you see why we don't need a lot of pie today," Becky whispered to her son as she set down the large cake.

"Now I see," he muttered in agreement.

"So now, there is cake and cobbler and homemade ice cream to go with either," Becky announced to all. "Come and get it!"

"Oh, it is just like a real *quinciañera*," Connie said with a soft sigh. "I never had one, you know." She looked up at J.C. with a melancholy smile that twisted his heart. "I think my mother felt worse that day than I did."

"What happened?" He asked, remembering that a *quinciañera*, a girl's fifteenth birthday party is the biggest event of a Hispanic teen's life, her coming out party, announcing to the world that she is no longer a little girl, but rather a young woman.

"We were in a pretty bad way at the time. My father was still in prison and we didn't know if he was dead or alive. There was no money for a party so it was pretty silly really. My mother and I sat in the living room, just the two of us, and we talked about the dress and the food we would have had, if we had the party. Of course, we ended up talking about the best food, Christmas food, like roast pork, *frijoles negras*-black beans, fried *plantanos*, yucca with garlic sauce, *flan, semillas de marañón*. You call them cashews, yes?"

"Yes, we do! Oh, Connie, all the foods of childhood, yes?" J.C. leaned his head back, looking at the sky. "We—your father and I—used to buy, what did they call them, *media-noches*, midnights, little Cuban sandwiches off the street vendors. They were made with Cuban bread and Swiss cheese, ham and butter or mayo. Oh, I can't remember the last time I had one of those but it sure brings back some memories!"

"The memory I am making today, it is the best one yet, yes?"

"Yes!" J.C. agreed with a hearty laugh. "But maybe you and I could work on those *media-noches* and some *mariquitas*. Not sure where we could find the plantains for those but if we look hard enough...."

"Oh, that would be wonderful!" Connie's eyes lit up. "We could share them with the others. And show them how to love real Cuban food, yes?"

"Hey, that sounds good!" Jamison Trundle came around the corner of the house, followed by Esther and three rambunctious boys. "Real Cuban food, huh? Today?"

"No, but maybe soon!" J.C. laughed again. "Come on in. Thought you were celebrating with the fireworks show in town?"

"Yes, well, we did, too, and then we got outvoted!"

"Outvoted?" Becky looked confused.

Esther grinned as she climbed up on the porch and sat down beside her mother who was still cutting the cake. "We got there and looked for the boys' friends and it turned out most of them didn't show up. We bought the boys hot dogs and the two older ones looked at me and Jamison as fast as they finished them and said, 'What else is there to eat? That isn't much and at Grandma Becky's we would have lots more good stuff.' Their dad began to tease and said if they'd rather we could come here and get some good eats but they would miss the big fireworks show. They looked at us very seriously and said they would rather be here so Jamison said, 'Come on, I don't need to be told twice!'"

"Now, that's funny!" J. Junior leaned back in his chair and roared. "But I got to say, Esther, it sounds to me like you are raising some very smart young fellers!"

"Of course, she is," Becky's smile was broad as she began to direct three young boys in the filling of their own plates. "They are my grandsons after all!"

J.C. cleared his throat loudly.

"Oh, yes, they are J.C.'s grandsons, too," Becky added as an afterthought.

As some finished dessert and others were just beginning to feast, Connie shared, "You know, J. Junior has a new job, too."

"You do?" Several sets of eyes turned his way.

"Well, I don't know if you'd really call it a job." He hid his face momentarily behind an empty paper plate before peeking out at his friends and family. "But it's kinda like Tabby, it's something I really enjoy. I'm tying flies for a couple of the shops. It's fun and they pay, so why not?"

"That's wonderful, J. Junior!" Becky was the first to speak.

"Congratulations!" J.C. lifted a glass of iced tea in his direction. "You know, the man whose work matches his God-given gifts never really works a day in his life. I've used some of your flies over the years, J., and they truly are a gift from above."

"Hey, well, how do we get in on this?" Jesse spoke up. "The Darling Family Campground won't be your biggest customer but we sell a few lures and flies, hooks and such. You and I will have to sit down and talk about some of those very special locally made flies, son. We can always sell a few here, you know?"

"Sounds good to me," the new entrepreneur answered, with a thumbs up sign.

Tabby walked toward the bathroom in the back of the house just as Esther, her youngest aunt, walked out. "Hey, I've been meaning to talk to you," Esther followed her back into the spacious bathroom. "Got a minute?"

"Sure. What's up?"

"Well, it's about your new boyfriend, Frankie. I just met him today for the first time but I've heard quite a bit about him from your mom. She's a little worried about you."

"What else is new?" Tabby rolled her eyes.

"No, I'm serious, Tabby. I know my big sister can be a little much at times but I think she has a legitimate concern here."

"Like what? Frankie? Aunt Esther, he's about the nicest guy I have ever dated. What's there to be concerned about?"

"Tabby, he's Catholic."

"So?"

"So, that can get to be a real sticky situation on down the road. Just be careful, will you? I mean, if you go falling head over heels for this guy and then want to get married, I'm just saying…"

"Married? Who wants to get married? I found this guy building a church across the road from my house. I would think that alone would be enough to keep my mother happy. I mean, most of the guys I've ever cared about going out with were more likely to be building a bar across the road, not a church, but now it's not the right kind of church. Good grief! And how come you of all people are the one delivering this message?"

"What?" Esther was surprised by the sudden twist in the conversation. "What is that supposed to mean?"

"Just what I said," Tabby shot back. "I've heard the stories over the years. Before you got together with Uncle Jamison, you had another boyfriend, a Jewish one. You even brought him to dinner at Granny Hannah and Grandpa Zeb's. Grandpa told me all about it. He said Granny Hannah nearly had a stroke when you wanted to bring a non-Christian to her dinner table, but you did. Now, if you didn't have to give up your Jewish boyfriend, what was his name? David? Do you really think it's fair to ask me to think about something like that with Frankie just because he's a Catholic? They still believe in Jesus and isn't that the important part?"

"Calm down, Tabby," Esther admonished. "I didn't mean to upset you. I just want you to think carefully about what you are doing, that's all. And David was never really my boyfriend, no matter what Pa told you. We were friends on the same ship during the war was all and he came through here once to visit. And you are right. He was Jewish but that's not why he didn't stay. Back then, when I was younger, I'd have been willing to fight for that, if he'd wanted me to."

"Really?" Her niece's interest was piqued.

"Yeah, I think I would have," Esther relented with a wistful smile. "But David had some hereditary medical issues in his family and by the time he visited here, he had already decided he was never going to marry and never have children. He had one dinner at the Darling household and looked around and told me that family was what my life was really all about and that I didn't have any business with someone who wasn't interested in that very same thing."

"And?"

"And he was right!" She reached over and tapped her niece on the tip of her nose the way she had so often done when Tabby was a grade schooler and Esther was a teen in high school. "He left here after a one day stay and he stayed at the old hotel, too, by the way. Ma managed to feed him dinner, kosher, no less, a meal with no pork but I wasn't sure she could have handled having a Jewish boy sleep under her same roof all night!"

Tabby giggled at her aunt's irreverence. "And what happened to him after that?"

"Oh, when he came here, he was on his way to California. He stayed out there for years and he did marry eventually, but not until much later and then he married a lady who already had a child. He never had any of his own."

"Oh, well, I'm glad you waited for Uncle Jamison."

"Me, too. And I'm not trying to tell you what to do here, either. Just saying be careful, okay? You do tend to be somewhat impetuous. You know, little things, like impromptu trips to California, that sort of thing."

"Oh, Aunt Esther. You do talk to my mother too much. Now go on, get out of here. I've got to go!"

Jesse was speaking primarily to J. Junior as she walked back out on the deck. "Now, to the important part of this evening. Exactly what did you all buy over there in Buffalo at Hale's? Did you get a good variety? A big piece of the Darling fireworks extravaganza tonight is depending on you!"

"Oh, now you tell me!" J. Junior half-whined as he leaned back in his chair with a tall glass of lemonade.

"What's he talking about?" Tabby looked from her brother to J. Junior and even to Connie, who smiled but said nothing.

"Well, it's been a busy year, you know," Jesse explained, "what with getting those new campsites up and running and everything else. I ordered new Darling Family Campground ball caps from Hale's Sportswear over there in Buffalo. Have you seen 'em? They came out real sharp. I guess I should be wearing one today, huh? Anyway, Bob Hale called and said they were ready and he could mail 'em over here and I said no, I'd come pick 'em up.

"Well, then I got busy and I also remembered about the fireworks. His wife, Jane Hale, and her son, Mitch, are running a fireworks stand over there again this year so I thought we ought to support our own business partners, you know? So I asked Connie as an employee of the campground to go over there and pick up the caps. J. Junior said he would drive her over and I thought while they were there, they could buy us a bunch of fireworks at the same time."

"Makes sense," Joey said with a nod.

"I thought so. I gave them the cash and now I'm just hoping they did a good job of selecting our fireworks tonight."

"I tell ya," J. Junior began with a deep breath and a smile. "Whatever we didn't get in quality, we more than made up for in numbers!"

"What does that mean?" His mother, Grace, asked.

"It means I took a woman shopping for fireworks who has never bought fireworks in her life and her helper was a twelve year old kid who know'd every kind of firework in the place and was more than willing to sell us two of everything!"

"Mitch Hale!" Jesse exploded in laughter. "That boy loves his fireworks, don't he?"

"Yes, he does," J. Junior agreed. "He was a hoot! Good kid, don't get me wrong, but what a little salesman! I was real glad I had that mad twenty on me."

"A mad what?" Grace leaned forward to peer around her husband with the question.

"A mad twenty, Ma," J. Junior explained. "It's a twenty dollar bill you keep tucked in the back of your wallet, like your own lil' emergency fund for when you need it. Learned to do that in the Army, don't you know." He grinned. "And it came in real handy, shopping for fireworks with this girl." He looked directly at Connie.

She squirmed as she realized she had been caught. "I was never able to buy them before," she began in her own defense. "It was very...." she hesitated, "very exciting!" she pronounced with a definitive bob of her head.

The rest of the family burst into laughter.

The kids scrambled off the porch as they finished eating. Matt, the oldest, went past the barn to pick up a coffee can with a neck strap on it and headed over to the far edge of the woods to try his luck at picking more blackberries. The two younger boys were content to romp in the field, chasing butterflies and in short order, fireflies that came slipping out of the woods as the sun set and the light of the day faded.

"Man, we used to spend some time climbing around in there, didn't we?" J. Junior's gaze rested on the weathered gray two-story barn behind the house.

"In the barn?" Connie looked at him as if he had made a

mistake.

"Oh, yeah." A look of contented reminiscences rested on his features. "Ain't no finer place to play hide n' seek than a loft full of fresh hay. We knew every inch of that barn and that loft, huh?" He looked at Tabby who smiled in response.

"Yes, yes, we did."

"Yes, you did," Grace nodded as she smiled at her son. "And it was all fine and good until the day you fell out of the loft and broke your arm."

"Yeah, well, I could still make it up the ladder in record time, even with a cast on my arm!" He laughed.

"Yes, you could," Tabby remembered with a moan. "I thought that cast would slow you down some when we raced but it didn't."

"No." J. Junior shook his head. "As I recall, it did not. It took a might more than that." He plunked his arms down on the arm rests of his wheelchair. "Oh well." He heaved a deep sigh. "No matter now. Getting to be an old man anyway, like somebody else I know." He reached over and pinched his dad's arm. "Probably couldn't have run too much longer, anyway." He grinned in his usual self-deprecating manner.

"Grace, what do you hear from your brother, Gabe, these days?" Becky asked. "He's planning on staying in Riverton now?"

Grace grinned. "Yes, I think he might. He went down there late last spring at the invitation of one of his friends from grade school for some big all-school reunion they were having at the little country school we went to years ago. They closed it, doing one of those school consolidations, so the little one room school house is no more. I was only in kindergarten there but Gabe was a little older and still remembered some of those kids so he decided to go. Well, seems he also remembered a gal named Jenny once he got there. He took a summer job at Hufstedler's, the store and canoe outfitter down there on the Eleven Point River, and I don't know. You know, he never married here but he might just do so yet."

Jessica chuckled softly. "Hufstedler's. Now that brings back some memories. My dad sold his last team of horses to those folks before he went off to St. Louis back during the Depression. My heavens, and now Gabe is working for them. How funny! They were always such good people."

"Well," Jesse added with a mischievous grin, "if he wanted to haul canoes and work at a store, he didn't have to go all the way to Riverton."

"Yes, well," his aunt replied, "I think it has a lot more to do with a woman named Jenny than it does canoes and camping!"

"Maybe so, maybe so," Jesse nodded.

J. Junior turned his eyes toward Jesse. "So how long before we check out those fireworks, Man? I mean, I can do the fireworks shopping, pickin' out and all, but I'll leave the setting up and lightin' to you, if that's ok. Ain't quite fleet 'nough to make that work anymore, if you know what I mean?"

Jesse laughed as he studied his old friend. "Not a problem." He stood up to go begin the set up work.

A half hour later, J. Junior, like all the rest of the family, relaxed in their chairs or on blankets on the hillside as J.C., Jesse, and Ben prepared to light off various pyrotechnic devices.

"Do we got firecrackers?" Mark, Esther and Jamison's middle-aged child, inquired as the little boys waited impatiently.

"Shhh!" Esther told him. "Just wait and see. Now what is here is what there is and just quit fussing!"

"Yes, ma'am," he replied, head down as he walked away. "Ain't no firecrackers this year," he mumbled under his breath, trudging back to report to his waiting brothers.

J. Junior snickered behind his own left hand. "Can't say I thought of that," he leaned over to confide in Frankie who was sitting on a blanket with Tabby on one side of J. Junior's chair. Connie was snugly tucked on the other side in a folding lawn chair.

"When we were over there in Buffalo and I seen all them fireworks but I just couldn't bring myself to buy none of that explosive stuff. I mean, if I never hear another thing blow up in my life, that'll be just fine."

"I understand that one," Frankie agreed with a twinkle in his eye, the two sharing their unspoken past.

"I figure the kids and the ladies enjoy the purty lights and bright colors but I don't need no more bombs bursting in air!"

Frankie nodded but was silenced by the first of the many high arcing brilliant displays of fire, color, and celebration.

"Happy birthday to you, Miss Connie," J. Junior whispered to the pretty Cuban girl on his right. "The whole country celebrates your birthday!"

* * * * *

"Tabby, are you leaving?" her father called the next evening as she was hurrying down the hall, blue denim purse in hand, digging in the cloth bag, after dinner. "Lend me the keys to Ben's truck before you go. I need to move a couple of those hay bales over by the barn."

As always, the keys had managed to slip all the way to the bottom and when she nearly collided with her father, the whole purse slipped out of her hands, part of its contents spilling out. A compact and Seeker's camera skidded across the hardwood floor. Tabby reached for the compact as her father picked up the camera.

"What is this?" he asked with a slight frown, as he turned it over in his hand.

"Oh, uh, it's from a friend in California…" She hesitated, wondering how much she dared to share about Seeker with her parents.

"Exactly, where did you get this?" J.C.'s frown deepened as he made no move to return it. Becky stepped up behind him from the kitchen where she had been cleaning more vegetables that Jesse had brought in from the garden. She peered around his shoulder to see what was so interesting.

"It's just a little camera. It belonged to a boy I met in San Francisco and he took a couple pictures of us on it and so when I left, I took it."

"He gave it to you?" J.C. persisted. "Where did he get it?"

"Well, he didn't exactly give it to me…" Tabby was scrambling mentally, trying to think of the simplest way to explain the camera's presence without giving them too many details.

"I had to box up his things after he was gone from the apartment," she began "and I didn't really think he cared about it anymore so I just took it. He said he got it from his brother. Why? It's so little. I just thought it was cute and I knew our pictures were on it. I wanted to get those developed."

"From his brother? And I wonder who his brother is." J.C. continued to study the camera.

"J.C., for heaven's sakes, it's a camera. What is the problem?" Becky cast a dismissive glance at the item in his hand and then looked at her husband's face, trying to determine what had him so concerned.

He sighed as he looked at both women. "The problem is that this isn't a little Kodak something or other that you pick up in the dime store. Tabby, I really don't think you could get these pictures developed down at the drug store, if you tried."

"Dad, what are you talking about?" She stared at him.

"I haven't seen a camera like this since I left Washington years ago but it's the last place I saw one anything like this. It's not a camera for family photos, sweetheart. It's a government camera, a spy's camera really, used to take pictures of things that others are often trying to hide."

"What? That's crazy! I assure you, Seeker was not a spy!"

"Seeker?"

"Seeker. He was my friend, the one who took our pictures. All I know is he said he got the thing from his brother but I never met him. Honest!"

"It's fine." Her father laid a calming hand on her shoulder. "I'm not accusing you of anything, I'm just puzzled is all. Listen, let me hold on to this for a little while. I'm pretty sure I can get it to someone who can get the pictures developed and I'll ask him to give us back the ones that you are interested in, all right? In the meantime, I'd very much like to know where this camera is really from and what other pictures might be on it."

Tabby let out a shaky sigh. "Sure." She tried to sound more confident than she felt. "That would be okay, especially if I can't get my pictures developed here. Thanks, Dad. Just tell 'em not to lose my photos, okay?"

"I'll tell them," he promised. "So, Tabby, this Seeker? What was his real name, his complete name?"

"Michael," she answered quickly. "Michael Miller from South Dakota."

Tabby stopped in the living room to give her grandmother a quick kiss on the top of her head. Granny Hannah was settled for her evening in front of a lineup of game shows and situation comedies.

As she walked down her drive that overwhelming feeling of being watched was back. This is ridiculous, she chided herself. Margie told her Diablo was in jail and she had convinced herself that her vision of Seeker under the dead tree was just that, a vision brought on by the stress of the tornado, nothing more. After all, when she thought about it, that man didn't really look like Seeker. He looked like a lumber jack or one of the locals, just something her imagination had conjured up after the storm. She tried to look around without seeming to do so. The long, tall grass waved in the gentle evening breeze. See? She told herself again. There is no one out there. Granted, there's lots of grass but no one could hide in that. And now Jesse is talking about mountain lions…no, no, no, she told herself again. It's just like Mama always says, nothing out there in the daylight or the dark. Just an occasional white tail deer and they wouldn't hurt a soul.

The taller grass reminded her that her father and Ben would be moving the cattle to the front pasture soon. In years past, that would have meant keeping the front gate closed but last year, J.C. and Ben had installed a cattle guard, so now the cows couldn't get out but they didn't have to worry about opening and closing a gate all the time. She tried to concentrate on that, the nice mundane sort of things instead of the scary stuff. Still, she quickened her pace to hasten her arrival to the perceived safety of the chapel and Frankie's calming presence.

She found him, sitting on the tailgate, looking over the nearly completed chapel.

"What's wrong?" she asked as she hopped up beside him.

"Oh, it's been a heck of day." He let out a long, measured sigh. "Just sitting here wondering how fast we can get this thing finished up. Getting worried is all."

"Worried about what? Thought you said you had more than enough money to finish up after the insurance settlement you got."

"Yeah, we do. It's not the money. It's Uncle Bob." He stared at the grass beyond his construction work boots, planted firmly on the ground.

"Is he worse or…" Her voice trailed off.

"I don't know." He shook his head. "The doctors don't say much. I'm not sure they know much, to be honest. The one doctor told me that sometimes so much damage is done by a heart attack that they can't fix it. Shoot, sometimes they can't even find the damage before it comes back to do more harm, like a second heart attack, and then it's all over."

"Oh, Irish, I'm so sorry. How is he taking it all?"

"Well, that's the truly frightening part. He's making plans."

"Plans? Well, that's a good thing, right? It means he's

thinking about the future, doesn't it?"

"Not the kind of future I ever figured on, that's for sure!"

"What do you mean?"

"I got called off the job site today to the house by Uncle Bob," he began to explain, pulling his ball cap off of his head and dropping it on the tailgate beside them. "At first, I was worried he was feeling worse but when I get there, he's got his lawyer sitting at the kitchen table and Uncle Bob is all smiles. I mean, the man had all kinds of paperwork waiting for me to sign." His voice rose as he finished and while she sensed his distress, she couldn't fathom exactly what it was all about.

She reached out to wrap her arms around him this time and waited.

He accepted her embrace but then pulled back. "He is turning the whole company over to me!" The emotion of the situation contorted his face. "I didn't know what to make of it. I didn't know if it meant he was giving up on himself or what. At first, I just sat there for a minute and then the lawyer finally said he needed to go get something out of his car. I realized later it was just an excuse to leave us alone for a few minutes which was fine. I mean, I wanted to tell Uncle Bob this was crazy. I can't do this. I don't know near enough to run his company and while we sat there, he told me why it was so important for him to do this.

"He said stuff like he's worked all his life to build up this company and he didn't want to just leave it or have it fall apart after he's gone. He and my aunt never had any kids and he said if I don't take it, it will do just that, fall to pieces. There are half a dozen to a dozen guys working for him, depending on the season, of course, and he said several of them have families and he didn't want to leave them out there, with no support. Then he told how he's been watching me ever since I got here late in the winter and he has total faith in me that I know lots more than he did when he started and that he believes I'll do fine." He took a deep breath. "So, I ask you now, how do you say 'no' to that?"

"I don't guess you do, unless it is something you really don't want to do?"

"Are you kidding? It's a dream-come-true, my own construction company, but the truth is it also scares me to death!" He sat there, dreams, delight, and terror all rotating across his face.

"Oh, is that all?" She giggled. "Life does that to me on a regular basis, not to worry."

He gave her a gentle shove. "Thanks a lot!"

"Honestly, Irish, if this is his wish and construction is what you do, it's perfect! So what did you do?"

"Well, I signed all the papers they laid out in front of me. It scares me in one sense but it's also pretty exciting. The bad part is that it makes me worry twice as much about Uncle Bob. It really makes me want to hurry up and get this place done because if his heart does give out, I want him to see it all complete before anything else happens."

She threw her arm around his shoulders as they continued to sit, side by side. "And you will! You and the Sugar Creek gang are so close."

"Yes, we are," he agreed, his eyes still on his feet.

"Look!" She pointed across the field, far to their left, along the tree line. A doe and her twin spotted fawns had tiptoed out into the open to graze on the fresh green grass.

"They are beautiful." He relaxed a bit at the sight. "Where do they go when they disappear?" he asked without expecting an answer.

"Watch," she instructed, still sitting close at his side. They looked on as the graceful woodland creatures grazed, yet wandered slowly back into the woods from which they'd come. "Come on." She jumped off the tailgate and headed across the field. "Come on," she repeated over her shoulder. "I'll show you."

She took his hand and they ran toward the spot where the deer had disappeared into the woods. She slowed as they reached the last place they had seen the animals before they vanished. "Through here." She beckoned him to follow, which he did, as she led the way into the forested back portion of the land donated to the church. Looking around as she moved cautiously through the underbrush, it occurred to her that no one had been through this part of the land in years, perhaps decades. She had really hoped to find one of the matted grassy stretches that served the local deer populations as bedding areas.

Still, he was right behind her and she couldn't simply turn around and leave him with nothing. He was so upset about his uncle and assuming command of the company, she felt compelled to try to find something, even the littlest thing, to take his mind off of his worries for at least a few moments.

She turned to look back and noticed he was a good ten feet to her right, not following her immediate footsteps. Before she could say anything, he caught his foot on an unseen obstacle and fell face first into a batch of thick brambles.

"Irish! Are you all right?" She turned back but he came up, sputtering.

"Tabby! This is nuts! I don't want to see where the deer go to bed at night this bad!"

She burst into peals of laughter. "Oh, I'm sorry." She tried to apologize as she reached up to pull bits of greenery from his hair.

"I'm glad you think it's funny. All this nature girl stuff is fine for you but it's not really my bag, if you know what I mean." He tried to move but his foot, the one initially caught, refused to budge. "Now what?" He reached down to free his boot and discovered it was wedged tight. "What the heck?"

"What's wrong?" She stepped in to take a closer look. Beneath the thick greenery, many of them covered in small thorns, she found his foot caught between what looked at first to be a pair of strong white stems of weeds or some other unknown plants. She ran her hands down on both sides of his boot and upon closer inspection, she realized she was actually looking at a pair, and then a set, of bones.

"Oh, my heavens, Irish! Your foot is caught up in bones!"

"Bones? What bones? Whose bones?"

"I don't know. Hold still. Maybe I can pull them." One of them snapped in her hands and his foot was free. He pulled it back but Tabby didn't let go. She began to run her hands over the other nearby bones in the tangled collection. "Oh, my...Irish, have you got a knife on you? Start cutting right here, will you? Cut this green stuff back so we can get a good look at what's here."

He did as she instructed, fearful that once again she was going to be contacting her uncle, the former sheriff, over their discovery. He cut away each place she pointed to and she tossed the cut pieces aside but what he saw slowly emerging had nothing to do with what he feared or expected.

Suddenly, she sat back on her heels with a huge smile on her face and wiped at the perspiration streaking down her neck. "Do you have any idea what we've found here? I've heard of this before but I've never seen such a thing. Wow! Wait 'til I tell, better! Wait 'til I bring Mr. C. out here and show him this. He's gonna freak! This is a once in a lifetime discovery. Do you realize that?"

"I don't have any idea what you are talking about!" Frankie laughed as he fell down beside her. "All I know is it's hot and I'm scratched and prickled all over and have probably found more ticks, chiggers, and mosquitoes than I ever knew existed! But for some reason, you think this is wonderful! You are, without a doubt, the craziest woman I've ever met!" He lay back on the forest floor and laughed so hard, it brought tears to his eyes.

CHAPTER 12

"They want to get married? Are you serious?" Becky stared open-mouthed over her coffee, at her husband.

"Well, *they* certainly are," J.C. shared quietly as he sat across from his wife one morning toward the end of July. "They showed up here as fast as you left with Marcia. Where did you go again, I forgot?"

"Oh, for heaven's sakes, J.C. I told you, Marcia said they are starting a new preschool in Lebanon at the Methodist Church and she thinks it would be a good thing for Adam. She asked me to go along with her to check it out and tell her what I thought."

"Oh, yes, that's right. And?"

"And what?"

"And what did you think?"

"It was lovely. It's clean and newly painted, lots of bright colors. We took Adam with us and he loved playing with the toys. They have a table full of cornmeal of all things, for the kids to play in like sand. The teacher told us they can reach in, run their toys through it to make roads and that sort of thing, but it is so much better because when the kids get it in their eyes, it doesn't scratch like sand. It softens and, well, it was all just very nice. Marcia enrolled Adam for this fall and he'll go two days a week. Now, stop it! You are making me crazy and you know it! Tell me this instant, what you are talking about?! Getting married, indeed!"

J.C. took a big drink of his coffee as he leaned back in his chair, a grin on his face.

"Sorry," he muttered with little sincerity. "After you left, J. Junior came by and of course, Connie let him in the side door. She sat in the living room while he came to my study and he told me he was here to ask for Connie's hand in marriage."

"Oh, my heavens, J.C., you weren't kidding."

"No, and neither are they. Of course, like you, I was pretty taken aback at first, wondering what they could possibly be thinking, but after listening to both of them, I have to say, it's not that simple."

"What do you mean?" Becky's expression had not changed. "You told him no, that they are way too young, didn't you?"

"No, I didn't." J.C. reached over and took both her hands in his. "I listened, first to him and then to the two of them together."

"Oh, J.C., what could they possibly have said?" Becky's concern now turned toward her husband as much as to the young couple involved.

"Well, let me start at the beginning." He took a deep breath. "Like I said, Connie waited outside and J. Junior told me he'd come to ask me for permission to marry Connie since her father isn't here." J.C. looked at his feet with a grin.

"And you know J. Junior, he can make anything sound like an invitation to a picnic. He told me that he and Connie had been spending most of their time talking, planning and thinking about what comes next for both of them. Heaven knows they've both been through some very rough times recently and maybe that is actually part of what has helped to form such a strong bond between them in such a relatively short time."

Becky nodded without saying anything.

"At any rate, he said he knows they are both young and that many will say, especially with his disabilities, that they have no chance but that they thought those things would actually help to strengthen them now and in the future. He told me a few things about his condition, including the fact that he wears a bag under his clothes because his bowels don't work right after what he went through in Viet Nam and the V.A. hospital. Of course, like everyone else, I had no idea. He said a week or so ago when he and she were over at the Catholic Chapel, she was showing him the new concrete floor and he realized his bag needed emptying. Not wanting to embarrass himself or her, he tried rolling off the concrete out into the grass a short distance to discreetly empty the bag. Well, he managed to get the job done but he also got his wheelchair stuck in the soft ground. Before it was done, he had to get her to help get him unstuck. When she quizzed him on why he went so far afield and he finally admitted why he had done it, she laughed.

"Oh no!" Becky clapped her hand over her mouth. "She didn't."

"Yes, apparently she did but she told him he was a silly boy and that the next time, he should just ask her and she *would* empty the bag! Of course, he told her he couldn't possibly ask her to do such a thing and she smiled and asked if he thought this was the only country in the world that had people with these sorts of problems. And with that, I learned a bit more of what has happened to my friends in Cuba after all these years." He rubbed his hand over his face before continuing.

"I knew she had referred to the fact that Miguelito had been in prison but it seems while he was there, he was beaten so bad, well, he just barely survived. He is back at their apartment now and has been for the last couple of years but he suffered a great many injuries and he, too, has this kind of intestinal damage. She told J. Junior she had often assisted her father in overcoming his many challenges and with much less professional medical assistance than is available here. She also told him that this is something she does for someone she loves and that there is no burden in that for her. As a matter of fact, after that, we invited her into the study as well and we had quite a little discussion."

"Are you telling me they convinced you that this would be a good idea?" Becky's incredulity continued.

"I can't say I'm completely there but I certainly can't dismiss it as a whim or adolescent fantasy. You remember last week she got a message back through the priest from her family and she was so elated about that?"

"Of course. She practically danced into the house after the Saturday afternoon Mass."

"I did find out the priest has connections with the church through Venezuela and the Dominican Republic and that's how the message got through. To be certain they all got it right with the message passing through a couple of hands, they wrote it down for her. Have you seen it?"

Becky shook her head.

"Well, she showed it to me. He produced a small notebook

page.

Dear Daughter,

We are thrilled to learn of your safe arrival. Our gratitude to our dear friends is without limits. Please let them know. Your brother is in the hills. We are well. We will always love you. Find your new life there. Your family

He continued, "Of course, even when we were in school, I remember that Miguelito could write a note that said everything that was needed without a single identifying word. He said that way if the teacher found the note, it couldn't be connected to him and he wouldn't get into trouble. Who knew such a skill might become a life-saving one a few decades later?" He snorted slightly at the thought.

"At any rate, she said that she and the rest of the family had long suspected Miguel Angel, her brother, had taken off to join anti-Castro rebels in the hills, one more reason her father wanted her out of the country. And she also said that last line means just that, to make permanent plans for her future to live here and in her heart and mind that means marrying J. Junior."

"Oh, J.C., but they are so young." Becky shook her head with worry.

"Well, I agree but then I started remembering exactly how old were you when we got married? Eighteen, wasn't it? And didn't we just celebrate Connie's eighteenth birthday with her, not that many days ago on July 4th? And I daresay, she's been through a lot more than either of us had by age eighteen and if that doesn't make you grow up pretty quick, I don't know what will."

"All right, fine but how are they going to make a living?"

"They had an answer or two for that as well. Of course, right now, J. Junior is living with Joey and Grace and he said they have discussed this with them and that they said they could continue to do so for a time. J. Junior is tying flies but that boy has plans. He's talking about the wholesale fishing equipment business, rods, reels, lines and like he says, he can fish from a chair just fine so he can sell equipment to people who are on their feet or on their butts, in his words, not mine." A burst of laughter surprised her. "They both also said that the two of them together have gone over the exercises he does at home, the therapies he has to have to keep his muscles in his legs from deteriorating. I'll say this, she isn't walking into this blind. She actually seems eager to take it on, right along with him."

J.C. continued, "He has disability benefits, of course, but he's also talking about accessing his V.A. educational credits to take business classes. Connie says she would like to teach school and wants to study to do that while working. I mean, I can't say they haven't thought about a great many sides of the different questions."

Becky stood up to freshen her coffee and poured a bit more in her husband's cup as well. "So, overall, what do you think? Are we really going to let them do this?"

He leaned forward and took her hands once again. "I'm not sure that is our choice. I think it is more likely to be, are we going to support them with a family wedding when they do this or we can refuse and I do believe they will run off and elope anyway, although J. Junior did say he really did want our blessing."

She looked at him for a moment before continuing. "I appreciate that, I really do, but there is also the business of the churches, the differences. I mean, Ma has been ridiculous in her opposition to the Catholics but is J. Junior really going to give up his church for hers? What will Grace and Joey think about that? I mean, J.C., there is just so much to think about!"

"I agree but again, it is not really up to us, is it? It is his decision, not yours or mine. I asked him about it, believe me, and while his answer was pure J. Junior, it was also pretty profound. Let's see, exactly how did he put it?" He leaned back in his chair and stared at the ceiling for a moment. "It went something like—'I talked to the priest. Father Clem and Connie both said I could stay in my church and she in hers but I don't wanna do that. I want to go to church each week and sit beside my wife, not in some other place. From what all the priest said, it seems to me that God and his Son, Jesus, and the Holy Ghost are still the three who head up the whole of their church. They really like Jesus' mother, Mary, but who doesn't? And they got a whole lots of folks after that in their line-up they call saints but they all sound like pretty good ones to me. It ain't like they've got somebody different heading up the whole works, now that would be a game changer, no doubt. But they still worship God and Jesus and pray to them and follow them same Ten Commandments. The Father said they tell everybody to love God and love your neighbor, take only one wife, and take good care of your family. I guess I just don't see what all the dust up is, J.C., and if'n all I got to do to marry this angel is go to a church with a different name over the door and a churchman that turns his collar around backwards and wears a long robe a little more often than Pastor Jamison does, that's a pretty small price to pay. I just can't see that the whole business might matter more than a hill of beans to the good Lord himself with all there is to say grace over, so why should it matter to me?"

"Oh, for heaven's sakes, J.C.!" Becky burst into laughter. "You are right, how do you argue with that?"

J.C. smiled with a shake of his head. "His last words to me were actually, 'God sent me an angel with a sweet little accent who loves me and knows how to do what needs to be done. She loves me and I love her and I don't think God would take it too kindly if I ignored a gift like that.' And finally he said he would do just about anything to marry her."

She shook her head again but still with a smile. "J.C., you are a romantic. You have always been a romantic ever since you showed up with your mother here in the fall of 1924 and asked me to marry you." She kissed him on the forehead.

"You're right," he agreed, as he stood up and pulled her to her feet. "And I can't say 'no' to true love." He wrapped his arms around his wife and kissed her with a passion that belied their forty plus years of marriage. "And I do think that this may be just that."

* * * * *

A few evenings later, the darkening clouds gathered, threatening rain and another summer Ozark storm. Frankie had called earlier to say he was exceptionally tired, trying to make up for the work he had missed earlier in the week and considering the impending weather, he was not coming out to the site tonight. Her parents had taken Hannah to Ben and Jessica's but then they were meeting Connie and J. Junior at Joey and Grace's house for dinner.

Tabby didn't really know what was going on there but something was definitely up. When she had inquired, her mother had made it clear that whatever it was, she had no intention of divulging the secret quite yet. She did promise after tonight, however, if Tabby would be patient just a little longer, her mother would tell her everything. Tabby had to admit she didn't like being left in the dark, so to speak, but if she only had to wait another day or two and if it would keep her mother in the good spirits she seemed to be enjoying, it was worth it.

She had to admit she truly wasn't unhappy at the prospect of an evening of peace and quiet, all by herself, in the house she had grown up in. She quickly found that the impending storm interfered with the television reception so after just a few minutes, she flipped off the set. She remembered some of the dozens of pamphlets she had found in boxes at work, including the ones she had loaded into her tote bag. Thinking she really needed to review some of those for work, she headed down the hall. Just as she reached into the bag on her bed, the lights along with the rest of the power in the house flickered and went out.

Flashlight, flashlight, her thoughts careened. Well, there were candles in the kitchen, she was sure of that. The hallway was inky black but that didn't stop her from hearing the eerie creak of the front door as it opened. She flattened herself against the wall but continued to listen with all of her being as the crack of lightning that lit the front room for a single second revealed the silhouette, standing in front of the living room window. The darkness returned and she slid along the wall, around the end of it, slipping in silence through the kitchen. She hit the back door on the run, tearing across the back yard toward the barn.

Fat raindrops pelted her, followed by stinging little balls of hail. If she could just make it to the barn and the hayloft where she had played all the years she was growing up, she knew she would be safe. She knew the barn and the loft, dark or light, and she was certain the man behind her did not.

And then she heard it, a savage cry, a scream, a terrifying sound like she had never heard before. It made her feet fly even faster. She heard the back door slam behind her and the pounding of his feet, splashing on the wet ground. The thunder rolled overhead and her feet slipped in the wet grass as she went down hard, knocking the wind out of her. She scrambled to get up but it was like her limbs had turned to lead with the fear that coursed through her. She heard the footsteps even closer behind her coming so fast, but it was confusing because it was as if they were coming from different directions. She expected at any moment to feel him knock her back to the ground. When she reached the barn door, she heard that savage cry once more. This time it was followed by an all too recognizable human sound, a short burst of foul language, a scream of pain and terror, and then, nothing but the pounding rain.

She collapsed against the door post, trying desperately to breathe, while shaking all over. She heard a vehicle pulling into the driveway and saw the flash of its lights, and then came the sound that made her knees buckle.

"Tabby! Tabby!" Her Uncle Benji's voice could be heard above the storm's fading fury.

"Tabby, where are you?" She heard her father's call next and she offered up a silent prayer of thanks.

"I'm here!" She voiced a weak answer at first and then stronger as she stood up straight. "I'm here, Daddy, Uncle Benji! I'm here!"

"Stay right there," Ben called out. "We're coming! Ugh!"

"Uncle Benji? Are you all right?" Tabby's sense of terror returned.

"I'm all right," he called but his voice was less strong and confident than a moment before.

"Here, Ben!" J.C. came up behind his brother-in-law with a

large bright flashlight in his hand. "Glory Hallelujah! Are you okay?"

"Yeah, I'm fine." J.C.'s brother-in-law picked himself up off of the wet ground. "What the heck…"

"Here!" J.C. shoved the flashlight into Ben's hand and scrambled on to find his daughter, still waiting in the safety of the barn door.

"Oh, Daddy!" The dam that had held to this point folded suddenly as did she into her father's arms, with wracking sobs.

"It's okay, baby. It's okay. We're both here. Are you hurt?" He wrapped her in a warm embrace that included tucking her inside his full length rain coat.

She shook her head, unable to speak.

A long, low whistle escaped Ben who was still standing out in the rain where he had fallen. "You won't believe this." He ran J.C.'s flashlight beam slowly up and down the length of the body that lay face down in the backyard. He checked for a pulse and breathing and found none. When he stood back up, he saw that his hand was covered in blood.

"Come on, you two." Ben called to J.C and Tabby. "Everybody okay?"

"I think we're fine," J.C. answered as they walked slowly toward Ben.

"Here, go around." Ben directed them toward the back door. "We can't help this poor feller anymore. I sure hope your phone is working, J.C., because I've got some calls to make."

* * * * *

An hour later, the three of them sat much more quietly in the living room as Tabby nursed another cup of hot cocoa, her favorite remedy in any crisis. The coroner and a deputy were in the backyard, removing the dead body that Ben had discovered there. Sheriff Francis Murphy came in the front door and shook hands with J.C. and Ben.

"Sorry it took me a few minutes to get here," he apologized. "I was on the other side of the county but when I realized what you all had going, I figured I better get out here. I guess the FBI boys will be here tomorrow morning."

"FBI?" Tabby's eyes flashed. "What has the FBI got to do with this?"

"Well, young lady, they've got a few questions for you and so do I."

He removed his sheriff's cap and sat down in the upholstered chair at the end of the couch where Tabby was sitting, wrapped up in the throw off the back of the couch.

"I don't understand." Tabby made a visible effort to remain calm.

"All right, well, neither do we," Sheriff Murphy replied. "Let's try this. I'll tell you some of what we know and you tell me what you know. Does that sound fair?"

"I guess, I guess so," she stammered, her eyes flitting back and forth between her father and her uncle.

"Listen, Tabby." J.C. spoke up. "We know this has something to do with where you were or who you were with in California. And I appreciate that you might be afraid you'll implicate someone else, get them into trouble and maybe you are even afraid you'll get yourself into more trouble but you must tell us the truth here. Do you understand? If you start lying or trying to cover things up, it will only make things worse. So let's get that straight from the beginning. I don't care what you've done or who you've been involved with but for heaven's sakes at this point, don't lie about it. As you've experienced tonight, this is a very serious situation and a man is dead. Let's get to the bottom of it right now. Agreed?"

She bit her lip as she nodded. "Yes, sir," was all she said.

"All right," the sheriff began. "This is what we know. That little camera that you gave your daddy. He sent it to a friend of his in Washington with the Feds and they looked it over real good. They developed the pictures in it and they dusted it for fingerprints and they found a couple real important ones. They belong to a man named Martin Miller. Ever heard of him?"

Tabby looked down for a moment before answering.

"Do you know him?" The sheriff asked again.

"I think I know his name but I never met him." She answered in a mere whisper.

"Did you know the FBI is about to put him on their Ten Most Wanted list?" was the sheriff's next question.

"No!" Her answer registered her shock. "He is Seeker's brother, from South Dakota. That's all I know. I never met him. Seeker told me his brother had come by to see him one night, that's all."

"So you never saw this man before?" the sheriff asked as he handed her a black and white photo.

"Oh, my heavens!" Her hand flew to her mouth. "He looks just like…"

"Like what?"

"He looks just like Seeker, his brother." A vision of a man in lumberjack attire under a dead snag of a tree flitted through her head.

"But you never met him?" The sheriff pressed again, making J.C. squirm in his chair, but despite his obvious discomfort, he maintained his silence.

"I....I," she hesitated. "I think I saw him once."

"Where? In California? I thought you said..."

"No, here," she whispered.

"Here?" The sheriff, J.C., and Ben all exchanged startled glances.

The tears welled up before she could continue. She blew her nose and tried again.

"The night of the tornado. Afterwards. I was looking out the side window there." She pointed past J.C. down the hallway. "I was just noticing how all the raindrops made everything outside glisten in the moonlight and then I saw him, back by the tree line, under that big snag."

"Tabby, you never said a word!" J.C.'s words came out more accusatory than he intended.

"Daddy, how could I?" she whined. "I didn't want to tell you any of this in the first place. Shoot, obviously, I didn't know half of what I should be telling you," she huffed and wrapped her arms around a throw pillow in frustration.

She took a deep breath and continued. "It scared me half to death because all I could think at first was that it was Seeker. I mean, they look so much alike. But there was no reason for him to be here at Bennett Spring, either of 'em. Seeker was the original live-and-let-live kind of guy. If he knew I came back here of my own free will, then with him

243

that would be it. He might call me once if he could find my number but he wouldn't come to my house and hang out in the backwoods. That wasn't the way he did things. Then when I looked back at the tree and he was gone, I decided maybe I just imagined the whole thing. The tornado that night was pretty scary even if I did try to make out otherwise, so as to not upset Connie any more. After a few days and then a week or two, I convinced myself, it was just a…what is it Mama calls such things? A figment of my imagination."

By now J.C. had his own question. "That tornado was nearly a month ago and our break-in was before that. Of course, your Deputy Franklin told me they never found any fingerprints after the burglary, despite their best efforts. He said the man probably wore gloves."

The sheriff nodded.

"So if he was involved, do you really think this Miller has been hanging around here all that time, biding his time?"

The sheriff shook his head. "No, no I don't." The sheriff turned his attention back to Tabby. "You said *was* more than once, when talking about your friend, Seeker. Why?"

A heavy sigh escaped her and she stole a sideways look at her father before continuing. "Seeker died the week before I left San Francisco. That's why I left as much as anything. I…I had been staying with him and he brought home some stuff—"

"What kind of stuff?" the sheriff interrupted.

"Some LSD, acid, they call it out there. He gave me a little of it and frankly, it was okay that night but it was terrible the next day. It really scrambles your brain. Anyway, he had done it before, lots of times, he said, but this time he took too much. The next day some of the others in the group were saying that it came from a guy called The Unicorn who had started messing around, putting stuff like other drugs, poison, I don't know what, in with the stuff he was selling. As some kind of sick joke, I guess. Anyway, Seeker didn't wake up after that night. He paid a terrible price for getting his stuff from The Unicorn, even after some of the others in the group told him not to deal with him anymore. The cops came and they took Seeker's body away.

"That's why it scared me so when I saw him or I thought I saw him outside under that dead tree. I saw his body wheeled out of that apartment in San Francisco so I knew it couldn't be him and yet, for all the world, it sure looked like he'd come back from the dead! I didn't even think of his brother," she finished with a whimper.

"All right." Sheriff Murphy bit the eraser end of his pencil for a moment before continuing. "So after this Seeker feller died and they took his body away, what did you do for the next little while? How long after that 'til you left San Francisco?"

She let out a long, slow breath. "I dunno. A few days, maybe a week. I had to beg the money for the bus ticket off the other kids in the apartment but they were pretty good about sharing what they had. The problem is nobody had much and then the landlord was throwing everybody out after Seeker died since his was the only name on the lease. So what little they had they needed to try to find another place. It took a few days to get the money and to get enough to have a little to eat along the way, too."

"I bet it did." The sheriff nodded with a sympathetic smile.

J.C. looked down, his stomach twisting at what she had been through and yet knowing somewhere in the back of his mind, she had learned some important lessons throughout all of this.

Tabby continued. "I boxed up Seeker's things for someone, like Martin, I guess, to come pick up later."

"And the camera?"

"When I saw it, I remembered the pictures that Seeker snapped of us the one day so I took it. I mean, it wasn't like he was ever going to need it again. I thought I would get the pictures developed and then I would have them, to remember him by, you know?" The tears began again as she reached for a tissue from the box on the coffee table.

"I knew it was his brother's camera but I never thought it was anything important. Seeker said his brother, Martin, came by the one night and asked him to keep it for him. He laughed at the time and said his brother acted like it was some big deal but Seeker said he was always going on about this or that conspiracy or some government plot. He said his brother said he'd be back for it in a week or two and that's all I know. But by then, Seeker was dead and it wasn't like there would be any of us left at the apartment anyway. I don't even know what they did with the rest of Seeker's things."

She added, "Seeker even said it was a very cool little camera. He said there were still plenty of pictures on the roll of film so he took some fun photos of us and that's why I took it. Those are the only things I have of him. Those pictures and these earrings." She flicked at her pierced ears.

"Earrings?" The sheriff raised an eyebrow as he looked up from the notebook where he had been scribbling.

"They are Chinese jade, these little green crosses. Seeker bought them for me in China Town when we went there one day. He wanted to buy little balls or Chinese gods but I told him I wanted the crosses instead and he smiled like I was silly but he bought them for me anyway." Her voice caught as she finished with a sniffle.

"Okay, I don't think we are worried about the earrings." The sheriff smiled. "So this Seeker? What's his real name?"

"Michael. His name was Michael Miller. He was Martin's younger brother."

The sheriff leaned back and after another moment, finally stopped writing. "Okay, here is some of what the FBI shared with us when they came here looking for Martin Miller. They've been trying to keep a tail on him ever since California, sometimes they managed and sometimes he gave them the slip.

"They knew the younger brother, real name Michael Miller—the one you call Seeker—was dead and like you said, a drug overdose, credited to some other fool out there with the name of Unicorn. I tell you, the names these kids come up with." He let out a short mirthless laugh. "They were watching that place, looking for Martin when Michael died. Anyway, they lost track of Martin more than once it seems and it shocked the fire right out of all of them when he turned up here, like you said, more than a month ago. Nobody expected that. I'm not even sure how they tracked him down here. I'll have to remember to ask that FBI agent in charge the next time I talk to him, but about the time they marshalled their forces and started looking for him serious-like here, he disappeared again. Apparently, he took a little trip back to South Dakota."

The sheriff looked up at Tabby. "I'm sorry, young lady. It sounds like you had a pretty rough trip out there to California."

"Well." She tried taking a deep breath. "Let's say, it

certainly didn't turn out the way I thought when I left here."

"I'd say that sounds about right," the sheriff agreed.

J.C. reached over from his place on the end of the couch and patted her knee. "You're doing fine, Tabby. Thank you."

"Daddy, I'm so sorry. I know you must think so much less of me than you did before."

His smile was tinged with only a little sadness. "No, darling, it's not like that. I think you've grown up and with that comes making your own decisions, not all of them wise ones. We all go through it and I'm sorry in one sense because I understand the pain and disappointment that comes with those poor decisions and frankly, the loss of innocence. But I could never think less of you, Tabby. I love you and mostly, I'm just so glad you are here right now and all in one piece."

"Sheriff, I'm sorry to interrupt, but I think you better take a look at this." The deputy who had been outside with the coroner came in the back door, dripping rainwater as he did.

"Sure. Excuse me for a minute or two, folks." He followed the deputy back out the kitchen door to the backyard.

"So, Uncle Benji, what is really going on here?" Tabby's question came out more like a whine than she intended but the fatigue and the strain of the entire situation was taking its toll.

"Well, let me see," he began. "Your dad sent that camera off to his friends in Washington and when they found Miller's prints on it, they called the sheriff here. He knew you were my niece so he called me once he realized how serious it was as a courtesy to a former sheriff, you could say. And also to see what else I might know, if you had been in trouble before, that sort of thing."

"So what is it that's got Seeker's brother in so much trouble? The FBI? What's he into?"

"Both brothers are from South Dakota. You knew that, right?"

She nodded.

"Well, they have some of those Minute Men missiles up there. As I understand it, that's where the main base is. That's one of our big defense systems against a nuclear attack to protect us from the Russians. The other pictures on that camera were of some of those missiles, their installation, that sort of thing and they aren't the kind of pictures a tourist would take. It seems Martin Miller has been involved with others who want to blow up these missiles, who are actually fighting against the US government, even though they are Americans and live right here in the US amongst us."

"Oh, my gosh!" Tabby dropped her head into her hands. "I heard about some of them out there. None of the people I was hanging out with were involved with them but you know, you hear about all these different groups. Some of them think they should be making war against our own government. I thought that was pretty crazy, even Seeker said so. I don't think he had any idea that his brother was involved in that sort of thing. Or if he did, he never said so and he sure didn't act like it. He made it sound like his brother was just sort of kooky and he laughed about it." She sighed. "It seemed so funny then. Not anything important like what you are talking about and sure not something worth getting killed over. I can't believe that man in the backyard is dead."

J.C. leaned over to pat her knee again. "What's even more frightening is that apparently he was here to harm you as well. Ben thinks he is probably the one who broke in here a couple weeks ago and tore up your room. The guess is he was trying to get his camera back."

"So that really is Martin Miller?" She asked, wide-eyed again.

"It makes sense, doesn't it?" Ben continued. "He was after the camera but it wasn't in your room when he broke in there, was it?"

"No, it was in my bag," Tabby said, thinking it over.

"Exactly. Once they got a look at those pictures, the FBI started putting more things together, too, like Martin Miller's movements. He came here to try and get the camera by breaking in and even kept watch on the place and on you, too, probably."

The feeling of being watched, Tabby thought to herself as a shiver ran up her spine.

"The only way he could get those kinds of photos was with help, inside help of someone else, working up there in South Dakota. When he couldn't get the camera, the FBI thinks he went back up north to try to take more pictures. By then, though, they had tightened up security and even more important, they caught the guy they thought was helping him. He talked and that is one more way, in addition to the photos, they knew what he and his friends were planning. At first, they thought he wanted the photos because they were so incriminating, but after tonight, as desperate as he was, I'd say they had bigger plans for those photos."

Ben continued, "When the sheriff called me and told me the kind of guy they were looking for, I called your dad over at Joey and Grace's house to tell him. We tried calling out here, but didn't get an answer what with the storm, so we decided we'd better come out to make sure you were safe."

"I'm so glad you did." Tabby sighed as she relaxed back against the couch with a small smile. "So where is everybody else?" She perked up a bit as she thought about the rest of the family.

"Well, I think Mom is just staying at our house tonight," Ben said, "and my understanding is that Connie is going to spend the night at Joey and Grace's house tonight as well."

"Really? What's up with that?" Tabby gave them half a smile.

"That's a kind of a different story that we will have to get into tomorrow," J.C. added with his own little smile, "but yes, she's going to stay over there. Grace said she was more than welcome."

"Okay." Tabby was still trying to follow that one but decided to let it pass, which was just as well as the sheriff came back into the room.

"So, now what can you tell me about the man in the backyard and exactly what happened to him?" He returned to his chair, notebook still in hand.

"I don't know," she said, turning a puzzled face toward the sheriff.

"The lights went out in the house with the storm, I thought. I started toward the kitchen to get a candle and that's when I heard the front door open. Mama is always telling Daddy that door needs a little more grease because it squeaks so but tonight I'm really glad it did. I was in the hall in the dark when I saw him in the living room because of the lightning. Quick as I could, I went out the back door, headed for the barn, because I knew I could hide in there. And that's when I heard it."

"Heard what?" All three men leaned forward.

"I'm not sure but it was the most God-awful screech I ever heard. It scared me so bad I could hardly keep moving after that and then I heard it again and then a bunch of cussing and a man's scream. The next thing I heard after that was Uncle Benji calling my name. That's really all I remember." She finished in a low voice. "Why? What happened to him?"

"Well, we're not entirely sure, but from what I've seen and what you've said....You all heard about the mountain lion tracks they found out by your mother-in-law's old place, right?" The sheriff turned his attention toward J.C. and Ben.

J.C. nodded, a deep frown on his face.

"The man those boys just loaded into the coroner's ambulance. If I don't miss my guess, he got on the wrong side of that cougar tonight and he's got the marks to prove it. You said there was quite a lot of blood, didn't you?" He cast a glance at Ben.

The former sheriff gave him a nod. "I didn't want to say anything earlier and add to the upset around here but yeah, from what I saw out there earlier, it looked pretty bad."

"It is," the sheriff agreed. "His throat was pretty well ripped out. He didn't last long once that cat was on him, that's for sure. And we found this. About six feet away from him. My guess is when he fell or got knocked down, it flew out of his hand and in the dark and the rain he didn't have a chance to look for it. At least not in time. This man wasn't out collecting for charity tonight. He meant business."

The sheriff held a heavy clear plastic bag with a large black leather-handled single-edged knife inside, with a wicked-looking long blade.

Tabby gulped and set her empty cocoa cup on the table with shaking hands. "Oh, my." She barely breathed.

"What else, Tabby?" J.C. gave her a strange look.

"Irish, what Irish said. He's always teasing, calling me Nature Girl. He said I protect the animals around here and that they protect me. Maybe he was right."

CHAPTER 13

―⊶⊷――

"All right," Sheriff Murphy sat back down. "The FBI has told us they want this kept quiet. We're pretty sure this man is Martin Miller and we think he came here for you." He turned to Tabby. "Or rather for the camera and if that is the case, the camera is gone and he's dead. There's nothing to be served by alarming the public by telling 'em we had some feller here that was threatening to blow up Minute Man missile silos. And if the Feds say we gotta keep it quiet, well, it's their case and that's that. We'll find out for sure once the coroner gets him back to his office and checks his fingerprints and then the FBI guys will be here tomorrow but I don't expect any surprises there."

For a moment, he studied the braided oval rug where his boots rested before continuing. "Now, as to this mountain lion business. The Feds don't want the man identified so I can't very well tell the local radio and newspaper reporters that we suspect we had a man killed by a cougar when the man isn't even supposed to exist. So, this is my way of thinking. We all need to keep this quiet. The conservation boys say they've seen this cat's tracks around here for a few days now and this is the first trouble we've had out of the animal. I haven't even heard of so much as a missing chicken up to this point. Maybe there is something to what you said, Miz Tabby, that this animal was acting out of protection for you somehow, but I sure don't want to start a panic and have people out there hunting for what they see as a killer cat with pitchforks, shotguns and what have you. We'll end up with a dead cow or horse or two, a bunch of mad farmers and, heaven forbid, somebody hurt or killed before it's all over!"

"Makes sense," Ben agreed as he leaned back, visibly relaxed. He looked over at J.C.

"I'm afraid it is the only thing that does," he sighed. "You already have the coroner, a deputy, all of us involved. It's going to be quite the job to keep it contained."

"Well, they better keep it contained, as you call it," the sheriff concluded as he stood up. "Or that deputy will be looking for a new job and find himself on the wrong side of a judge. The coroner, he knows how to keep his mouth shut. As long as you folks can handle your end of it, I think we can make it work. Now if that cat will just cooperate a little. Best for him and all of us is if decides he had enough excitement tonight and goes on back out west or wherever he came from. Say a little prayer for that and we might just slide by on this whole thing."

Tabby collapsed into her bed as fast as the sheriff was out the front door. She heard her mother come in with her Aunt Jessica moments later. Her bedroom door swung open and she saw the feminine silhouette, the light in the hallway shining all around her. Tabby was already more asleep than awake but she couldn't help thinking it looked like a guardian angel was standing in her doorway. Now, she didn't mind that kind of being watched at all. Her mother turned off the hall light and the last thing she heard was Becky's words to Jessica. "Poor thing, she was so exhausted she is already sound asleep."

It seemed as if she had only been asleep a few moments when she was nearly jostled right off the bed when Connie came bounding onto it.

"Tabby!" She shrieked in delight. "I am sorry but I could not wait any longer to tell you!"

"What? What's going on?" Her friend stared at her through half-opened eyes. "Is it really morning?"

"Yes, it is and you must wake up so I can tell you. We are going to marry! J. Junior and me, and I want you to be *mi madrina*, how do you say it, my maid of honor!"

"What?" Tabby shot up straight and wrapped her arms around her friend who was, by now, kneeling at her side. "What? Wait…." She grabbed Connie by her shoulders and shoved her back to look her full in the face. "Are you crazy? You and J. Junior?"

"Yes! J. Junior and me. We are going to be husband and wife. I will be Mrs. J. Junior! It is wonderful, yes?" Connie's face was so alive, her eyes aglow with elation.

"Oh, Connie." Tabby threw her arms around her friend again and rocked her gently side to side in her delight at the other's happiness. "If you are sure this is what you want."

Now it was Connie's turn to look at her roommate. "I have never been more sure of anything, my friend. I know others will look at him or even at me and see a man in a wheelchair or a girl who lost her country and her family, someone who is trying to fill empty spaces in the heart, but it is so much more than that. Oh, Tabby, we have such plans and especially J. Junior. It is wonderful to listen to him and he laughs when he listens to me, but not like he is making fun, you know? He tells me he likes to listen to the way I sing when I talk, that is what he calls my accent. He said it is like an angel singing."

Tabby leaned back in the bed, tucking a hand under her head, with a genuine smile on her face. Especially after all of the distress of last night, it was so uplifting to share in Connie's delight. She listened as Connie talked about everything from tying flies, or fishing bugs as she called them, to J. Junior's plans for a fishing equipment business.

"And what about you, Connie?" Tabby asked. "What do you want to do?"

"Oh, I have always dreamed of teaching the small children." She leaned back as she explained. "J. Junior says there is no reason I cannot go to school, too and become a teacher. Oh, Tabby that is the best because you know, I would never be allowed to do that in Cuba now. Because my family is against Castro, well, only his people are allowed to teach the young ones. To twist their minds as my father calls it. But here, I can be a school teacher. Now that is a real dream to come true and to do it with someone who loves me like J. Junior. Well…" She stopped speaking, wrinkled her nose, and squeezed her shoulders together in a little girl's expression of glee.

"Then I am truly happy for you." Tabby continued to relax. "So when? What do we have to do first? And a ring? What kind of ring are you getting?"

"A ring, yes. One that matches his ring."

"Well, yeah, but I mean, a diamond one. An engagement ring."

Connie sat up and gave a little shake of distaste, like a dog ridding itself of a flea. "No," was all she said. *"No diamantes."*

"All my friends in college who got engaged got diamond rings, big tradition here, so I just thought you would want one, too. If you don't, that's fine, but I gotta ask—why not?"

A demure little smile crossed her friend's face. "My family, by the time I was old enough to remember, had many fine things, the hotels, the houses, the cars, but they did not start out that way. My grandfather began as a *mozo,* the boy who carries your bags, in the same hotel he would one day own. He worked his way up and even when my father was old enough, he made him do the same thing. Some people talked badly about my grandfather for making his son work that way since he was the owner's son but my grandfather said it was the best way for him to learn, to learn to work hard and to learn to have respect for the people who had to work that way every day to feed their families. He also said it would teach him the hotel business in the very best way. And it must have worked because both my father and grandfather made a very good success of their business and I have to say, they were very much loved by their customers and their employees both."

She smiled. "That is how my father met my mother. She was a maid there but she came from one of the poorest families and she really needed the job. My father fell in love with her but she would not have him! In the beginning there was a little resistance from his family, but she was the one who fought against the marriage most of all!" She covered her mouth as she laughed out loud. "My father would tell me stories about how he would chase her, literally, through the hotel and she kept screaming she would not marry a rich man and all kinds of crazy things. But he is, of course, very charming, like your father. I can see why they were, still are, such good friends because they are such good men.

"But the one thing my mother told my father is that she would never wear diamonds. She loves the colored stones, the cheap ones as she calls them, that the people wear.

They are bright and they are beautiful and she always liked to go and buy them in the market and from the street people. She told my father she would not wear a ring or a necklace that could feed a family for a month or a year but that she would only wear the type of glass jewels she has always worn. My father agreed because he said she is his true jewel. And that is her real name. Everyone calls her Pilar but her full name is Gema Pilar and *gema* means jewel or gem."

"Oh, Connie, that is beautiful. Your mom sounds like quite a lady."

"Oh, she is. I miss her, now that I do not see her, but like you with yours, we often seemed to trade sharp words."

"Yes, well, maybe it is just the curse of being mother and daughter."

"Maybe so."

"So, no diamond ring."

"No, we will both have a ring that is the same, yes? We have to go find those but I imagine they will be simple, like a gold band. He said that was fine with him. Besides, diamonds are so expensive and I think we will need to spend our money on more important things. I am used to that in Cuba, believe me!"

"Okay, so what's next? Who is going to be J. Junior's best man?"

"He is asking his father, Joey. He says the tradition is to ask your best friend and he says that truly is his father. That is good, yes?" Connie bobbed her head with the question.

"That is very good, yes!"

"We will talk to Father Clem and see but we hope very

soon. We want to be the first wedding in Frankie's new chapel. That will be wonderful, yes?"

"Oh, yes!" Tabby sat up straight. Oh, she couldn't wait to share that news with Irish!

After some breakfast, she left Connie in the kitchen when she heard her mother calling her from her own bedroom. Tabby found Becky with a mound of clothes piled on the bed. An amused smile crossed her face as Tabby poked at her own christening dress and other special items her mother had saved from her childhood days and those of her sister and brother.

"What are you looking for?" her daughter asked as Becky finished unloading the old camel back trunk that sat at the end of her bed.

"Here." Becky straightened up with one last garment in her hand, wrapped in a gauzy white covering. She laid it gently on the bed, without unwrapping it. "Sit down, Tabby. I've got a question."

"Connie has told you about her and J. Junior's plans?"

Tabby smiled.

"I heard the squeals," Becky grinned. "He came and asked your father for permission to marry her a few days ago and then, of course, there's been lots of discussion since. We were at Joey and Grace's last night, all of us talking it over. I can't say I'm not worried about them but they are determined and if God blesses their union, well, then it will be good. Heaven knows your daddy and I didn't have any more than they do when we started. Of course, your father wasn't in a wheelchair but somehow, I do believe...." A happy little sigh escaped her.

Becky gave herself a little shake as she changed the

subject. "Here is my question. This is my wedding dress." Becky turned and pulled the cover down on the last item she had pulled from her trunk. She revealed a champagne-colored dress of lace from the 1920s, with a high collar, buttons down the front, with a skirt of tiny pleats that stopped at the mid-calf.

"Oh, Mama. I remember you letting me and Lizbeth look at this when we were little." Tabby lightly fingered the heirloom dress.

"Yes, we looked at it a time or two and the truth is I kept it all these years, thinking that Lizbeth or you might want to use it. When Lizbeth got married, she thought it too old-fashioned and I was wondering if you wanted me to try and keep it for you, although honestly, I don't know that it would fit..." She looked at it doubtfully as she unwrapped it fully.

"Mama, I don't want to hurt your feelings but like Lizbeth, it's not really my style, if you know what I mean."

"Oh, that's fine, I know. It's old and I don't remember it being nearly such an ivory color but maybe with age. But it does seem to be the same all over so I think it would be all right."

Tabby cocked her head to one side, surveying the still elegant dress as she tried to determine just exactly where her mother was headed with all of this.

"So I was wondering...." Becky plopped down on the bed, beside the pile of old cloth memories. "Do you think I should offer it to Connie? I mean, she's little enough to fit it but I don't want her to take it because she thinks she should or she has to. If she wants her very own dress, we can go shopping for one. Can you talk to her about it?"

"Oh, Mama, of course, I will," Tabby laughed out loud.

"Let's just ask her. She might surprise you. She often does me, that's for sure."

Tabby stepped out into the hall and beckoned Connie inside. "My mother has a question but first you must make a promise."

"All right," Connie answered as she looked from one to the other, mother and daughter. "What is the promise?"

"You must promise that your answer to the question," Tabby explained, "is completely honest. If you don't like what we are about to ask you or you want something different, you must promise to say so."

Connie's confusion deepened, but the delightful expectancy she saw on her friends' faces let her know that whatever the question, it was all hemmed in love.

"Oh, Tabby, I don't know if you make things better or worse," Becky laughed. "Connie, I was just wondering. This was my wedding dress from many years ago when I married J.C. and there is a tradition here that some brides follow to use their mother's dress years later. Many brides do not follow it though because they don't like the old style or they want their own dress. For instance, neither of my girls want this dress but I did want to offer it to you, in case you might be interested…" She watched as the young girl reached out to touch the dress.

"Oh, *Niña Becky*," Connie's words came out in a soft rush. "This is so beautiful! We, too, have that same tradition in Cuba but as you said, many choose not to follow it." She looked up, her face luminous. "It is almost golden. You would let me use this for my wedding? It would be…." She swallowed. "It would be such an honor."

"Well, thank you, but the honor would be mine, Connie. I thought we could cut down the neck here and open it up to show off your pretty shoulders. We can shorten it, too, if you like."

"Oh, no." Connie shook her head. "It is good a little longer, I think. But to change the top a little, that would be nice. Oh, it is just so special!"

"Well, here, let's be sure." Becky lifted the dress from the bed and its wrapping. "Go try it on and then we'll see what we have to do after that."

"I think that was a pretty honest answer," Tabby laughed as Connie stepped into their room to change. "Even if I did mess it up, in your opinion." She tossed a throw pillow at her mother.

A few moments later, a truly radiant young woman from Cuba stepped back into the room.

"Oh, Connie, it is perfect!" Tabby exclaimed.

"Well, it certainly is." Becky's hand suddenly flew to her lips as her eyes filled with tears. "Oh, the memories this brings back…Connie, you will make such a beautiful bride. Now, let's see what we can do with that neckline."

* * * * *

After the tumultuous events of the night before, Tabby called into work and begged off for the day. She told Mr. C., as she called him, a lot had gone on at her house the night before with her family and no one had gotten much sleep. He told her not to fret.

"Your timing is good, kid," he laughed over the phone. "Not a lot going on today anyway. Take it easy, catch up on your rest and we'll see you tomorrow."

"Thank you," she told him, her smile evident in her voice. "I'll come tell you all about it tomorrow." She figured by then, half the valley would know about J. Junior and Connie but it would make a nice story anyway and an even nicer cover for her absence today.

Connie went on to work at the campground and Tabby ended up on the couch, taking a nap before noon. Afterward, she made herself a sandwich for a late lunch and then wandered down to see what Connie was doing.

A glance across the road told her once again that the new Sportsman Chapel, as she had now heard it called, was very close to completion. She took unconscious pleasure in the yellow brown-eyed susans with their upright dark centers, that had popped up seemingly overnight and were now sprinkled along the roadside.

Tabby was vaguely relieved to find Connie alone in the store. "Where is everybody?" she asked when she finally located Connie along one of the back aisles, stocking shelves.

"Oh, Jesse is down below as they finish out the new trailer sites. Marcia went to town to get supplies for this weekend and she took Adam with her. Did you know he is going to start pre-school next month?"

"Oh, yeah, I heard something about that, in between a marriage announcement and some other stuff. So, are you going to keep working here?" Out of habit, Tabby picked up a rag from behind the counter and began to dust the tops of the items on the shelves. With so many dirt roads in the campground and summer breezes, dust was a constant, making it look as if the place hadn't been cleaned in a week instead of a day.

"For now, yes. I cannot stop now, how do you say, in the middle of the season?"

"In the middle of the season?" Tabby raised an eyebrow,

amused at how well the Cuban teen was adapting to her new environment.

"That is what Jesse calls it. Is that not right?" Connie asked.

"Oh, that's exactly right," Tabby smiled. "Was he giving you a bad time about leaving or something?"

"Not really." Connie concentrated as she marked the price on a couple boxes of graham crackers. "He only asked if I decide to leave, to let him know as soon as I can."

Tabby shrugged. "That's fair."

"Yes, I think so," Connie agreed as she moved on to pricing marshmallows and chocolate bars. She finished and stood up. "I am so hungry. Do you want to eat?"

"No, I already had something at the house. It is really late. You miss lunch?"

"I was not hungry before," she said with a shy smile. "I think I was too excited to tell you about our plans and then when your mother showed me that dress. It is so beautiful!"

"You are so beautiful." Tabby gave her another quick hug. "This is going to be such a special wedding. I will make you the best maid of honor ever, I promise. Oh, I've got to find out exactly what all I've got to do for that!"

"Well, I do not know about that," Connie laughed. "I imagine I better find out what all the rules are for the bride."

"The good thing is that it is all changing nowadays." Tabby leaned over the counter as she watched Connie assemble a small sandwich of brown bread, a slice of ham, and one of cheese.

"What do you mean? Changing how?"

"From the old traditions. It's easier here anyway, in the country. In the cities and even in the bigger churches, there were some pretty strict rules, traditions really, but it's like they had made them into rules after so many years. Now, it is less strict as more people want to wear their own clothes, not such fancy and expensive wedding clothes or write their own vows, things like that. If you have your wedding across the road, then the rules will depend on what the Catholic Church says but I imagine it will still be more laid back, being outside."

"Laid back?" Connie wrinkled her nose.

"Hmm, laid back. It means more relaxed, fewer rules, more casual. Does that make more sense?"

Connie nodded, her mouth full.

"Hey, I think I'm going to go." Tabby stood up straight. "I'm just going to walk on down to the park, to the spring and all."

"Everything good with you?" Connie gave her friend a serious look.

"Sure." Tabby wasn't quite truthful. "I just haven't really taken a relaxing walk down there in a while so thought I would today since I have the day off."

"Yes, you do." Connie's attention went back to her sandwich. "Why is that?"

"Oh, no reason." She flat out lied this time. "Just a schedule change. Hey, I'll see you later."

She wondered if that was fair as she walked on down the hill but she just couldn't bring herself to rain on Connie's best day right now with all the disturbing occurrences of last night. Besides, she was supposed to be keeping it a secret, right? She wondered what, if anything, her parents had shared with Jesse.

The afternoon sun was bright but the gentle breeze was strong enough to make for a most pleasant walk, as the oak leaves whispered answers to the winds. She often heard her parents and others make comments about the days flying by too fast, but now, thinking of the last time she had been right here, she discovered she was experiencing the same thing, a slightly disturbing phenomena.

As always, with the exception of the occasional seasonal flood, the clear blue-green waters of Bennett Spring slipped along the peaceful spring branch. She thought again of the last time she had walked here, weeks ago, actually a couple of months ago, and how much more turbulent her heart and her thoughts had been that day. Once again, just like that day, she recalled Grandpa Zeb's words about the waters of Bennett Spring and their miraculous power to heal souls. Maybe he was right, she mused. It hadn't been all that long but she certainly felt better now than she had back then.

A vehicle pulled up behind her and she turned to see Frankie climbing out of the driver's seat.

"Hey, what are you up to?" he asked as he ambled toward her with his unmistakable gait.

"Oh, not a lot, just walking, thinking a bit, I suppose you could say."

"Want some company?" In his own way, he fell into step beside her.

"Sure. I was just thinking, the last time I walked down here like this was the day I met you."

"Really?" He looked at her. "Let's see. I think that was the day you were mad at your mother and we had a discussion about a house a-fire."

Her laughter was as pleasing as the riffle of water over the nearby rocks in the stream. Their steps turned toward the spring. "Yes, it was." Her eyes sparkled with mischief as she looked up at him. "And by the end of the walk, we were back at your new building site which wasn't really a building site at all yet. You introduced me to Father Clem and your uncle so you all knew my name but you drove away that day and I still didn't know yours. That's when I started calling you Irish. You don't mind that I still call you that, do you?" She watched him from the corner of her eye.

"No." He reached over and took her hand as they walked. "I don't mind. It's sort of sweet that you have your own name for me, different than anyone else's."

"I think so, too but I just wanted to be sure." They fell silent for a few steps. "Did you hear about J. Junior and Connie?"

"Hmm, let me guess. Are they seriously dating now?"

"No, more than that. J. Junior asked my father's permission to marry her and it took a little convincing on J. Junior and Connie's part but they are going to allow it."

He let out a long, low whistle. "You're kidding? Wow! There's a lot involved in that one, huh?"

"What do you mean?" Tabby squinted, bringing her hand to her brow to shade her eyes from the sun so she could get a clear view of his face as he spoke. Her heart quivered momentarily as she feared he might say something awful that would shake her faith in this man she had truly begun to trust.

"Oh, just everything. I mean, first he's in a chair so he's got medical issues and believe me, after some of what I saw in the V.A. hospital, you never know how that is all going to turn out. He seems like he's good mentally. As a matter of fact, he's one of the best I've ever seen to come through all he has, but still. I know that jungle on the other side of the world leaves you with a lot to think about, a lot to haunt you long after you leave there. Then you've got her status, whatever that might be, with immigration and I imagine she's still terrified for her family in Cuba. Then there's the whole business of how old they are or rather, how old they aren't. I mean, what are they, both a couple or three years younger than us, right? Plus, they just met. It's only been a few what, weeks, couple of months? Does seem kinda fast and then it's not like either of them has a real job or anything. Where are they gonna live? How are they gonna make ends meet? There's just all kind of stuff to think about there. Don't you think so?"

"Is that it?" she asked in a most sober tone.

"What? That's not enough? I can tell you, it would be enough to keep me awake nights, if I was in his place. Why? What were you thinking?"

"Nothing." She gave him a huge smile and offered up a silent prayer of gratitude. "Nothing more. You are absolutely right on every one of those points but it seems like they have thought about all of those, too. They've been talking to his parents, Joey and Grace, and to mine, of course, and they seem to think they have most of it worked out. It may not be a perfect plan but they are so very happy. It's amazing really. I'm like you. Part of me wonders how can they be so sure, so quick and yet from what I've seen and heard so far, they really are. Even my mother has gotten on board. Of course, from what I've heard over the years, it isn't like she and my father knew each other all that long either, a summer and fall was about all it was. She brought her own wedding dress out of her old trunk this morning and offered it to Connie, with some alterations, of course. And Connie was thrilled. It does look awfully good on her."

"Wow," he nodded. "That really is something. And your dad?"

"Daddy is the romantic in the family. Mama always says so. He may have started out as a senator's aide but he came around before Mama and I think he really believes they will be able to make it work. Of course, like Joey and Grace, I think my parents are planning on being real help to them in whatever they need but you know, J. Junior is pretty darn independent, like a lot of folks around here. He has his own plans, which include classes on business, using his V.A. benefits. They are both talking about her studying to be a grade school teacher. They aren't exactly walking into this without thinking of lots of angles."

"Man, they really have been making plans." He started to laugh.

"What's so funny?"

"Oh, I was just thinking of that night a couple of weeks ago. Remember when we all went to the drive-in movie over there outside of Lebanon? They were in J. Junior's Jeep and we went in my truck and parked next to each other. I remember you went over to their Jeep and were teasing them because you said they were talking an awful lot and not much else. As I recall, you were telling them both that the drive-in was for more than just talking and J. Junior ended up throwing a bunch of popcorn at you to run you off, telling you to get back in my truck and leave 'em alone. He said they knew exactly what they were up to and they didn't need your help!"

Her laughter sparkled once again. "You're right! I forgot about that. I guess they have been making plans for a while now."

"It would seem so." He was quiet for a moment before asking again. "So what do you think?"

"What do you mean?"

"Just what I said. What do you think about them getting married?"

"Well, I dunno. It's up to them, right? Connie is truly the happiest I've seen her since she got here and I really do think it's genuine. Did you see that message the priest wrote down for her last week, from her family? The last line says she is to find her life here in her new home. She says that is her family's way of telling her to stay and not to even think about coming back. She says this is part of that, to make her life with someone she really loves and that's J. Junior."

"Wow," he repeated.

"Yeah, wow," she echoed. "I just can't imagine it right now."

"What?"

"Getting married, for me, I mean." Before he could say anything, she switched gears on him. "You were right, you know."

"I was? About what?"

"When you said I should tell people, teach people about this place, the animals, nature, everything here."

"Okay...." He spoke slowly in a doubtful tone.

"I love what I'm doing now," she explained. "It's like teaching but so much better because I'm not stuck in the same classroom day after day. There is some class-type teaching on tables or in a room but so much of it is outdoors, walking around, looking, touching, smelling, even tasting. I went back and checked out some things in my college catalogues. I think in two semesters, three at the most, I can complete a major that I could use to get a permanent job with the park here or in some other aspect of conservation. There are even private concerns that hire people to be naturalists, outdoor educators, nature interpreters. Depending on which agency you work for, they call it different things. So you were right."

"I see." He frowned. "I'm going to have to think about this. Savor this moment, so to speak."

"What are you talking about?"

"Well, it's not every day that a woman tells a man he was right about something. I probably need to circle today's date in red on my calendar or something."

"Oh, you are so ridiculous!" She took a fake swing at his head which he easily ducked.

They stopped as they reached the spring, surveying the calming waters of the deep blue hole. Tabby's attention focused on one of the nearby fishermen as his graceful moves with a fly rod dropped a dry fly exactly where he intended. After less than a half dozen casts, a large trout accepted his invitation. The fisherman played his catch for several moments, in no particular hurry to bring the experience to any sort of hurried ending. When he did have his quarry close, he reached down and grabbed the fly, and, with a quick flip of his wrist, released the fish, without ever completely removing it from the icy waters. A catch and release fisherman, she thought, her father's most preferred way to trout fish.

"J. Junior says he's already tying flies for a couple of the shops here and he's talking about a fishing equipment business," she continued after a few more moments of silence.

"Well, that's pretty cool," Frankie nodded. "Kinda like Jesse, making a living from what he knows and what he loves. Like you, too, it sounds like." He leaned over and planted a soft kiss on the top of her blond head.

"So what do you think?"

"About what?"

"You know what." She gave him a look of exasperation. "The same thing you just asked me, about marriage."

"Well, about marriage, I think, over all, marriage is a good idea although I have to say, so far, I haven't gotten around to trying it out myself. Kinda busy right now, trying to figure out how to run a construction business and—"

"That is not what I meant and you know it. Honestly!"

"Well, that is what you said."

"Oh, all right, about the two of them, J. Junior and Connie getting married!"

"Yes, well, that's different. I think if they are ready for it and it sounds like just maybe they are, then it's great and I'm happy for them. I guess my thoughts on this one run a little like yours. You say they sound sure and I just hope they are, you know? There is so much to it and these days, you got all kinds of folks just moving in together rather than getting married. I guess that started in California and New York but now it seems to be everywhere. I suppose it's all right for some people but I don't think I would like it."

"You wouldn't?" Now she was truly surprised as she thought shacking up, as so many called it, was every man's dream.

"No." He shook his head to emphasize his words. "I mean, if you think enough of a woman to want to be with her like that, then you should think enough of her to make her that promise, to love her, take care of her, be there for her, and offer her your name. And frankly, I want her to make that same promise to me. I want something to back me up when she's mad at me or I'm mad at her or everything goes wrong, like you lose your job, run out of money, when the kids are really sick, or you are facing other hard times. Jesus promises to stick by us through thick or thin and I think if you love someone enough you want to live with them, it should do the same thing. You should make that promise and stick by it. I hope that's the way J. Junior and Connie are thinking."

Tabby's heart skipped a beat as she listened to this amazing man. She swallowed hard. "I hope so, too," was all she managed to say.

CHAPTER 14

"Did you know they want to get married here?" Tabby sat on the end of Frankie's pickup tailgate again, parked beside the new Sportsman's Chapel, which seemed to have become their favorite place to sit and talk of late.

"What, really?" Frankie snapped his head around and gave her a brief look.

"Connie said they were going to talk to Father Clem and see if they can be the first wedding here. I think J. Junior has already talked to the priest some about taking classes to become Catholic but they are hoping to get married before the end of the summer."

Frankie kept staring at the ground. "Well, we are basically done here. Father is talking about having the dedication soon. I'm just not sure exactly when." Even as he spoke, he didn't look up.

"What's wrong?" She reached over to run her hand along the inside of his arm as he sat with his palms planted on the tailgate at his sides.

"Huh? Oh, I'm sorry." He sighed softly and then leaned back a bit, trying to relax but doing a poor job of it. "I went by to see Uncle Bob tonight before coming out here. He just doesn't look good, you know? He says he's all right and that the doctors haven't told him anything new or different but he just looks....kinda pale and weak."

"I'm so sorry." She continued to stroke his arm as she leaned up against him. "Should I go by to see him again in the next day or two when I'm in Lebanon?"

"Well, that probably wouldn't hurt anything." He gave her a weak smile.

"I wish there was something else I could do," she added.

"I'm not sure there is anything anybody can do, except finish this up and talk to Father Clem about getting that dedication date set pretty soon. I just don't want anything to happen before..." He left the thought unfinished. "So they want to get married here? Well, that will be pretty cool, if we can pull that off," Frankie commented with a small but genuine smile this time. "Pretty cool indeed."

"Listen." She moved a little closer to him, pulling tighter on his arm. "I have to tell you about last night, what happened out here during the thunder storm. But it also has to remain a secret."

"What?" He looked at her sideways and then realized how serious she was.

"Okay," he tried again. "What happened?"

"Well," she began. "It all started when everybody left. I was at home by myself which was fine but then the lights went out and..."

When she had finished sharing every detail, she leaned heavily against him as a little shudder escaped her.

"Oh, for the love of the saints, girl!" He managed to

breathe as he hugged her close. "You are one tough little Nature Girl, aren't you? And to think you laughed at me when I said you protect the creatures and they protect you. I am so glad they do!" He laughed with relief. "And now? Are you all right, really all right?"

She nodded as she ducked her head and simply leaned into him. "I think so. Maybe now, the feeling that someone is always watching will finally be gone. I think if that is done, I can feel like I am really home."

"Oh, you are home, girl. I have no doubt of that, no doubt at all, and your creatures as well as your family are your proof."

She smiled without saying a word.

* * * * *

Father Clem scheduled the dedication of the new chapel two weeks later. Tabby helped Frankie wrap the new structure with a long stretch of ribbon, which Father Clem and Bob McCleary cut together, although Bob did so from a wheelchair. Several different ones from the church spoke and even the Bishop from Springfield attended and blessed the new structure.

The Reverend Jamison Trundle from the Bennett Spring Church of God was an honored guest along with his wife, Esther, and many others from his wife's family, members of the Shine and Darling families were also in attendance. Even Hannah Darling came with her son-in-law and daughter, who kept an exceedingly close eye on her mother for the afternoon. While the interaction between Catholics from the town of Lebanon and area Protestants was somewhat strained at moments, Father Clem managed to conduct a Saturday afternoon Mass, much like any other he had done this summer and last, the only difference being an extra large crowd. Ladies from the St. Francis de Sales Church in Lebanon passed out tiny squares of an all white cake with white icing at the end of the Mass with small cups of punch for everyone.

"It truly is a beautiful structure," Jamison Trundle complimented the priest at the end of the service.

"We had an exceptionally good building crew." Father Clem immediately passed the compliment on. "I think you know the head of the construction project, Frankie O'Donnell from our church and of course, as I understand it, Tabitha is your niece, right? She was quite the helper as well and we have a whole crew of volunteers from Lebanon as well as the town of Sugar Creek up close to Kansas City. With such good help and God's good blessing, it was bound to come out all right. Even with that initial setback from the tornado at the beginning."

"Oh, yes, I heard about that," Jamison replied. "Good thing for good insurance, heh?"

"Certainly. We have Bob McCleary and his construction company to thank for that. Bob had us covered all along under his company's policy so we managed even when we thought we had been hit by a total disaster. I'm not telling you anything you don't already know, Pastor. God takes care of His own."

"Yes, he does, Father. Yes, he does."

After the service, the nurse who brought Frankie's Uncle Bob said it was really time to get him back to the house to get his medication and some rest and Bob McCleary smiled but didn't argue. Tabby and Frankie slipped away to the Dining Lodge for a quiet little dinner all by themselves.

"Is this okay?" he asked as he escorted her to the same table they had dined at with Father Clem and Uncle Bob at the very beginning of the building project.

"It's fine, just fine." Tabby smiled as she accepted the chair he pulled out for her.

"So now that it is all done, the chapel is all built and dedicated—how do you feel?" she asked him.

"Relieved," he admitted with a sigh and a smile. "More than anything, just relieved. We got it done and Uncle Bob got to come and see it and be there for this day. I'm just so grateful that he lived long enough to see it."

"Oh, Frankie, you really don't believe he's going to live much longer, do you?"

He shook his head as he answered softly, "No, I don't and I don't think he does either. That's what all that paperwork was about a month ago, I'm sure. There doesn't seem to be much more the doctors can do for him. I've asked about specialists and the like and they said there are some but Uncle Bob said no, he wasn't interested."

"Wasn't interested? How can that be?" Tabby squinted at him.

"He just said if this is the way it is meant to be, then so be it, but he said he didn't have any interest in chasing around the country to see this one or that one. He said he was tired and he was just happy to be at rest in his own home. He doesn't seem to be in any pain and I'm thankful for that so I'm like, well…what else can I do? The man is 67 years old and he knows his own mind so…"

She rested her hand on his wrist for a few moments until the waitress came to take their order. They enjoyed a meal, just the two of them, of fried trout and all the fixings and, of course, a slice of pie. They talked about brighter things and laughed about the fact that Granny Hannah actually attended the dedication of the Catholic chapel she had objected to so adamantly at first.

"I'm not sure she had a lot of choice," Tabby chortled, "between Uncle Jamison scolding her gently as a good Christian and Mama just downright threatening her that if she didn't behave she wouldn't hesitate to treat her just like a child and whip her right out of there. I think that probably moved her more than Uncle Jamison's preaching. Mama can get pretty scary when she gets a full head of steam going."

Frankie laughed. "I could see that. I'm sure I wouldn't want your mama mad at me, that's for sure."

"I don't think you have to worry about that," Tabby assured him.

"Hope not," he added, as he picked up the check and they turned toward the door.

* * * * *

Two weeks later, another mixed crowd, Catholics and Protestants alike, almost as big as the one for the chapel dedication, gathered once again in the now officially named Sportsman's Chapel.

Father Clem stood before the multitude as two of the young men from the Cat Hollow Barn Dance strummed guitars behind him.

"We gather here today in the Lord's house in his magnificent chapel known as the woods and fields of Bennett Spring. We are here to celebrate the marriage of two young people just beginning their lives and yet in another sense, both have already lived, suffered, and triumphed over more of life's obstacles than many of us have experienced in more decades than they have been alive, more of life's challenges than most of us can even imagine.

"Generally, I'm not much for sharing a message at weddings other than the sanctity of the blessed sacrament given by God to unite two of his people forever in love. But as we know and can plainly see this union is a little different than most and these two have graciously given their permission to share something more with all of you."

The priest continued, "Joseph Jacob Schultz Junior and Maria Consuelo Rios. We know they are both quite young and it would be easy to dismiss their desire to wed as impractical or some whimsical fantasy that will pass but I have spoken at length with both J. Junior and Connie, separately and together, and I find in them a deep love for each other and also for God and His Son. With a basis like that, I think they have what it takes to forge a life together.

"I spoke a moment before of the challenges they have faced. Both have been in some very dangerous parts of the world. J. Junior joined the Army last year and went to Viet Nam and as he puts it, came home with a souvenir wheelchair. Connie grew up in Cuba which I understand from friends of mine was once a beautiful place. But like Viet Nam, life there has been disrupted and many have died as a result of civil war and the conflicts that continue. Her family sent her to live here rather than to continue to risk her life there in her own homeland. Can you imagine, upon arrival here, she could not even tell her family that she had arrived safely? There are so many things we don't have to deal with on a regular basis."

He was quiet for a moment as he looked out at those gathered before turning his attention back to the pair in front of him. He continued with a more traditional wedding proceeding, mentioning each of their names, helping them to repeat their vows to one another. He brought out a small ceremonial Communion set which he also used for the couple to share their first communion together as J. Junior had been busy in recent weeks, studying privately with Father Clem, receiving instruction on converting to Catholicism.

Hannah squirmed a bit standing between her daughter, Becky, and her son-in-law, J.C., at the slight deviation from her own faith's practices. J.C. reached over and patted Hannah's hand where it rested on his forearm. "It'll be fine, *Mamá*," he assured her. She smiled up at him and then looked down at her feet. Becky gave him a silent wink of thanks.

The priest continued the ceremony, speaking privately to the new couple at a couple of points. Then he looked up with a wide smile. "Ladies and gentlemen, there are a couple of new customs we bring here this evening, from Connie's homeland of Cuba. First, J. Junior...."

J. Junior reached into his pocket and produced a small black velvet bag, loosened the drawstring at the top and emptied a dozen tiny coins into the palm of Connie's waiting hand. "These coins represent J. Junior's promise to always provide for his bride, their family and their home, to work and make certain they are never in want. As the head of the household, this is, after leading his family as the head of a Christian household, his first and foremost responsibility, to see to the welfare of his family."

Connie turned and gently laid the tiny bag and the coins on the altar.

"And then Connie…" the priest continued.

Connie turned back to Tabby, her maid of honor, who handed her a small package, wrapped in a miniature embroidered cloth. She opened it, revealing a palm-sized loaf of bread, which she handed to J. Junior. "This is Connie's promise to always provide food in their home, nutrition for her husband and their children to come one day."

J. Junior accepted the bread and then laid it beside the coins on the altar. At this point, Joey Schultz, J. Junior's father and best man, stepped forward, unwinding a silver cord and with Tabby's help, he laced it over Connie and J. Junior's shoulders, figuratively as well as literally binding the two together before the wedding guests.

"And this is called the *investidura*," Father Clem continued, "a silver cord that literally binds these two together before God and all these witnesses from this day forward and for the rest of their lives."

Connie knelt down for a moment beside J. Junior's chair and the priest rested a hand on each one's head as he pronounced the final blessing. Joey helped his new daughter-in-law to her feet when the priest finished and removed the cord, which he carefully rolled up.

"I would like to present to you today, Mr. and Mrs. Joseph J. Schultz Jr. but before I do, I have been asked by this new and very wise couple to point out an unusual display at today's ceremony.

"Outside here," and he pointed to a set of trees just past the chapel, "you will see what looks to be a set of bones, complete with not one, but two full sets of antlers. If you look even closer, you will see that those antlers are locked together. These two white tailed bucks were apparently fighting with one another when they locked antlers in a battle and could not separate from one another. The tragic truth is that they both died in mortal combat, dying, starving perhaps because they could not separate, a direct result of their duel with one another. There is a lesson for all of us here and it is one this new couple has asked me to share today.

"For those who insist on fighting one another, whether over political, religious, or philosophical differences, we risk ending up just like these two great bucks. Think of all the beauty, the majesty, the magnificence that was lost here in this clash. We must find a way as people of Christ, our savior, to avoid a similar fate. We must find a way to live together in love. That is the lesson that Mr. and Mrs. J. Junior leave with us today and I cannot imagine a better life lesson, a better gift that they could have shared with all. God bless them! God bless you! J. Junior, you may kiss your bride!"

The new young bride leaned over as J. Junior reached up, taking both sides of her face gently in his hands. Those gathered erupted in applause and cheers, including the priest himself. Tears of joy slid down Connie's cheeks and several stepped forward to clap J. Junior on the back.

"And now let the celebration begin!" the priest announced loudly.

The next half hour or better was spent as a makeshift receiving line formed and everyone filed past to hug and congratulate the two. Folding tables and chairs appeared in the field in front of the chapel and all around as food of all sorts suddenly covered them. Becky, Hannah, Grace, Tabby, and many others unloaded coolers, picnic hampers, and boxes of all description with foods of the same depiction, including ham, turkey, and fried chicken. Side dishes, fruit dishes, and all the trimmings materialized into a huge church dinner on the grounds and mushroomed into a joyous wedding reception.

Becky and Tabby had spent the last couple of weeks making plans with Connie and the congregations of both the Bennett Spring Church of God and Father Clem's church, St. Francis de Sales in Lebanon. Everyone brought food and everything needed. J.C. and Jesse even brought out a beautiful white wedding cake at the end of the dinner. J. Junior and Connie cut the cake together and tenderly fed a piece of it to each other as everyone watched and cheered. Continuing in joyous traditions, J. Junior slipped a blue garter off of his bride's leg just above the knee and threw it over his shoulder to his gathered single friends, including some of his fellow musician friends from the Cat Hollow Dance Barn.

With more cheers and whistles, the single young ladies also assembled for Connie to toss her wedding bouquet of multi-colored wild flowers, the ones she said she most preferred over any from a florist. She closed her eyes and said a silent prayer as she pitched the flowers overhead. The gathered ladies jostled for position and much to her surprise, the bouquet landed directly in Tabby's hands!

"Oh!" was all Tabby could say and everyone laughed at her wide eyes and startled expression. Everyone except Frankie, who watched quietly with a small smile, but looked away quickly in embarrassment when several other faces turned toward his. Other traditions were also observed such as the pickup truck parked discreetly a short distance away under the trees where small plastic glasses of beer were offered to the gentlemen who quietly made their way to its tailgate.

Frankie and Tabby made their way out to take another look at the mass of bones they had discovered in the woods weeks ago, now that they had been mounted on a huge board by the park naturalist team.

"When I got my foot stuck in that bramble patch that day," Frankie shook his head, still in wonder, "I never imagined this is what was under there. It's still pretty amazing!" He snickered a bit. "You had me chopping away at those long prickly stems and I really thought you had lost your mind but then I was afraid to quit because I thought I might never get my foot out. Who knew it was rib bones holding on to my ankle at the moment?"

"I can't say I knew right away what it was but I knew it wasn't just undergrowth." She, too, continued to marvel at the display. "I could see the bones and I knew something didn't fit. And then when I realized what it was….well, I knew it was incredible to find such a thing. Didn't Mr. C and the girls do a great job of getting this on display? He said this was temporary so we could bring it out here today but then he has plans to get it done by the professionals in a display case that can travel. The only bad part is that they are going to put it on the road and not leave it here, but the good side is that more people will get to see it."

Footsteps turned both their heads as Hannah joined them. "Hey, Granny," Tabby welcomed her with an open arm she slipped around her grandmother's waist. "Did you come to see the Battling Stags? That's what my boss, Mr. C. calls them."

"I heard stories about bucks like these when I was a girl," Hannah stood, staring, "but you know, I don't think I ever believed it. I thought it was just one of those old tales the hill people tell but now I see it is true."

"Yes, it is," Tabby nodded.

After a few more moments, Hannah kissed her granddaughter on the cheek and turned back to the celebration behind her.

Frankie looked at Tabby, who simply shrugged with a surprised expression on her face, watching to make certain her grandmother safely joined the others. He and Tabby also returned for more punch and separated to talk with the many guests.

As the different ones milled about visiting, Frankie casually made his way over to the groom, determined to ask him something he had long wondered about. "How you doing?" Frankie asked his smiling friend as he pulled up a chair beside him.

"How am I doing?" J. Junior repeated the question with a broad smile. "I just married an angel, sir. I think I'm doing purty good."

"Yes, you are. As a matter of fact, J., you've been doing pretty good ever since I met you."

"Meanin'?" A slight frown creased his brow.

"Oh, nothing bad," Frankie hurried on to reassure him. "Truly! But I wanted to ask, if you don't mind...I saw a lot of guys in chairs when I was in the V.A. hospital, amputees, and all and none of them had an attitude like yours. I never even met anybody with that kind of— I don't know what you call it, other than the best dang demeanor I've ever seen in anybody on two feet or four wheels!"

J. Junior dropped his head with a smile. "Oh, that," he finally said.

"Well? Is there an answer to the question? 'Cuz if there is, I'd really like to know the secret to it."

"Well, I don't know if it's any kinda secret," J. Junior sighed softly, "but I can tell you what little I know and what happened in the hospital, after getting on the wrong side of a grenade over there."

"If you don't mind...I mean, maybe this isn't the time or place—"

"No, no, it's all right," J. Junior reached over and cupped his friend's shoulder. "After I landed back in the states, in the hospital, I wasn't much different than anybody else there, you know? I mean, I was always a pretty easy going type. Not taking things too serious or nothing but once you get your legs blowed off of you, like some of those guys, or you find out from the doctors, like me, that you still got yours but they ain't never gonna work again 'cuz some piece of shrapnel cut through your spinal cord, the happy-go-lucky side of you goes pretty flat. I guess I was as angry as any of the rest of 'em. And then one of the guys in the hospital unit with us there, he up and died. Kinda surprised us all because he seemed to be doing okay and then it was like all at once, he just gave up. I guess they didn't realize how bad he was, in the head, and they wasn't watching for it. Anyway, he did himself in one night. Got a razor, went in the bathroom in the middle of the night, and left a real mess, they said.

"So, several of the guys decided to go to his funeral 'cuz he was from right there in the city where the hospital was. The orderlies said they would take any of us who wanted to go. I wasn't like the guy's best friend or anything but I seen it as chance to get outside the hospital for an afternoon so I said, yeah, I'd go."

He took in a breath with a funny little smile before continuing. "So we went to a funeral. They wheeled me up to this paved graveside area outside where they had it in this little memorial garden. Guess they have a lot of them there 'cuz it was all set up real neat for those of us in chairs and there was probably half a dozen of us there that day like that. But I ended up sitting right across from his mama and daddy and let me tell you, that was a real eye opener. 'Til that day, I guess I'd never really thought about how hard we are on our folks sometimes. To sit there and watch those folks suffer, to just fall apart right in front on my eyes as that funeral went on...." He stopped speaking for a moment and wiped at his eyes before he went on.

"Maybe it didn't help that they were about the same age as my folks, I dunno. I just know that before that service for some guy I hardly knew was finished, I was praying to never put my folks through that kind of misery. I bowed my head and thanked God for saving my miserable life and even if it was gonna be lots different from now on, I was just that, alive and able to still do lots of things. Maybe not everything I could before but there was still plenty I could do. I would just have to learn to do it sitting on my butt! So, I got busy on every rehabilitation exercise and therapy they would let me have. I worked my butt off in some ways and by the time I told my folks I was ready for them to show up to visit me for the first time, I was already working on getting my head on straight. They came and saw that I was really doing okay and that first day, my dad and I already started figuring out how to retrofit that Jeep! And I been making plans ever since!"

"Well, I just couldn't help but wonder." Frankie shook his head, sitting there beside his friend. "So that's where it comes from."

"It?"

"The attitude, your attitude."

"My attitude? Oh, no, my friend, not MY anything," J. Junior grinned. "Anything I got in the way of attitude comes from the same place as that little lady I am now blessed to be married to." He cast his eyes straight up and pointed in the same direction. "Right from heaven and the good Lord above, there's no place else for you to get great gifts like that!"

"Oh, J., we are so blessed to have you." Frankie stood up to move on as he saw others loitering nearby, waiting to speak to the new groom. "You are gonna fit right in with us Catholics!"

"Amen to that!" J. Junior raised his glass of punch in toasting fashion.

Tabby sat in the driver's seat of yet another pickup truck. The music and dancing for the evening was something that had greatly concerned Connie. She had fretted about making her new husband feel awkward in any way even though when she tried to discuss it with him, he had simply shrugged and said whatever she wanted to do was fine with him. Tabby's idea had been to have different vehicles alternate playing tapes in their vehicles' tape decks, providing background music, and the two girls decided that would work the best. Tabby worked it all out with various friends. Without making a big announcement, they could just skip the dancing issue altogether and that seemed to work well, as people enjoyed simply visiting with one another after eating.

J. Junior looked around as he visited with those who stopped to chat but when he noticed that a few were beginning the packing up process to leave, he beckoned to the pair of musician brothers who played at the Cat Hollow Dance Barn with him. They brought out their box guitars as Tabby turned off the last tape deck. J. Junior rolled forward, a guitar player on each side of him.

"'Scuse me." Carl, the taller of the two guitarists, called out to the assembled guests. "Now we all know this is a different kind of wedding for lots of reasons. And as a few of us remember, even from before J. Junior went off to Viet Nam, well, like some of the rest of us, he wasn't much of one for dancing. But he said he figured every girl has it in her heart to dance with her groom on her wedding day and he said this wedding shouldn't be no different in that regard."

By now, Carl had the undivided attention of all those assembled, including Connie who was on the other side of the chapel where she had been chatting with J.C. and Becky.

J. Junior looked at his bride and held out his hand.

"J., what are you doing?" She asked in a stage whisper as she drew close to his wheelchair. "Please…"

"Shh," he responded as Carl's youngest brother pulled a flat lace-trimmed cushion from behind his back and handed it over to the man in the wheelchair. J. Junior plopped it onto his knees and took his bride's hand, pulling her into his lap.

"So at his request, we have a special song for the bride and groom." Carl finished and began to strum his guitar.

The strains of the long familiar melody of the world's best known Cuban song, *Guantanamera,* echoed throughout the chapel as J. Junior slowly rocked his chair back and forth to the Latin rhythm. Connie slipped her arms around her husband's neck and momentarily buried her face in his shoulder. When she lifted it, it was damp with tears that were instantly dimmed by the bright smile on her face.

"Oh, J." She barely breathed his name. "How did you know?"

"Hey, I got friends who study up on this kinda stuff, don't you know?" He grinned at her, tucking one hand around her waist while barely keeping the chair moving with the other.

She leaned over, a dreamy expression lighting her face. "With this soft night air and this music, it is like my heart is home."

"Baby, you are home." He gave her a squeeze as they shared yet another tender kiss.

Her head continued to rest on his shoulder as she sang soothingly next to his ear, *"Yo soy un hombre sincero, De donde crece la palma, Y antes de morirme quiero...."*

The guitarists played on and those gathered, watched, many misty-eyed while others swayed to the gentle beat.

J.C. wrapped his arm around Becky, pulling her close. "You know," he spoke quietly so as not to disturb the others. "Those two are going to be all right. I was still a little worried up until a week ago but not anymore."

"Not anymore?"

"Not after what I just saw. The boy never did dance and he certainly doesn't know Cuban songs but he came to me last week and asked me to find him one that she would like and that his friends could play on guitars. He wouldn't tell me exactly what he was planning, just that it was a surprise for the wedding and—"

Becky put her head down to hide a smile of amusement.

"What's so funny?" J.C. asked.

"Well, J. Junior asked Grace to make that pillow for him but he wouldn't tell her what it was about, either. I had the lace from the sleeves we took off of the dress so it matched perfectly. It worked out well, but like you, I had no idea what he was up to. What a lovely couple they make." She reached up to her shoulder and took her husband's hand.

J.C. continued, "the best part is that no matter what happens from here, they will take good care of each other and that is the most important part," he added.

"Yes, it is," she agreed. "I was just remembering…"

"Remembering what?"

"A Bible verse, of all things. In the Book of Luke, after the birth of Jesus and all the visitors, it says…and Mary pondered or treasured these things in her heart. That is how I'm feeling, as the one filling in for Connie's mother tonight, like I want to forever treasure this night in my heart."

J.C. smiled. "And so you will, hopefully, so you can tell Pilar and Miguelito all about it someday."

"Oh, from your lips to God's ear," Becky whispered.

J.C. was pensively quiet for a moment, watching the young couple like everyone else when his attention was distracted by another couple at the far side of the chapel. "Look right over there," he whispered in Becky's ear.

Hannah was approaching Father Clem as he also watched the wedding dance. She held out her hand in a delicate gesture as she stopped to speak to him. He took her hand, sandwiching it between both of his and leaned forward to listen. He laughed heartily and shook her hand in introduction and then released it. They both smiled and continued to chat.

"I believe your mother just introduced herself to the local priest," J.C. whispered once again.

"Well, hallelujah," Becky responded with relief. "It truly is a night of miracles."

"Yes, it is. It is still so difficult to believe it has been over forty years since the first time I came to this valley. Do you remember what I told you back then was the most special thing I found here, besides you, of course?"

"Hmm." She smiled at the memory of the tall blond boy back then who was, in her eyes, still just as handsome and charming today. "Yes, I believe I do," she answered. "The very first time you walked me home from the hotel after that big meeting the senator hosted and we stopped at Bennett Spring in the dark. You told me that night that the true heart of the spring is the people here."

"Yes, I did," he replied as he nuzzled her ear. "This bride and groom and even your mother tonight are proof that all these years later, that hasn't changed."

Watching from a short distance away on the other side of the chapel, Frankie stepped up behind Tabby, encircling her in his arms. "What a nice wedding," he said softly.

"Oh, it was," Tabby agreed, a faraway timbre to her voice as she leaned back against him. "I talked to Connie a few minutes ago and she is so happy."

"Good," Frankie replied. "J. Junior is busy telling everyone he's married an angel so he's a happy groom as well. You know, I have a lot to deal with over the next couple of months, what with taking over the construction business, watching over Uncle Bob and all." He continued to hold her while he spoke into her ear, his breath tickling the back of her neck.

"Uh-huh," she answered.

"Well, I want you to think about something."

"What's that?"

"I want you to think about next summer."

"Next summer?" She turned around, his arms still around her.

"Yeah, next summer," he repeated, kissing her on the lips.

"Think about next summer and we'll do this all over again."

"Another wedding?"

"Yes, you go to school this year and finish up your degree so that you can work as a park naturalist or something similar and share Bennett Spring and all of the Ozarks with the people who come to visit and learn. I'll get a handle on running this construction company full time and next summer, we'll have another wedding, yours and mine. Will you marry me then, Miss Tabitha Shine?"

Her eyes shone as she answered, raising up on her tiptoes to put her lips next to his ear.

"Yes, yes I will," she answered and kissed him. "Next summer."

The music had stopped and folks were forming another line, this one leading to J. Junior's Jeep which was appropriately decorated with attached tin cans and tissue paper streamers. As the new couple made their way to the vehicle, those surrounding them tossed rice and cheered. J. Junior started the engine with a noisy flourish and they roared off into the night, with cheers and best wishes of their family and friends echoing behind them.

A great blue heron sailed above the trees, across the face of the full moon as it shed its angelic pale light across Bennett Spring, its waters, its woods, and, most of all, its blessed residents. Those in attendance gathered up their leftover containers, folded up their tables and chairs, and soon left the new chapel just as they had found it earlier in the day, a simple yet beautiful structure, resting and waiting in God's natural cathedral for the next great celebration of His Love there.

HISTORICALLY SPEAKING...

- The Sportsman's Chapel, constructed by volunteers from outside the area as well as from the local St. Francis de Sales Catholic Church, began in 1972 and was completed in the spring of 1974. Father Clem Ilmberger of the Lebanon church spearheaded the movement along with a local resident, Ben Shanoski and his wife, Jennie, and a group of fishermen from the Kansas City suburb of Sugar Creek who also worked in the building trades. Ben Shanoski became seriously ill before the chapel was completed and passed away December 19, 1973, shortly after the statue of the Virgin and the altar were laid in place. All funds used in the construction of the chapel were donations specifically for that purpose and did not include funds from the local church.

- Ralph and Willa Jean Ursery owned cabins, a campground, and a small horse barn just to the south and east of the spring at Bennett. They provided guided trail rides for Bennett Spring visitors along the spring branch into the 1970s. Kay Peace was once one of those trail guides for the Urserys in years past. Along with her husband, Larry, and her son, Kelly Peace, their family has operated Larry's Store and Cabins, located just before entering Bennett Spring State Park, from the 1970s well into the 21st century.

- George Kastler worked five summers at Big Spring State Park, before coming to Bennett Spring in 1969, to supervise the building and establishment of the current Bennett Spring Nature Center. He worked at Bennett until 1978, as the full time naturalist. From there, he moved to Jefferson City, to become the state's fifth chief naturalist, a position he held until he retired in 2010. He was awarded various awards over the years, including Master/Distinguished Professional Interpreter Award from the Association of Missouri Interpreters, the Bob Jennings Meritorious Service Award in 1998 and 2006, and the Fellowship/Lifetime Achievement Award. The character of Richard Campbell represents George and his work in this fictionalized account of the naturalists' work, efforts that still benefit visitors to Bennett Spring in the 21st century.

- Over the years since Bennett Spring State Park was officially established in 1924, a great many private concerns—campgrounds, canoe rentals, motels, convenience stores, gas stations, cabin rentals— have sprung up around the famous park. A few have endured for decades, like the Sand Spring Motel, celebrating its 50th anniversary in 2015, but most have come and gone, with the seasons, changed hands and names a few times over the years and often simply disappeared over the years. Several of those in closest proximity to the park, have been purchased by the state, their buildings razed and the lands absorbed into the park itself. Such has been the fate of the Bramwell cabins, the Ursery campground, cabins and horse barn, the Vogels cabins and several others over the years. Likewise, Albert and Flossie Baird's farm located off of the west side of Highway 64A, was purchased by the state park system. The Bairds are also the family that donated the original land where the Sportsman's Chapel now stands just outside of Bennett Spring State Park on the east side of Highway 64A.

- A number of international, national, and historically significant events are mentioned throughout this story as they impacted the lives of folks at Bennett Spring at this particular time and that includes: the Summer of Love in 1967, which was the arrival of thousands of young people, known by some as Flower Children, spilling onto the streets of San Francisco; the Viet Nam War, which ran from the early 1960s through 1975, killing and injuring hundreds of thousands of Americans during that era, a legacy we all still grapple with today; the Cuban revolution, bringing Fidel Castro to power in 1959, a regime that is finally changing and once again recognized by the US government for the first time in over 50 years; Minute Men missiles, an American defense system once thought essential by the US government; and long-time conflicts between members of Christ's church, specifically Catholics and Protestants.

A BRIEF HISTORY

The first visitors to what we now call Bennett Spring were barefoot and later moccasin-footed. Members of the Osage, the Delaware and Kickapoo tribes were known to have hunted, fished and camped in the area. There is some conviction amongst early historians that the People of the Middle Waters, as the Osage called themselves, did not actually live at or around the spring, but rather simply passed through, believing this to be a sacred area, a place they held in high respect.

They shared a legend that described the original site of the spring as a small pool of great depth. Their best divers could not reach the bottom, despite its calm waters which produced only a small stream of water. Their stories relate that those original native people forgot their traditions, who they were and where they came from. They became proud and arrogant, forgetting their daily prayers and neglecting their responsibilities as stewards of the land that had been entrusted to them by the Sacred One. They killed other Indians and took the scalps of those who were not worthy. One night, after they had returned from yet another shameful raid, the Sacred One's wrath was felt by all as the ground shook, nearby trees tumbled and the earth as they knew it changed forever. The quiet pool became a boiling spring, as ceaseless tears began to flow from the eye of the Sacred One, creating a full and flowing stream that followed along the valley floor all the way to the Niangua River over a mile away. Bennett Spring, the spring we know that produces 100 million gallons of cool fresh water daily, was born.

By the early 1800s, the Osage, the primary Indian tribe of this area, left of their own accord as their chief, Pawhuska, moved his people to lands in Kansas. Many years later, the Osage moved on to what is today still Osage County in Oklahoma. By the 1830s, the U.S. Army made certain that all other Indians had been pushed westward, leaving behind only thousands of arrowheads, souvenirs that today decorate the mantels of many local residences and on rare occasion, still delight a sharp-eyed tourist.

In 1837 James Brice, originally from Virginia, and his wife, Ann, of Kentucky, arrived in the valley from Illinois. The forest of oak, hickory, black walnut, elm, maple and dogwood grew dense with underbrush and bears, wolves, panthers, wildcats and even the occasional buffalo were also common. Smaller animals such as raccoons, rabbits, squirrels, deer, fox, beaver, mink, muskrat and wild turkey, most of which can still be seen on occasion, abounded.

In the early 1840s James Brice, then 50 years old, built the first of several mills in the Bennett Spring area. As other settlers moved into the valley the area became known as Brice Spring. The small village that sprang up on the site of today's Bennett Spring State Park Store was later called Brice, Missouri beginning in the 1860s after the death of James Brice.

Within a few years other settlers and families moved into the valley—Hawk, Brown, Conn, Clanton, Henson, Lomax, Mullicaine and Bennett. Peter M. Bennett constructed a second mill at the confluence, where the spring waters meet the Niangua River, but within a few short years, both mills were destroyed by flood waters.

James Brice's daughters, Jane and Anna, grew up and married others in the valley; Jane to Asahel Bennett and Anna, per her father's wishes, married John Clanton, a young wagon maker from North Carolina. He and Anna had two children, Nancy Jane and James Madison Clanton, before John Clanton's death in the winter of 1856 at the age of 30. Shortly afterwards in early 1857, Anna Brice Clanton gave birth to her third child, Anna Caroline.

By the 1860s the country as a whole was engaged in the Civil War but the spring area and the tiny town of Brice were protected by their secluded location and lack of a nearby railhead.

The widow Anna Brice Clanton remarried, to Peter M. Bennett Jr. this time. The 427 acres of property, including the spring itself that had once belonged to her father and had been willed by him to her first husband, John Clanton, now reverted fully to her. Upon her marriage to Peter Bennett Jr., all of her property became his and soon the general area became known as Bennett Spring. Peter and Anna Bennett had six children but only two lived to adulthood, William Sherman and Josephine Bennett.

In 1894 the Rev. George Bolds, his wife, Mary, and their four children, the oldest being a 17-year old daughter, Louie Bolds, came to Bennett Spring and held the first of many old time revivals. At their first meeting, 38 men and women were saved and baptized including 29 year old William Sherman Bennett. A year later, he and Louie Bolds were married. In the years to come, Louie and later her son, Paul, would become well known ministers throughout the area.

The record is vague as to exactly how many mills were eventually built in the valley. The two original grain mills were both known to have been destroyed by flood and the last mill built by Peter Bennett was constructed close to the village of Brice. It burned in 1895. The last Bennett Spring mill, a grist mill, stood near the location of the previous mill, across the section of land that today holds the concrete hatchery pools built in the 1960s. This mill was a partnership amongst J.H. Hensley, a local cattleman, and Dr. John B. Atchley, Arminta Atchley, John B.'s wife and J. H. Hensley's sister, and Freeman Atchley, a brother-in-law to Hensley and Arminta Atchley.

The new mill partners took out a ninety-nine year lease with W.S. and Louie Bennett for use of the wheel left from the 1895 mill that had burned, the dam floor, water and roadway use rights necessary for the operation of the mill.

The new mill, opened in 1900, once again drew people to Bennett Spring to fish and camp while they waited in line for their wheat to be ground. Meanwhile, a report in the *Laclede County Sentinel* in January 1900 stated that the Missouri Fish Commissioner deposited 40,000 mountain trout into the spring branch, brought from west of the Continental Divide. While several others, visitors and residents alike, expressed an interest in stocking more trout in the area, an Oklahoma dentist, Charles A. Furrow, and an unnamed business partner were the first to actually invest in the idea by establishing a hatchery at Bennett Spring in July 1923.

Others began to come to Bennett Spring driving Model A's and Model T's or a rented buggy from Lebanon to picnic, visit or even spend a night or two at the Brice Inn, run by Josephine "Josie" Bennett. The residents of the village of Brice, never prosperous by any stretch of the imagination, continued in their daily lives and welcomed the growing number of visitors to their valley.

According to an article that appeared in the December 12, 1924 issue of the *Laclede County Republican*, A.O. Mayfield, the president of the Lebanon Chamber of Commerce, requested that state officials consider Laclede County as a possible site for the first state park.

Soon after negotiations began however, they were publicly

called off as the parties involved could not agree. They began again shortly afterwards and on December 27, 1924, Josie Bennett Smith sold the state their first acquisition of land, 8.5 acres for the new Bennett Spring State Park.

In April 1925, William Sherman Bennett sold 565 acres of land to the state that would become the heart of Bennett Spring State Park and 427 of those acres could be traced directly to his grandfather, James Brice, the original settler at Bennett Spring.

The state gave full power and authority over the new lands to the Lebanon Chamber of Commerce to collect and receive rents on current leases until the state could take proper control of its new property. Arlie Bramwell, a great-great-grandson of James Brice, was hired as the first superintendent of both the park and the hatchery. Life in Brice, Missouri continued basically uninterrupted for a few more years, despite the change of ownership of the land.

The Great Depression changed many things in America and by 1933, one in four persons throughout the U.S. had lost their job, their home or both. The Civilian Conservation Corps, one of several Federal programs designed to put people back to work and put the country back on sound economic footing, provided hundreds of workers with desperately needed work with many different projects and Bennett Spring Park was one of them.

The CCC work at Bennett Spring is well-known and well-documented. In 1938, the year after the CCC left the area, records indicate 53,762 persons visited Bennett Spring, ten percent of the total visitors that year to Missouri's twenty-five state parks.

In 1940, a report prepared for the Missouri Park Board by a Kansas City landscape architectural firm made several recommendations, including several that were never carried out. Those that were included more acquisition of private lands around the park and the repositioning of roads that ran too close to the stream and therefore, were more prone to seasonal flooding. Within a few years after the passage of the Civilian Conservation Corps from the area, America was involved in another great struggle, World War II. Money and effort went to the war effort and little was expended elsewhere.

For the next two to three decades, most of the development around Bennett Spring took place outside of the park's boundaries as private individuals built cabins, hotels and campgrounds. For the next many years, people planning a summer weekend or vacation to Bennett often did so at Bramwell's Cabins, Usery's Cabins and Campground, the Sand Spring Resort, Weaver's Campground, Splan's Resort, Vogels—the list of private campground owners was long.

Beginning in 1969, the state began to buy up many of those private enterprises, one by one. Arlie Bramwell sold his wood and stone cabins to the state. For many years, they had graced the hillside across from what is now known as the Bramwell or lower entrance to the park. Ralph and Willa Jean Ursery's cabins and small stable, located near the spring, were also purchased and used by the state for a time, before they were razed and replaced by new structures in the mid-1980s.

Improved Federal and state highway systems in the 1950s and 1960s brought a growing number of visitors to Bennett Spring each year until the yearly average during the 1970s was a million fishermen, their families and other tourists.

Bennett Spring State Park, since the first lands were purchased from members of the Bennett family in the mid-1920s, has been a jewel of the Missouri State Park system and continues in that role ninety years later.

OTHER BOOKS BY
LAURA L. VALENTI

Novels

The Heart of the Spring
The Heart of the Spring Lives On
The Heart of the Spring Comes Home

*

Between the Star and the Cross: The Choice
Between the Star and the Cross: The Election
Between the Star and the Cross: The Promise

Las Palomitas: The Little Doves

www.ingramcontent.com/pod-product-compliance
Lightning Source LLC
Chambersburg PA
CBHW071103250626
47159CB00002B/583